APPARITION ALLEY

Katherine V. Forrest

BERKLEY PRIME CRIME, NEW YORK

APPARITION ALLEY

A Berkley Prime Crime Book / published by arrangement with
the author

PRINTING HISTORY
Berkley Prime Crime hardcover edition / September 1997
Berkley Prime Crime mass market edition / October 1998
All rights reserved.
Copyright © 1997 by Katherine V. Forrest.
This book may not be reproduced in whole
or in part, by mimeograph or any other means,
without permission. For information address:
The Berkley Publishing Group, a member of Penguin Putnam Inc.,
200 Madison Avenue, New York, NY 10016.

The Putnam Berkley Inc. World Wide Web site address is
http://www.penguinputnam.com

ISBN 0-425-16632-5

Berkley Prime Crime Books are published
by The Berkley Publishing Group,
a member of Penguin Putnam Inc.,
200 Madison Avenue, New York, NY 10016.

The name BERKLEY PRIME CRIME and the
BERKLEY PRIME CRIME
design are trademarks belonging to
Berkley Publishing Corporation.

PRINTED IN THE UNITED STATES OF AMERICA

10 9 8 7 6 5 4 3 2 1

For Eugenia Lowe
with love

Acknowledgments

To my indispensable support team: Montserrat Fontes and Clarice Gillis, Michael Nava, Cath Walker, Sherry Thomas, Phyllis Burke and Lynn Hendee. To my editor, Natalee Rosenstein. To Charlotte Sheedy, with many, many thanks.

To Sergeant Mitchell Grobeson, who suggested the original concept for this novel. Police procedure hurdles were particularly daunting in this story, and I owe many thanks for his technical expertise and experience, his great patience when the novel veered off on its own tangents, his unfailing generosity of spirit, and his friendship. *Vaya con Dios*, my friend.

To Jo . . . for everything.

1

"**Z**IPPED up tight, Kate," Sergeant Fred Hansen said, moving past her, holding his nine-millimeter slanted downward and close in to his body, trigger finger laid along the gun frame. Standing sideways, he peered up the hallway, presenting, LAPD Homicide Detective Kate Delafield thought, an unmissable target for the poorest shooter; his body, bulked up by a bulletproof vest, took up most of the hall doorway.

The team moved quietly along the dingy, dimly lit second-floor hallway of the dilapidated fifties-era apartment building, the intricate, yellowed plaster moldings a doleful remnant of the structure's former stylishness.

Adrenaline surging through her, Kate reached for the holstered gun underneath her LAPD raid jacket to again test the motion that her own vest would restrict. She nodded to Hansen and to her partner, Torrie Holden, and then stepped in front of Officer Alicia Perez. "Ready," she said to Torrie.

"Let's nail this scumbag," Torrie said with the cockiness of the patrol cop she once had been, a hand in the shoulder bag that contained her gun. Mirroring Torrie, Kate reached into her own shoulder bag, but to touch the arrest warrant.

She braced, reaching for her gun as a door opened ahead of them. She was pleasantly assailed by the oniony vapors of soup as a white-haired old woman clomped into the hallway in ankle-high lace-up shoes. Alicia Perez moved quickly to the woman and spoke to her in a low tone.

The old woman, with hanging jowls and wearing sequined fifties-style glasses, a threadbare yellow sweater pulled over a housedress laundered clean of color, scowled at Perez. "Takin' men's work, shame on you," she pronounced, her jowls quivering, and then she clomped back into her apartment.

Perez winked as Torrie and Kate moved past her. "Forgot to mention my grandma lives here."

Torrie and Hansen stationed themselves on either side of apartment nine, and Hansen extended an arm and rapped on the door. Kate reached into her jacket, positioning her thumb on the snap of her shoulder holster.

"Who is it?" a querulous female voice inquired.

"Police, ma'am. Please open the door."

"If it's Darian you want, he's not—"

Kate heard a *click*, and in a blood-freezing instant she understood what it was and that it came from behind her.

Adrenaline kicked in sky-high, but the next events seemed to advance one by one, like frames of a film. Whirling to the sound, at the same time shoving aside Perez, who stood between her and the sound. Snapping open her holster, the restriction of the vest, grasping her .38, ripping the gun from its holster.

Imprinted on her vision as if illuminated by spotlight: glassy blue eyes staring out between dark, greasy strands of hair over a pale forehead. A white shirt so pristine that Crockett must have just donned it. Jeans with a huge silver buckle. New, white jogging shoes adorned with a bright red Nike swoosh. The gun in his left hand silver, toylike.

From somewhere a shout of *"Police!"* An exploding string of firecrackers *splat! splat! splat! splat!* filling the hallway.

"Fuck!"

"Jesus Christ!"

A scream.

Crockett flying backward, his white shirt blossoming with red flowers, Nikes lifting off the floor, plaster raining down as his gun spewed fire into the ceiling, his greasy hair flying forward and his head flung backward as if it would detach from his shoulders.

Her shoulder erupting with pain, the impact of the bullet so forceful that she spun in a full circle to once again face Crockett before the *whump* of his body as he crash-landed onto the hallway floor.

The strength in her legs vaporizing, the floor coming up at her before she could hope to extend her gun hand to brace herself, the dark floor mottled and coated with some sort of sticky fluid as her face struck it . . .

An instant of silence echoed in her ears like thunder.

"Shit, shit, fucking shit—" Hansen.

"Kate! Oh my God, Kate!" Torrie.

Torrie on her knees beside her, her face filled with such fear that Kate for the first time felt her heart accelerate with alarm at the possible extent of her injury.

A dimming of her senses that was not a drift into unconsciousness but a less distinct awareness of her surroundings. The search for strength in her legs produced nothing more than a twitch, and more alarm: her legs seemed unhurt but she had no hope of getting up. Was she paralyzed? Focusing her willpower into her right arm, she pushed herself over onto her back. Found her voice. "What—"

"Kate, don't, easy, don't try to move—"

She managed to move her head to see the rapidly darkening stain on the left side of her tan jacket. How bad am I hit? she wondered. And then: Aimee will have a fit.

She could scarcely make out Torrie's face, but saw that she was unhurt. "Anybody else . . . hit?"

"We're all okay." Torrie said urgently, "Don't move. You'll be fine, Kate."

The crackling static of a police radio: "... officer *down*, do you copy?" Perez's voice was filled with such rage that Kate scarcely recognized it. From somewhere the piercing wail of a female voice. Doors opening. Screams, male and female. More male voices, shouting orders.

"Crockett," she uttered.

"Motherfucker bought it good." The savage growl from somewhere above her, from Hansen.

She closed her eyes. She felt no satisfaction. Only deep, heavy pressure in her shoulder.

Sirens screamed in an onrushing chorus. More commotion in the hallway, shouted orders from Hansen.

When the smooth-faced young African-American man knelt beside her, Kate realized that she had passed out, lost track of time. "You're gonna be okay," he said with soft huskiness. She recognized the dark blue uniform shirt: a paramedic. His partner, small and blond, efficiently cut fabric away with angled scissors, packed a pressure bandage into her shoulder.

"Looks to be a flesh wound," she said to her partner as she worked.

Despite herself, Kate grinned at the woman paramedic, who grinned back and nodded reassuringly. Torrie said in a relieved voice, "Can't be all that bad if you're smiling, Kate."

"A flesh wound," she managed after sucking in a breath; pain had kicked in full force with Torrie's words, searing agony that seemed to intensify with every beat of her heart. "When I was a kid . . . it's what they said about wounded good guys . . . in every western I ever saw." But she could easily be dead, Crockett could as easily have killed her. . . .

"We'll take good care of you," the male paramedic said. "Start an IV to help you with that pain."

"The pain doesn't need any help," Kate joked through gritted teeth. She would be okay. She was alive.

"Torrie," she said.

"Right here, Kate," Torrie answered from beside the woman paramedic.

"Tell Aimee. You tell her. No one else. Tell her I'm okay."

"You got it. I'm staying with you. I'm staying right here with you."

"Get everybody out of here, the scene needs to be protected. Secure the area. Call Robbery-Homicide, they'll be taking—"

"I think I can handle all that, Kate." A masculine voice from above her.

"Lieutenant," she uttered, shocked to see the broad-shouldered figure of Mike Bodwin looming above her.

He hunkered down beside the male paramedic. She rarely saw Bodwin in such casual clothes—jeans and a faded blue polo shirt under a short jean jacket; he must have picked up the radio call and responded immediately. "They tell me you're gonna be okay." His eyes were narrowed in concern in his acne-scarred face, but his voice held an easy warmth. "Don't worry about anything, Kate. Just take care of yourself. You'll get all the time you need to come out of this good as new."

I'll never be as good as new, she thought, never. She would be a symbol of every cop's nightmare, a cop who got shot. . . . And her next stop in all this was the Officer Involved Shooting team from Parker Center.

She was lifted onto a stretcher. Carried downstairs, blue uniforms and sympathetic faces all around her, lining the entire path, some of them calling encouragement. Outside, the dark, cold street had become brilliant with flashing light bars on black-and-whites, and was filled as far as she could see with blue uniforms. My God, my whole family's here, she thought, tears leaking from her eyes. My whole police family is here.

Loaded into the paramedic unit. Torrie climbing in with her, pulling a mobile phone from her shoulder bag as she sat on the bench beside Kate's stretcher. As the doors slammed closed and the siren opened up, pain declared a temporary truce, and Kate drifted into blackness.

2

"THE date is February 5, 1996. Present at the Wilshire Division station are Detectives Wayne McMillan and Jim Phillips, to conduct an interview of Detective Kate Delafield. Detective Delafield has waived her right to the presence of a Police Union representative. Would you confirm that that is correct, Detective?"

"That's correct," Kate replied.

The three detectives were isolated in the office of Lieutenant Bodwin, who had extended this courtesy for the purpose of the interview. On the table before Mc-Millan lay a stack of files and a tape recorder, its reels moving. They had arrived here from the crime scene on Gramercy, where Kate had quickly led them through the shooting of Darian Crockett.

McMillan said, "Detective, we'd like you to mark on this sketch of the second floor exactly where everyone was in the hallway as Crockett came out of that apartment."

Kate nodded assent to the square-faced, husky blond who addressed her from across the small, round table. To his right, his partner on the Officer Involved Shooting team from Robbery-Homicide at Parker Center sat attentively forward in his vinyl-backed chair. He was considerably shorter than McMillan, a skullcap of black fur lacquering his bulletlike head under the office lights.

With the fleeting thought that McMillan and Phillips's dark gray suits, blue shirts, and dark ties were similar enough to be considered uniforms, Kate stationed her otherwise useless left arm to steady the sketch on the table and diagrammed with her pen. The two men held notebooks propped against their crossed knees as they watched her; she had neither notes nor notebook to rely on. "Just tell it like you remember it," Phillips told her.

Remember it she did. The events from the night of February 1—four days ago—held for her the vividness of photographs.

Pointing with her pen to two of the boxes she had inked on the sketch, Kate told McMillan, "Sergeant Hansen was here, to the left of the door to apartment nine, my partner, Detective Holden, to the right. I was just behind Hansen, right here." She pointed to a third box, placed her initials within it. And a fourth: "Officer Perez was here. Do you want the location of the backup unit?"

McMillan's square-jawed face was impassive as he asked, "Did you actually see them in place?"

"The backup unit was in direct communication with Hansen."

"We want to know only what you actually witnessed and what you actually did," Phillips said.

Perfectly polite, she thought, but the two of them could deflect a heat-seeking missile.

"So all of you were in your assigned places," McMillan said. "Correct?"

"Correct."

Phillips asked, "In retrospect, was there anything to warn you that this arrest would be anything out of the ordinary?"

"No. We picked up Simms on a stakeout. But Crockett wasn't a high-risk warrant. His sheet was all drug possession, not sales. The arrest looked to be routine. Still, it was orchestrated, tamped-down. Tactical."

"So what happened next?" McMillan asked.

"Before we could act on the warrant, a woman came out of apartment twelve. Officer Perez asked her to step back inside her apartment; she complied.''

Phillips flipped back pages in his notebook. "That would be the charming and lovely Mrs. Corsella. Go on.''

"We approached the subject's apartment, number nine. Sergeant Hansen knocked, received a verbal response, and identified himself as police. Then,'' she continued somberly, "as you know, the subject came out of apartment seven. From behind us.''

"Why wasn't a uniform stationed at the entry to the hallway?''

Kate was astonished. "You mean an officer wasn't there?''

"You tell us, Detective.''

"Someone was there,'' she asserted. "When Hansen told me everything was set up to go, then everything was set up right.''

"No shots were fired from that area.''

"The officer probably took cover—I don't know. Look,'' she said doggedly, "I've worked with Fred Hansen for years. He knows the routine. His tactics are very, very good.''

"Meaning that nothing like this had happened before.''

Don't be defensive, she told herself. She answered evenly, "Meaning that it was tactically sound.''

"Detective Delafield, did you actually see an officer behind Detective Holden and the suspect? Can you name that person?''

Kate bowed her head to concentrate. In the melee had she seen anyone, anything, any motion, in the hallway door behind Crockett? Just as importantly—and in all objectivity—had the circumstances of this case led her to assume anything, take anything for granted? She remembered thinking, outside the apartment building on Gramercy, that this arrest should be routine. Crockett would be unaware he'd been linked through Willie Simms to a crime that had no witnesses. Even though a print had been lifted from the glass counter and traced through AFIS to career criminal Simms, by itself it was insufficient proof; any defense attorney would argue that Simms could have left the print prior to the holdup. And so two full months had elapsed since the holdup at Pete's Liquors, the delay caused by the FBI's Special Photography Unit, which nonetheless had produced results more quickly than an overloaded L.A. crime lab could have, had the equipment even existed at Piper Tech for anyone to perform the necessary work.

Simms had blasted the liquor store's surveillance camera after first blowing away the victim who had made the mistake of removing a .38 instead of money from the cash register drawer. But bad luck for Simms too, and now for Crockett, the driver of the getaway car: Simms' shot had destroyed the camera and singed the film, but Kate had sent it to the FBI lab. The lab had managed to reconstruct four usable frames from the tape and had computer-enhanced one to produce an identifiable image of Simms, whose white 'do rag had framed his face perfectly as he looked straight into the camera, .32 in hand. As part of a plea bargain down from murder one with special circumstances, which carried the death penalty, Simms had fingered Crockett.

"I can't tell you that I saw an officer there," she said to McMillan. "But I know Hansen, and so I know an officer was there." She was not about to use the all-time cliché that she didn't notice everything because it all happened so fast.

McMillan said with something close to sympathy, "Everything happened pretty fast, didn't it."

Kate could not prevent a smile. "It did."

"Then what, Detective?"

She quickly sobered. "I heard a click. I knew the cocking sound had to be a gun. I turned, saw the suspect. All hell broke loose."

"How did you know the click didn't come from the police officer you claim was outside the hallway door?"

"I just knew."

"Did you hear the door to apartment seven open?"

"No. It's a front apartment. Crockett must have seen us on the street. He must have eased it open thinking he could sneak out or—well, God knows what he thought."

"How did he know you were police?"

"We wore raid jackets."

"Did you have your raid jackets on before you entered the building?"

"We put them on just inside the building." Then she remembered: "When Crockett came out, one of us even shouted, 'Police!' "

"Which one?"

"I don't know—one of us."

"Was the voice male or female?"

She remembered. "Male. It must have been Hansen."

McMillan nodded, checked something off in his notebook. "Who fired first?"

"I don't know. I don't know why it matters."

McMillan sat back, crossed his arms. "You don't? Why?"

She said with quiet force, "I know an investigation is required. I don't mean to seem . . . in this particular case, what's to explain? The suspect had a gun, he opened fire. It wasn't up to us to introduce ourselves to someone with a gun, to wait until he shot one of us, even though that's what happened."

Phillips said, "You did not fire your gun, Detective."

She focused on the tape recorder. "No, I did not."

"You didn't get a chance to get off a shot—correct?"

Poor questioning technique for someone from the elite Robbery-Homicide Division, she thought. Especially for so crucial a part of their investigation. But all to her benefit. "Yes." Technically, that was true.

"You had your gun in your hand. You fell on it."

"Correct."

"We'll come back to that," McMillan said.

His eyes, she thought, were so ice blue you could skate

on them. Phillips, even with his skinhead haircut, seemed diminished by his partner.

McMillan asked, "What do you remember about being shot?"

"It hurt," she said with a smile. "It was one hot slug. I did a complete three-sixty." She touched the healing bruise on her cheek. "Broke my fall with my face."

McMillan asked slowly, "In your opinion, how did the officers under your command conduct themselves?"

"In exemplary fashion," she said promptly. She added, "There are always things you think of after the fact that you could have done better."

"Such as?"

"I'm not in any position to make those judgments, I was out of it too fast, but there's always something you can critique. I'm sure Detective Holden and Sergeant Hansen have their opinions."

"You were damn lucky," said Phillips.

"You're damn right," Kate agreed fervently. "They tell me a quarter-inch difference in trajectory and I could have a shattered bone or permanent nerve damage."

McMillan offered, "You weren't so out of it that you couldn't issue orders."

His smile was too scant to really qualify, Kate thought, but at least it was an attempt, and so she smiled back. "If I was conscious, if I could function at all, the scene was my responsibility. And it was now a homicide scene. But I had a lot of help—Lieutenant Bodwin arrived."

McMillan indicated the sketch. "Now show us where Crockett was when the shooting started."

"Right here." She drew a fifth box in the hallway.

"Detective, on the sketch you show Officer Perez between you and the subject. But you were shot, not Officer Perez."

Kate braced herself. "I shoved her out of the way." She assumed that Perez and others had also told the truth of what had happened.

Phillips nodded. "Okay. Why?"

"Pure instinct," she said.

"Trying to be a hero?" Phillips suggested.

"Not hardly. I wasn't trying to be anything. The whole thing was over in seconds. Whatever I did, I did by instinct."

"Detective Delafield." McMillan raised a pale blond eyebrow. "What kind of instinct would lead you to shove another armed police officer out of the way?"

Kate spread her hands. "It was unconscious. I didn't know if she'd heard that click. She's new to the Division—"

"Detective, she's been in patrol at Central, at Newton—she's been on the street seven years, she was caught in the riot, in that firefight on Normandie—"

Kate was nodding as he spoke. "I know all that. And I was never in patrol, if that's what you're driving at." She looked pointedly at the files that sat in front of McMillan. "As you know, I was promoted to the detective ranks out of Juvenile."

"So why use the excuse that she was new?"

"I'm not using any excuse," she said heatedly. "She was new to *me*. I work with a detective partner, we know each other's judgment and reaction levels. In that instant, all I knew was that I didn't know hers."

"She's an Academy-trained police officer, she's—" Phillips began, then asked, "Were you trying to be chivalrous?"

"Was I trying to be *what*?" She told him with undisguised contempt, "That's ludicrous."

He said, almost idly, "The fact of the matter is, three of the four police officers involved in this shooting are women."

"Meaning exactly what?"

Phillips said with a bland smile, "I was simply stating the obvious."

Baiting me, the turd. She struggled to control her ire at Phillips and at herself for falling into such an easy trap.

McMillan had been writing in his notebook. "But you knew your own reaction level," he said to Kate, as if he hadn't heard the exchange between her and Phillips.

"I knew my own," she said.

"Do you think shoving Officer Perez aside cost you a shot?"

"No, I don't."

Because at that point she was still yanking her gun from its holster. A fact known only to herself—and to a dead man. Hansen and Torrie had been in front of her, their attention focused on the door to apartment nine. Perez had been in no position to observe much of anything. She had been behind Kate, and then Kate had turned and flung her aside.

"But you didn't fire," McMillan said.

"I didn't have to, as it turned out."

"But you did draw your weapon."

"You know very well that I did." But only as she was confronting Crockett . . .

"No one drew it for you, after the fact?"

"Is that a serious question?"

"Answer it, Detective."

"No."

"Did Detective Holden have her gun in her hand?"

"Yes."

"That's not what she told us."

"My recollection is that she had her hand in her shoulder bag where she carried her gun."

"Detective, that's not the same thing as having her gun in her hand."

"You're right. It's not. She did not have her gun drawn." Of course it wasn't the same thing. Having to yank a gun out of a shoulder bag took just that extra split second. As did having to pull one out of a shoulder holster.

"Did you do the same thing—have your hand on your gun in your shoulder bag?"

"No, I did not."

At one point she'd indeed had her hand in her shoulder bag, on the arrest warrant. But she had nothing more to say to these two detectives. She should have had her gun drawn when Torrie knocked on that door. She'd taken a bullet for her lapse; she deserved to. The situation could have turned out much worse; she was grateful it had not. She'd paid dearly enough. She wasn't about to let herself be pilloried in the public square because these two men thought it was a good idea.

"Why are you trying to cover for Detective Holden?"

She said emphatically, "I wouldn't do that, and she doesn't need me to. She did have her hand on her gun—it's all just semantics."

McMillan said, "I hope you're not shading any of your other answers with what you justify as semantics."

She stared at him in open animosity. He held her stare. She had conducted hundreds of interviews and interrogations during her career, had withstood the most abusive cross-examinations from defense attorneys in court proceedings. Never had she dreamed that she would be on the receiving end of so hostile a grilling from her own people. She said, "I'm a police officer—"

"A man is dead from police bullets," McMillan countered sharply. "Police officers aren't exempt from tough questions, and under no circumstances should they be. They should be questioned more thoroughly than any civilian."

"You're right," she conceded, a thread of respect for him glimmering though her antipathy.

Phillips said with a half-smile, "It's hard for anyone to contend with criticism, Detective, real or implied."

"Something doesn't add up in all this," McMillan said.

Kate shook her head. "If I may say so, I can't figure out where you're coming from." She looked at the tape recorder, then pushed on. "Granted, you have to thoroughly investigate any officer-involved shooting. But this is cut and dried."

"Okay," McMillan said reasonably. "You've had a few days to think about it, you tell us how cut and dried it is."

She pointed to the sketch. "We were all in place, with a properly executed warrant. Sergeant Hansen sought entrance to apartment nine. The subject came out of apartment seven, behind us. A cousin lived in that apartment. We had no way of knowing that. Crockett had a gun, he cocked it, I heard it. I turned to him, he shot me in the shoulder, Hansen and Torrie Holden shot Crockett."

McMillan did not change expression. "As such things go, do you think this was a good shooting?"

Kate sighed, looked down at her useless left arm. "Darian Crockett was seventeen years old."

"Exactly seventeen," Phillips said. "It was his birthday. The white shirt he wore was a gift from his mother."

His words had been spoken paternally, with an overtone of sadness. Kate looked at him to see that he wore a wedding band.

"Answer the question, Detective," McMillan said. "Was this a good shooting?"

McMillan also wore a wedding band, Kate noted. She wondered what kind of woman would marry so robotic a man, and if he had any children. She said, "It was in policy. Crockett fired his weapon at us. As such things go, and if anything could be called a good shooting, I guess this one could."

"What if we told you that Crockett wasn't the one who shot you?"

She sat perfectly still.

"The hit in your shoulder was through and through. The emergency room doctor told us the entrance wound was at the back, exit wound in the front. Holden, Hansen, and Perez support your account that they were all behind you when you faced the subject. You were hit by friendly fire.''

She was stunned. It had never occurred to her to question any of her doctors about the physiognomy of her wound. ''You're telling me that Fred Hansen or Torrie Holden shot me.''

''Or Alicia Perez. Despite your action against her, she also fired her weapon.''

''Do they know about this?''

''Of course they know. They're a little anxious about how you'll react now that *you* know. So,'' McMillan asked in a passable imitation of James Cagney, ''you gonna take revenge?''

''They're dead meat,'' Kate said in matching vein.

McMillan's appreciative chuckle was low and oddly attractive.

She was still trying to harness her emotions. ''Who—''

''We don't know who shot you yet. We dug slugs out all over that hallway. We're still running tests. All three officers fired nines. Crockett's weapon was a .38, like yours.''

''I'm old-fashioned, I guess,'' Kate muttered. The Smith & Wesson had always been her only gun; she had resisted the department-wide rush to greater firepower to compete with the arsenal that was out on the street. She said slowly, ''I don't know why I'm surprised. I don't know why I hadn't considered the possibility . . . I guess you always figure it's the bad guy. Being shot by your own people, you just . . . But still . . . I was in the line of fire.''

McMillan leaned forward. ''Given this information, are you clear in your own mind that it was an accident?''

She sat back in her chair. ''Are you serious? Are you implying that one of my own people took an opportunity to settle a score?''

''A fragging, you Vietnam vets would call it,'' Phillips said, drumming his blunt fingers on the table until Mc-

Millan frowned and inclined his head toward the tape recorder.

"I feel reasonably confident it wasn't a fragging," Kate said dryly.

"You never know," McMillan said. "Everybody has enemies."

Yours would line up around the block twice, she thought. No one from OIS would ever win a popularity contest.

McMillan asked, "How do you feel now toward your partner? Not to mention Hansen and Perez?"

"I wish one of them had been a better shot," Kate said.

McMillan again gave her his chuckle. He tapped the top file in the stack in front of him. "Fourteen years in homicide, hardly any paper on you. Lots of commendations."

McMillan seemed to appreciate deadpan, so she tried more of it. "I'm just your friendly garden-variety homicide detective."

But McMillan did not react to it. He leaned forward and shut off the tape recorder. "You're damn lucky. They've finally stopped calling us out every goddamn time a cop pulls the trigger, even if nobody gets hit. IAD's still up to their asses in bullshit complaints. Everybody's getting them these days."

Kate nodded. Civilian complaints had escalated against patrol officers and the detectives on all the tables. In these days of continuing damage control post–Rodney King, post–O. J. Simpson, the embattled LAPD was particularly sensitive to complaints against its officers and Internal Affairs investigated the most frivolous allegation. Some people were using the complaint process as a weapon of revenge against law enforcement. The record of an investigation in an officer's file, even if he or she was cleared, meant some trace of the mud would remain.

Phillips said, "You've never even had a stress leave."

"You know what a picnic it is for homicide cops," she offered. What did he expect her to say? Her shoulder was beginning to hurt.

"Yeah, you should hear the guys in Robbery-Homicide these days," McMillan muttered.

Kate did not pursue the comment, she did not need to. It was common knowledge that after the savaging administered at the O. J. Simpson trial by defense attorneys on the case detectives, morale had hit rock bottom among LAPD's elite homicide unit at Parker Center.

Phillips turned the tape recorder on again. "You've been a cop a lot of years not to have a stress leave," he said.

And there I was, she thought caustically, one of the three obviously inferior women involved in the shooting on Gramercy.

"The streets are a dangerous place these days," Phillips said.

The remark did not merit a reply. And her shoulder had begun to hurt in earnest, and she would die before she took a pain pill in front of these two men.

"You seem to be turning defensive, Detective."

"Of course the streets are dangerous," she snapped. "Do you think I spend my days inside my desk drawer?"

"Just stating the obvious, Detective."

"You seem to make a habit of it."

Smiling, McMillan picked up a file, opened it, wrote in it. "BSS will provide a further evaluation on you."

"Meaning what?" she demanded. "What are you trying to do to me?"

"Trying to take care of you, Detective. Thank you for your time. You're to continue on paid administrative leave."

"For how long?"

He looked at her blandly. "Till you're cleared to return to duty."

McMillan switched off the recorder and got up from

the table. Phillips scrambled up after him, hastily gathering the files.

Kate remained sitting at the table as McMillan and Phillips left the office.

Her next stop was the Behavioral Sciences Service Section for psychological counseling. Shit, she thought, a shrink.

3

THE therapist, an African-American woman, rose to an imposing height behind her desk and strode out to greet Kate. "I'm Dr. Calla Dearborn. Feel free to call me Calla. Should I call you Kate? What do you prefer to be called?"

Kate uttered a perfunctory "Kate will be fine," shared a firm handshake, then glanced around the office for a moment to adjust her expectations. She had been certain that the therapist would be, as she had informed Aimee, "some skinny little touchy-feely twit."

The office was an admirably aesthetic composition of blues and dark browns accomplished on a low budget. The walnut-veneer desk and credenza matched the file cabinet, coffee table, and end table; the blue sofa matched two armchairs upholstered in a basket-weave fabric; a tall, healthy ficus in a white ceramic pot rested on a brown-flecked Berber-style carpet beside a window looking out over nondescript downtown rooftops and drab building facades. Other than a large gray-blue abstract watercolor and a half dozen diplomas and certificates of achievement hanging on the wall behind the desk, there was scant evidence of anything personal to reflect the occupant of this room.

"Sit wherever you like, Kate."

Wondering whether the woman expected her to stretch out confessionally on the couch, Kate unhooked the shoulder bag from her immobilized left shoulder and slung it into a corner of the sofa, then pulled one of the wheeled armchairs closer to the desk and sat down. Noticing a few dark scuffs on the desk's legs, she wondered if they might be kick marks.

Calla Dearborn settled into her tall-backed chair, opened a black leather binder to a lined yellow pad, and said, "To begin with, I need to give you some general information about why you're here and what you can expect from our time together."

Kate nodded. The single piece of information she wanted to know was how long she would need to endure this business.

"Of course I've heard about what occurred. If you're like most police officers, you don't want to be here—and you may be one of those people who recover quickly from a traumatic event. But we've learned from considerable experience with other police officers that stress after a traumatic event is very common, has many levels and symptoms, and may be considerably delayed in its reaction. So it's important for you to talk about the event as soon as possible to identify and understand your own reactions. On the job, you're the expert in physical tactics, and what we hope to do here is to equip you with some emotional tactics so you won't be derailed if you happen to have a delayed reaction somewhere down the line."

Kate nodded. She was hardly a novice in the trauma department. And, from the many interviews she had conducted, the psychology department either.

Dearborn continued, "Some reactions may be physical—and anything you experience physically is a normal reaction to what happened to you. Everything from nausea and diarrhea to sleep disturbance and fatigue to getting the shakes. You may feel a need to eat more, drink more. Any of those things—they're normal." She looked expectantly at Kate.

"I haven't had anything like that," Kate said. *And I wouldn't tell you if I did.*

"I'm not here to evaluate your job performance in any way," Dearborn assured her. "I have nothing to do with that. At the end of our time together I'm required to give feedback by phone to your captain. So our sessions are not fully confidential in just that one respect. But I promise you, whatever I tell him will be brief, no more than a sentence or two, and what I say to him I'll say to you first, so we can discuss it as much as you wish. You needn't worry about being told one thing in this office and having your captain be told something else. After I give my verbal report, if you elect to continue therapy with me, our ensuing sessions will have complete confidentiality."

Nodding, Kate thought, The day I elect therapy will be the day there's a snowball fight in hell.

As Dearborn picked up a slender, green malachite roller ball pen and made a note, Kate studied her. A two-inch nimbus of dark hair with frosty hints of gray framed a face neutral and composed, giving away nothing beyond the surface detail of its features. She was at least three inches taller than Kate, and younger, late thirties maybe, although that was hard to gauge. Her mature, solidly padded figure was clad in a simple, well-fitted toffee-colored two-piece dress with a thin gold chain at the throat. The left hand holding the malachite pen bore a wedding band and a modest diamond engagement ring.

Kate said, disarmingly, she hoped, "My only physical complaint is my shoulder."

"How's your shoulder doing now?"

"Good," Kate said heartily, not wanting this woman to use physical impairment as any excuse to keep her off duty. "In good shape. I was lucky. They tell me I'll be as good as new."

"I'm glad to hear it. Other reactions can be cognitive: absent-mindedness, having trouble concentrating, preoccupation with what happened, flashbacks, feeling vulnerable, being acutely aware of and suspicious of your surroundings—"

Kate shook her head. "No. None of those things."

"Any bad dreams, Kate?"

"So far I'm sleeping just fine."

"I'm glad you said 'so far.' An officer-involved shooting is especially rough. For some police officers, it can be like they've been hit by a train. A friendly fire incident makes you a special concern—"

"It was bad luck." *And damn stupidity by whoever shot me.* "An accident that happened in seconds. I understand that," she said. "I accept it." *Except for the fact that it's put me in this room with you.*

"Intellectually, I'm sure you accept it. But you can still experience an entire range of emotions: grief, numbness, anxiety, a more intense emotional reaction to what's going on in your life . . ." She paused, looking at Kate over her steel-rimmed glasses.

"You're right—what happened was hard," Kate said cautiously. She did not want her to think she was an emotional robot. "But I seem to be dealing with it okay."

"Some behavioral reactions can be subtle. Withdrawal. Or the opposite extreme—making light of what happened, being more hyper than usual. Outbursts of anger . . ."

Kate shook her head. "Nothing like that so far."

"Kate, it's important that you understand this: You're not here because of anything you did wrong. Any reaction you have to what happened is neither bad nor wrong. Any reaction you might have is a *normal* reaction to an *abnormal* event. Do you hear what I'm saying?"

"I hear you." Calla Dearborn's tactics were nicely polished, Kate thought. Similar to an experienced detective establishing rapport with a suspect in an interview room.

"I'd like you to tell me about the incident," Dearborn said.

The incident. A flashfire of offense enveloping her,

Kate tried to keep her anger out of her voice. "I'm sure you know all about it. It was all over the papers."

Dearborn looked at her sharply. "Of course it was, complete with photos. But only you know what happened, and I'd like to hear your own words about what you saw and heard."

Kate sat resignedly back in her chair and related what had happened in the hallway on Gramercy, her recital identical to the one she had given that morning to McMillan and Phillips.

Dearborn listened in a stillness of attention, then made a note, saying, "We'll come back to what happened. How long have you been a homicide detective?"

"Fourteen years," Kate replied and extracted a business card from a Lucite holder on the desk and glanced at it:

> *Calla Dearborn, Ph.D.*
> *Licensed Psychologist*
> *Lic. # PSY 705536*
> *Se Habla Espanol*

She slipped the card into her jacket pocket. Now that Calla Dearborn, Ph.D., had gone over the ground rules and the basic facts of the shooting, she was choosing questions to which she knew the answers from Kate's service record, indicating she probably followed a routine road map toward issuing a clean bill of mental health. It was already evident that there would be an inquisition to withstand, an outrageous violation of privacy.

"A rhetorical question," the psychologist said, "but you have to start somewhere. Fourteen years is a long time to be in a division like homicide."

Kate did not reply.

Amusement touched Calla Dearborn's dark eyes. "Experienced police officers—you're so used to testifying in court, you always give the most minimal responses. How many death scenes would you say you've been at in those fourteen years?"

How many police officers have you force-marched over the coals during your career? she wanted to retort. She said, "I don't know."

"Dozens?"

Kate shrugged. "Obviously." She hated this. Hated it.

"Hundreds?"

"Over that period of time there would be more than a hundred."

"As many as two hundred?"

She struggled with her irritation. "I don't know."

"You don't know, Kate, or you don't want to say?"

"I do know. I just don't see that it's useful to add them up."

The psychologist made so brief a note on her yellow pad that Kate assumed she used shorthand. She said, "Or you simply don't want to."

"Would you?"

"Would you mind answering the question?"

Yes I would. Do I have a choice? "To add them up is to remember them."

"Why don't you want to do that?"

God, how she hated this. It was even worse than she expected. She said to the psychologist, "Would you mind telling me how long this business will take?"

Calla Dearborn glanced at her watch. "Another thirty-five minutes. For this session."

Gaining a measure of control over her temper, Kate said evenly, "I mean all told."

"When can you get back to work? Your captain is eager to have you back, as you can imagine. I have absolutely no investment in keeping you off the job, Kate, but we have a number of issues to cover, especially in an officer-involved shooting. So we'll play it one session at a time. Each session will determine what happens in the next."

Kate looked at her then, sizing her up as she would a hostile subject in an interview room.

The features, she grudgingly conceded, were interesting. High forehead, smooth almond skin warming to pink-brown on the cheeks and on the broad nose, darkening in a fold of skin on the eyelids and in faint delineations that would someday deepen to permanent creases around the mouth. Wide, full lips, slightly deepened in color by pale plum lipstick. Eyebrows as if a fingertip had traced a scarcely visible arch so that the widely spaced, sable-brown eyes, flecked with green and framed by steel-rimmed glasses, dominated the face with their intelligence.

The psychologist calmly watched Kate's scrutiny of her. "You don't like answering questions."

"Let's just say I'm used to asking them."

"You don't like answering questions," the psychologist repeated, "and you don't like to talk about your work."

"Neither supposition is exactly true," Kate said mildly.

Calla Dearborn smiled, a tiny dimple emerging in her right cheek. "Whom do you talk to about your work?"

"A great number of people. My partner. Other police officers. Assistant DAs . . . lab technicians . . . relatives of victims . . ."

"Of course. Who in your personal life?"

Kate gritted her teeth. This was the worst invasion, and the worst thing about it was that she did not know if or how the answers she gave might damage her. She shrugged as she answered, "Lots of people."

"Your parents?"

"They're deceased."

"Both of them? When?"

"Years ago. My mother in sixty-three, father in seventy-seven."

Calla Dearborn shook her head. "You lost them so

young. You've never been married—what about a significant other? A partner?''

"What about it?''

"Do you have one?''

Kate tensed. "Yes.''

"And you bring the job home, you talk about it.''

The tension eased. "Some of it. The good parts. Well, let's say not the worst parts.''

"What about friends? Do you share your work with friends?''

"Some of it.'' Maggie Schaeffer and a few regulars at the Nightwood Bar were pretty nonchalant about her job, thanks to shared history—although after all these years the emotion-charged investigation of Dory Quillin's death in the parking lot behind the lesbian bar was more lore than history. But the friends Aimee brought home were something else. Young women from another generation, staring at her as if she were a fascinating fossil. Their diffident questions about her work were probes for stories with horror movie details, and she was sure that outside her presence they accorded the same mockery to her and her freakish occupation as they would to a mortician.

Calla Dearborn finished a note and asked, "How come?''

"How come what?'' She had lost Dearborn's question in all her woolgathering.

"What are your friends for? Why not share all the tragedy of what you see with friends who care about you—not to mention a significant other?''

"My job isn't anything anyone would thank me for sharing.''

"I'm sure they'd tell you differently.''

"I'm sure they would. But they only think they want to know.''

"What makes you so sure about that?''

The woman was being intentionally obtuse. Surely she had heard the same answers from cop after cop. Kate said, "Two weeks ago I caught an accident scene. Hit and run, an old woman on Hauser and Eighth—maybe you read about it."

The psychologist, brow knitted, slowly shook her head.

You probably *did* read about it, Kate thought. Scanned the few lines about Vera Cowley in your *L.A. Times* and then put it out of your mind the same way everybody clucked over and then forgot atrocities that did not directly affect their lives.

Kate had to reach inside herself as she related, "The van hit the victim at a speed of approximately sixty miles an hour and flung her forty-seven feet. You may know that the body liquefies when it's hit with that kind of force. Every bone in her body was smashed: arms, legs, spine, shoulders, hips. Her skin was nothing but a purple-black sack filled with bone shreds and blood. Her face was shredded completely away by the pavement, her skull pulverized like a dropped egg."

Calla Dearborn looked gratifyingly disconcerted.

Kate said, "You're saying I should bring this home to friends and family."

Her dark eyes fixed on Kate, the psychologist said softly, "That's a very hard thing for you to have to see, Kate."

"It's what I'm paid to do."

"You're paid to do a very difficult job. But the expectation that you need to carry such . . . horrific things alone . . ."

She did not continue, and Kate did not respond. What was there to say? Everyone edited their lives, everyone. What she chose to edit was hers to factor, no one else's.

Her face again expressionless, Calla Dearborn made another brief note. "So are you close to any of your professional colleagues?"

"I have a friendly relationship with most of them."

"Do you socialize?"

"LAPD has all kinds of activities. Athletic leagues— everything from running to baseball."

"Do you participate?"

Making an attempt at lightness, Kate pointed to her immobilized arm. "Not at the moment."

Rewarded with an indulgent smile, Kate muttered, "Those are young people's activities."

"Do I take that as a no?"

"Not an entire no. I like to swim; I should do it more often."

"Swimming is a solitary sport," Calla Dearborn commented, turning her pen in her fingers as she contemplated Kate.

Kate said in irritation, "Sometimes I attend an interDivisional baseball game"—Torrie had dragged her to the last one—"have a beer with everyone afterward. Socializing is a little harder these days under the new regime."

"You mean Chief Williams?"

"No—well, indirectly. I meant the pilot program, the new hours."

"Oh yes, you're one of the four Divisions on it. How's it going over?"

"Patrol officers like it—all that time off. Except for the equipment shortages when we have to call extra officers in on a shift."

The new sixteen-month pilot program required patrol officers to work three twelve-hour days followed by four days off—an attempt to cut sick days, overtime costs that were draining the city budget, and most of all, to improve morale after the recent high-profile trials. New officers were being hired on a crash basis, but the Police Academy graduates had not kept pace with "the blue angst"—more and more police at all levels opting out of an organization where morale had sunk lower than the Dead Sea.

Kate added, "Detectives work four ten-hour days instead of three, but they bitch all the time over losing continuity with their cases." Not to mention overtime. Many officers and detectives had factored their overtime checks as a permanent part of their salary structure and standard of living. Ten- or twelve-hour days could throw a monkey wrench into locating part-time work to compensate for overtime loss.

"Do you like the new hours?"

"They don't affect homicide much—we need to work what we need to work." Her rank as a D-3 gave her complete flexibility. But she was already unhappy at losing continuity with her caseload.

Dearborn asked, "Would you say you're a competitive person?"

Struck by the question, Kate reflected over it. "I think mostly with myself. With my own expectations."

"What's your home situation, Detective?"

Kate stirred in her chair, aware of a vague pain in her shoulder. God, she hated this. She said, "Will that information leave here?"

"I explained about giving a brief statement to your captain. Otherwise, what's said in this room stays in this room."

"Am I being recorded?"

"Absolutely not." Clearly offended by the question, Calla Dearborn said, "Kate, I'm no more eager to protract this than you are. The department needs you, and I have plenty of claims on my time."

Kate knew that Calla Dearborn's Behavioral Sciences Service Section was also hiring more psychologists to handle all the stressed-out officers. She gestured to the leather binder lying open on the desk. "What happens to your notes, your file?"

"They're for my own use. I guarantee you confidentiality."

This whole business should be perfunctory, Kate thought angrily. Other officers involved in shootings did a quick visit to a psychologist and were right back on the job. Torrie was back, so were Hansen and Perez. She hadn't done anything wrong, a goddamn stray bullet from her own people had landed her here. But as sure as she sat here in this office, her badge and gun were at stake. If she revealed anything of a nature that led this psychologist to believe she was in any degree unfit to perform, something would go in her file, and hell would freeze over before she could regain credibility with her supervisors, before she could lift the cloud of suspicion over her job and her performance.

She said, "I don't understand why I need to discuss my personal life with you."

Calla Dearborn put down her pen, spread her hands on the desk, and leaned forward. "Let me ask you a question. What outcome would you like to have from our sessions?"

"That's easy. Very simple. I want my job back."

"You haven't lost it."

"Right. It's sitting across the desk from me, tucked in your back pocket. I understand there's nothing I can do until I go through with this."

The briefest glimmer of a smile crossed Dearborn's face. "Your job is actually tucked in your own back pocket, Kate. You've been seriously injured in the line of duty. My job is to make sure that a very valuable member of our organization returns to duty with her health restored physically, and with information on how best to take care of herself in the future."

"I'm recovering physically; I've never given a reason to anyone to think I'm unhealthy mentally."

"I know you don't believe this, but at the moment you're not in the best position to judge that. Don't be in such a hurry to return to duty, Kate. A lot of officers end up wishing they'd given themselves more time. Make sure you take all the time you need."

"I assure you I'm perfectly fine about what happened to me."

"A lot of officers—too many of you—think you're perfectly fine . . ."

Calla Dearborn put down her pen and massaged her eyes, fingertips lifting her glasses as she rubbed. "Do you know how many of you have committed suicide?"

Kate swallowed her ire to answer somberly, "I've gone to many police funerals."

"Four to six of you a year."

Kate wondered if some of those four to six had been treated by Calla Dearborn. And if any of them had been gay . . .

Dearborn said tiredly, "You're killing yourselves faster than the bad guys can shoot you down on the streets. You're in one of the highest-stress professions in the world, and as for you, you work at the very highest-stress level of that profession—"

"I don't know how you can say that. I'm not in the line of fire," Kate argued. "I do make arrests, but getting shot making an arrest—that's really freakish. I don't have to walk into firefights, I don't have to answer domestic disturbance calls. I don't hear any screams, the cases I investigate have victims who are dead."

"Right, all you have to do is look at dead bodies like the one you just described. All you have to do is deal with people in agony—parents, wives, husbands, children—"

To Kate's relief, Calla Dearborn's phone buzzed. With an expression of irritation she snatched it up, listened intently, and said. "I understand. Two minutes."

She hung up and said softly to Kate, "I'm afraid I have to cut this session short. I'm truly sorry, but it's unavoidable."

"It's okay. I assume it's somebody who really needs your help."

Dearborn closed her leather binder and said firmly, "Kate, get used to the fact that I won't be responsible for allowing something to happen to you that I could have prevented by giving you the time and treatment you need. I won't have you on my conscience."

"Doctor, I guarantee you I won't be on your conscience."

"Then put this in the same category as going for an annual physical checkup. All I ask is the chance to verify your own diagnosis."

"And then I can go back to work?"

"And then you can go back to work."

4

SANTA Ana winds blowing in off the desert had raised temperatures into the mid-eighties, unseasonably warm for early February, the *Los Angeles Times* had reported. Kate knew better, marking the time of year from a particularly memorable investigation in a Wilshire-area high-rise that former partner Ed Taylor had dubbed "Amateur City." Every February since then had brought the same "unseasonably warm" Santa Ana winds.

Car windows rolled down to welcome the hot, dry gusts, Kate turned off Melrose Avenue onto Kings Road. She slowed, drifting the Saturn to gaze at the profusion of trees—date palms and fan palms, silver poplars, laurels, pines—frenzied in wind that wrenched them away from shading the large condo units. The prismatic greens along this particular wide stretch of the street had been a prime factor in her agreeing with Aimee that they should buy the condo, and while the three- and four-story buildings might not be in the same league with the quietly costly edifices lining Burton Way, this street was an oasis in a city that exposed the vast majority of its structures to unsparing sun.

After nearly two years, she still found agreeable her own simply designed white stucco three-story building, its dark wood trim and large windows open to the filtered sun through the trees, its balconies artfully recessed and private, its front garden overflowing with great mounds of red, pink, and white impatiens. She pressed the remote control to open the sliding gate into the garage, reflecting that she had liked living in Glendale and Santa Monica during the years she had spent there, but the city of West Hollywood suited her like a perfectly fitted pair of gloves.

Pulling into the cavernous subterranean garage, she saw that she was not the only one home on this early afternoon of a work week: Aimee's red Ford Escort occupied one of the two parking places allotted to their condo.

Kate let herself into the apartment and went immediately into the kitchen, knowing Aimee would be there; at home, Aimee always preferred to do her paralegal work at the breakfast bar instead of at the desk in the den.

Clad in a blue Dodger T-shirt that reached to midthigh, Aimee was perched on a bar stool, the balcony off the dining room behind her open to the warm day.

Fingers poised over the keyboard of her laptop computer, eyes narrowed in scrutiny of Kate's face and the sling on Kate's left arm, Aimee said, "I told Lou if he wanted this done, I had to get out of there to do it. You're home early."

"She had to cut the session short today."

"So the skinny little touchy-feely twit turned out to be a woman."

"A very scary African-American woman about six feet tall." Kate moved to her, kissed the top of her head. "She means to dangle me by the feet and shake my insides out before I get to go back to work."

"Sounds like she's well-equipped to do it. Is she really terrible?"

Kate deposited her shoulder bag on the breakfast bar. "She figures to be a royal pain. She won't understand anything from my point of view. A psychologist—you might as well try convincing a gopher that some things are better left unexhumed."

Aimee grinned, then said seriously, "Honey, maybe

right now she knows better than you. Maybe it's good she's checking you out. After all, the human mind is her field of—''

"It's mine, too," Kate said in annoyance. Was it too much to expect a little support from the home front? She pulled off the sling supporting her left arm, wincing at the pain and disgusted with herself for causing it. Gingerly, she began to shrug out of her jacket. "The people I see are in a state Calla Dearborn can't begin to imagine."

"That's really unfair," Aimee said, climbing off her stool to assist Kate. "The people she sees hurt like hell." She added, "She has an interesting name. Calla, like the Easter lily."

Pulling her good arm out of the jacket, Kate said sarcastically, "And Dearborn, like the Detroit suburb that's always kept out people of her color."

"It has? How come Farrakhan isn't holding one of his Million Man Marches there?"

"He should. All this hypocrisy over places like Bosnia—bad enough that people can't live in our own country without wondering if they'll be firebombed or hit by bullets from a passing car."

"Bad enough living with someone who's been hit by bullets from a passing cop." Looking into Kate's face, she raised both hands. "Hey, just kidding."

But Kate was infuriated by the jest. "The hell you are," she snapped. "I don't know why you won't understand it was an accident."

"I do understand. I don't understand why you won't understand I find *that* more horrifying than you being taken down by one of your criminals."

"Drop it, okay?"

Aimee shrugged and muttered something about having no choice and reached for the pad beside the portable phone on the breakfast bar. "A couple of calls came in for you."

"Torrie?"

"Nope." Aimee ripped the page off the pad. "Louisa from the insurance company about a revised bill from the hospital—"

Kate groaned.

"—and some guy named . . ." She looked at the page, "Luke Taggart."

"Luke Taggart?"

Startled, Aimee checked the page again. "Yep. Luke Taggart. The name sounds familiar. Should I know him?"

"What on earth did he want?"

"He didn't say. Who is he?"

"A cop. A rotten cop who pursued an unarmed suspect into a dead-end alley and blew him away."

"Oh yeah, now I remember, it was right after New Year's—"

"Another lousy cop," Kate fulminated, "one more story in the papers about all the Nazis infesting the police department—just what we need more of these days."

"What's he want with you? He's not even in your division, is he?"

Kate shook her head. "Hollywood. He's relieved of duty, of course. Till he's prosecuted and fired. I can't imagine what he wants with me." Or how he got her home phone number. Presumably through channels—and when she got back to work she'd make damn sure to close down the channel.

"So call him."

"No way."

"Aren't you even curious?"

"I don't want anything to do with him. All I want right now is to get into some shorts."

"Damn, just my luck to not have any on," Aimee said, peering impishly down at her bare legs.

The quip broke Kate's sour mood. Smiling, she glanced at Aimee's computer screen. "What are you working on?"

"The same old, same old." Aimee's slender shoulders rose and fell in weary resignation. "The case that ate downtown L.A. I need to E-mail this stuff to the office by four-thirty. So do you know this Taggart guy?"

"Only by sight." Just one time, couldn't Aimee let something go? "Remember the Ferrera funeral?"

Aimee shook her head. "You've been to too many."

Even one was too many from Aimee's perspective. Police funerals were the nightmare reminder of what lurked around any corner for any police officer, Kate's shoulder wound being proof positive. But to Kate, each funeral was a death in her police family, the ritual surrounding each one gut-wrenching but necessary. Rank upon rank of silent, solemn-faced uniformed cops, all the brass present including the chief, the row upon row of motorcycle cops, the roar of their engines as if they could rev open the gates of heaven. The bagpiper's wail, the riderless horse, the lamenting bugle call of *Taps*, the white-hatted, white-gloved honor guard, their rifles at the ready for the final salute, the flag sliding off the coffin and folded and given to a young family as wall-eyed and stunned as if they'd been poleaxed . . .

Gazing out the balcony door into the filtered sunlight, Kate said, "At the funeral Torrie pointed out this great big guy and said he was Luke Taggart, Tony Ferrera's partner the night he died."

"Jesus. Taggart was responsible?"

"Not that I heard. Ferrera got caught off duty, in a liquor store robbery gone wrong. All I know is, anybody involved with Luke Taggart somehow ends up . . . I don't know, he's just bad news. Back in Vietnam, we'd have called him a shitbird. Never been on any department promotion list, he's been stuck at Hollywood as long as I can remember."

She changed the subject. "Torrie didn't call?"

Aimee shook her head. "Kate honey, your people are trying to tell you they want you to take it easy till you get well."

"I *am* well. I have investigations under way—"

"They're being taken care of."

Not the way I'd be taking care of them. "I could lead an investigation right now."

"You're being ridiculous."

"Let's not argue, okay?"

"Who's arguing? Haven't you figured out why Torrie doesn't call? It's very simple."

Kate was fully aware of her own irrationality as wrath engulfed her: Aimee had not been snide, she hadn't been anything but Aimee. But Kate still said, "Why don't you put it in teeny little words so that my teeny little brain can understand it."

Aimee's violet-blue eyes darkened, but her tone was even: "Torrie knows she might have been the one who shot you. She doesn't know how to deal with it."

"Did she tell you that?"

"It's what I think. It's not something she'd ever tell me."

"Well, it's ridiculous. She's paid enough—an official reprimand for improper handling of a firearm during an arrest."

Aimee shook her head as if trying to dislodge a buzzing sound. "That's crazy. You have rules as crazy as the military."

"We *are* the military," Kate said impatiently, and then softened her tone. "We might as well be. The rules are pretty much the same." Police departments everywhere were modeled after the military. Police rankings—sergeant, lieutenant, captain—were hardly an accident.

Aimee said, "How would you feel if Torrie's shoes were on your feet? How would you feel if you'd shot Torrie?"

"Wouldn't have happened."

"How do you mean?"

"I mean it just wouldn't happen. I wouldn't have fired my weapon in that hallway unless I had a clear shot at Crockett."

"For God's sake, Kate. With everything happening in a split second? How can you know what you'd have done?"

"Training."

"Training? You haven't even had Police Academy—"

"Okay, bad choice of word. Experience. Discipline."

Aimee said incredulously, "If Torrie and those other two cops had waited for a clear shot, that man might have shot you dead."

"Not true. Someone would have got him. It's set up that way, it's what backup units and teamwork are all about. We're like soldiers in a foxhole. One thing we know for sure—we can absolutely depend on whoever's guarding our back."

Aimee's brief head shake was her only comment.

Kate said with finality, "I would never have shot another police officer." And she walked off into the bedroom to finish changing her clothes.

Never, she thought, pulling a pair of white shorts out of the drawer. Never would she have risked a shot in that hallway without both hands steadying her gun and anyone other than the suspect in her gunsights. Whatever she lacked in street experience, she made up for in concentrated sessions at the practice range and complete immersion in her profession. She had come to police work knowing combat technique from years in the military, and she had learned from every postmortem analysis of shoot-outs what had gone wrong and why there were dead suspects and dead cops. She was a damn good shot; she knew what her weapon could and couldn't do; she handled it with expertise and the proper mind-set.

Civilians were the real amateurs. They thought carrying a gun afforded them personal protection when the truth was, they risked worse trouble. A civilian pulling out a gun was no different from somebody commandeering a fire truck to put out their house fire without any concept of how to handle a fire hose or attack a fire.

Proper action in an emergency had to be preprogrammed, ingrained, founded in knowledge and pure discipline.

Pulling on a tank top, she walked into the living room, her skin prickling in the dry heat. The palm trees rattled in the erratic wind, Aimee's computer keys a rapid *tick-tick-tick* of accompaniment. Kate stopped to ruffle the gray fur of Miss Marple, who was curled up as usual in her favorite armchair, white paws covering her eyes. The startled cat seized Kate's hand and then licked her knuckles.

Kate withdrew her hand and said softly, "I bet your day's been better than mine." She added, "And Aimee's."

She'd been really hard on Aimee lately, her temper on a hair trigger. Maybe she was more on edge than she realized. Maybe there was something to what Calla Dearborn had said about reaction to stress. Or maybe it was the devil riding in on these Santa Ana winds.

"Honey," she called, "what do you say we go away for a few days? Maybe even a week?"

The *tick-tick-tick* halted. "You're kidding, right?"

"Name the place." Kate strolled into the dining room and stood in the balcony doorway for several moments, enjoying the sunlight on her bare legs. Then, coming up behind Aimee, she snugged her good arm around her shoulders, buried her face in Aimee's hair. "You're always complaining about my court dates messing up our vacations. Now's our chance."

"Your timing is impeccable," Aimee said, stiff within Kate's embrace. "The Acme case is due in court in a month, and you know it. Twelve-hour days, weekends—I can't go anywhere."

Kate released her and walked into the kitchen. "Guess it's too early for the cocktail hour. Want a beer?"

"Uh-uh," Aimee said distractedly, peering at her computer screen. Kate took a Foster's from the refrigerator and popped it open.

The phone rang. Aimee, still focused on her computer screen, groped for the receiver. Kate put down her beer, picked up the receiver. "Kate Delafield," she said automatically.

"Detective Delafield," an authoritative male voice said, "I've officially requested you as my representative at my Board of Rights hearing."

Grimacing at Aimee who was looking at her inquiringly, Kate said into the phone, "Officer Luke Taggart, I presume."

"You presume right."

Kate closed her eyes. *What the hell was in the bullet that hit me? Why has my life all of a sudden veered off toward a corner of hell?*

5

SET in from the street and above sidewalk level, Venetio's had placed half a dozen of its tiny complement of tables on a weathered gray plank terrace overlooking the cars cruising Santa Monica Boulevard and the passing pedestrians. The West Hollywood restaurant was quiet; the lunch-hour crowd had vanished.

A small, darkly tanned waiter, his black pants and T-shirt covered by a white apron, hoisted a large tray of dirty dishes onto his shoulder and then halted to cast a raised-eyebrow glance at Taggart. "Sit anywhere," he said, and quick-stepped into the kitchen.

"Outside okay for you?" Luke Taggart asked Kate.

"Suit yourself," she answered curtly. She would quickly dispense with this brazen man and expend minimal effort doing so.

Striding to the edge of the terrace, Taggart pulled back the chair Kate would have chosen from the table where she would have sat—directly facing the street and its activity—and made himself comfortable, his loose-limbed posture conveying total relaxation. Irked as much with herself as with him for surrendering protection of her back to a man she neither knew nor trusted, she conceded ruefully that the only danger in this section of town lay in being swept aside by men wanting to get a better look at her companion—at a face that belonged in a male action film, and a set of shoulders usually seen on a football field. She dropped her shoulder bag beside the chair opposite him and sat down, awkward with her shoulder sling.

"I have a right, Detective," Taggart said grimly, placing two smooth, mammoth hands flat on the table. "You know the rule."

"I don't have any problem about your rights or the department's rules, Taggart. But this is crazy. We have a whole department of defense reps who specialize in what you're asking me to do. You don't even know me."

"I know you the same way most other cops do. Reputation."

"The same way I know you," Kate said tartly.

"Insults will get you nowhere," Taggart said, his dour expression lightening with what might have been a hint of amusement.

Kate studied his broad Slavic face, the Schwarzenegger cheekbones and pale skin tones, the bristle on his cheeks and chin slightly darker blond than the hair buzz-cut to a half inch from his scalp. His green-blue eyes watched her frank evaluation of him from a cool, self-contained distance.

She said, "I can't imagine why you want someone to represent you who doesn't want to."

"I did a pin-the-tail-on-the-donkey and you got it."

Kate sighed. Indifference in an adversary was always the slipperiest of slopes; there was little leverage to be had. Thus far, Luke Taggart appeared to be the epitome of indifference, beginning with his phone call and proposal for an immediate meeting—she could designate the place. She had tested that open-handedness by naming this restaurant and location. Most male cops, unless in uniform and on duty, would not be caught dead in Boys' Town; they would have insisted on an alternate meeting place. But Taggart had agreed with a succinct "Fine." Thus far she had not picked up anything about Taggart as a gay man on her radar, she had never heard that he was, and she was connected fairly well, she believed, into that particular gossip pipeline. If his obliviousness to his surroundings was an act now, it was a good one.

Menus in hand, the waiter quick-stepped to a halt beside Taggart.

"Just iced tea," she said. She would give Taggart the space of a drink to come to his senses and get out of her life and what could only be equally foreign territory for him: West Hollywood.

"Coke, lots of ice. Thanks." Taggart did not appear to notice that the waiter's limpid, blue-eyed gaze was fixed on the biceps exposed by Taggart's white, short-sleeved cotton shirt; Taggart was watching a battered red pickup make its backfiring way down Santa Monica Boulevard.

As the waiter nodded and left, Kate noted that Taggart wore a pair of dark blue cotton pants with his white shirt, and leather sandals crisscrossed with elaborate latticework. The sandals didn't go with the pants and shirt or with Taggart. Nothing about this odd man seemed to quite fit in with anything else. So far, she liked nothing about him. He was a big body mass who had blundered into her personal space, and she didn't want to know him or anything about him.

"Why did you call me?" she asked.

"I've been set up," he said.

She managed not to snort or to roll her eyes. Innocent as a lamb, just like every other piece of offal caught in the jaws of the criminal justice system.

"The suspect I followed into Apparition Alley was a druggie. He had a gun, a .22 I'd say, holding it on a woman and dragging her in there with him. The guy that got shot in there was some other guy I never saw before."

Apparition Alley? A new and different corpse? She shook her head. Here was a tale as tall as any she'd heard in any interview room. She skipped ahead to the key question: "Why did you go in solo? Where was your backup?"

"I knew I could handle the guy."

Another cowboy cop with his own rule book. "Completely against regulations," she said.

"Do you go strictly by regulations, Detective? Never deviate, never let judgment come into play?"

Kate looked at him, interested in this perhaps inadvertent slipping away from his macho posture. She said, "This isn't about me. It's not about what I would or wouldn't do."

The slight movement of his massive shoulders was not quite a shrug. "Let me put it this way. I've learned to handle most things pretty well myself."

"You didn't handle this thing pretty well." His imposing physical presence was an advantage that would lend him a greater degree of authority than most cops, but an advantage was all it would give him. Physical invincibility belonged only in comic books; reliance on it was an arrogance that always landed you in trouble.

"Let me put it another way," Taggart said coolly. "I've made enemies along the way."

"Haven't we all. What does that have to do with this situation?"

"It has to do with you asking about backup."

"Are you telling me when you call for backup nobody comes?"

His shoulders moved again, this time in impatience with a question to which she knew the answer. "Of course not. Rodney King taught even the nitwits that what you send over the MDT gets recorded. It's an open book that can hang you."

She nodded. In the aftermath of the Rodney King trial, Internal Affairs had questioned a number of patrol officers, including several dozen at Wilshire Division, over racist remarks transmitted over their Mobile Digital Terminal computers.

"Backup," Taggart said, "it's how long it takes and who it is."

"So you're saying you get hung out to dry." She did

not automatically disbelieve him; she had heard rumors for years about backup arriving late or not at all as a forceful hint to targeted individuals that police work was not their healthiest field of endeavor. She could never imagine participating in such a vendetta—it would be like a soldier intentionally abandoning a comrade.

He said calmly, "What I'm saying is, I'm more worried about cops with guns at my back than not having anyone there to help me. Just like you."

She sat up straight. "What the hell are you talking about?"

He pointed to her shoulder. "Friendly fire, I hear."

"An *accident.*" Kate realized how much she had raised her voice when a woman swathed in saggy leotards and a black leather jacket stopped in the street to look up at her.

"So you say," Taggart said easily. "Have it your own way if it makes you feel better."

She struggled to control her temper. "Give me one good reason why should I have it any other way."

"Department scuttlebutt."

"Such as what?"

Taggart stirred in his chair. "I called your place—"

"How did you get my number?"

"Come on, I'm a cop. Until further notice."

She did not reply. Someone would be called to account over this.

"Anyway, a woman answered. From what I hear, a woman always answers."

Kate leaned aggressively across the table. "So?"

"So you've found your way into a particular section of the LAPD rumor mill."

"Which particular section is that?" She intended to expose every corner of this cesspool.

"To quote someone else, the muff diver section. Rumor has it a real looker's been your special muff for a long time."

She wanted to reach across the table and slap him.

"So your nimble mind has made the reach that this is why I took a bullet."

"It hasn't occurred to you?"

It had never occurred to her. She covered her outrage with an elaborate shrug. "Whatever the reason for my being shot, what does it have to do with you?"

"It's something in common. I figured the experience would give you some insight, some understanding of where I'm coming from with all this."

So this was the reason he had chosen her. The poor misguided bastard.

As the waiter served their drinks, Kate made the grudging concession that she would need to spend more time with Taggart. She asked him, "You hungry?"

"Yeah, as a matter of fact."

"I'll get menus," the waiter said cheerfully.

"Just tell us what's good," Taggart said.

The waiter placed a hand on a hip. "The rock shrimp on angel hair pasta and the quiche of the day, which today is spinach."

Taggart nodded. "You have any hamburgers?"

"I'm sure we could make one up for you." Looking with admiration at Taggart, he asked archly, "Anything special you'd like on it?"

"Whatever's lying around."

"We'll do our best to look. Would the lady like something equally butch?"

Unable to prevent a grin, Kate said, "The lady will have the quiche of the day."

"Here's hoping that injured arm heals soon, dearie," the waiter said, and left.

Kate, still grinning, picked up her iced tea. She loved living here in West Hollywood. Loved it. A gust of wind snatched her napkin and she grabbed for it with her free hand, yelping with pain as her shoulder sharply reminded her of its damage. Taggart rescued the napkin before it vanished over the railing of the terrace.

"Never been shot before, I take it," he said.

"No." She gritted her teeth, waiting for the pain to subside. "Have you?"

Taggart shook his head. "Not even a broken bone. Lots of pulled muscles, stuff like that. When I was . . . young."

"Football?"

"Wrestling." As if sensing that his allotment of small talk had just run out, he flicked the straw out of his Coke and picked up the glass. "I was on patrol—"

"Alone?"

"Alone."

"In a black-and-white?"

"Yeah. Sure. In uniform with my badge on." Taggart took a long drink of his Coke.

She closed her mouth firmly. She would cease her questions until they were absolutely necessary.

"It was ten-fifteen. I called in code seven. I came out of the Burger King on Hollywood Boulevard and there they were, two very stupid guys in big, hooded sweat-shirts, doing a deal right out in public, and big for this territory—a baggie the size of a book bag stuffed with pills every color of the rainbow. They see me, take off like jackrabbits."

Taggart drank more Coke. "They split up, natch. No decision—I go after the guy with the baggie. He legs it down Stewart to Wheeler, I'm yelling all the way for him to stop or I'll shoot." He gave a self-deprecating shrug. "I like to think I'm in good shape, but this guy's Carl Lewis. Half a block away on Wheeler, I spot him outside Apparition Alley, he's grabbing this woman in a head-dress—"

"A headdress?"

"Yeah, a veil, a robe, the whole Indian magillah."

Kate shook her head.

"He turns his gun on me. I do a swan dive behind a palm tree. He drags the woman into Apparition Alley—"

"Wait." She had vowed to not interrupt him, but this

was right out of the theater of the absurd. "What on earth is Apparition Alley?"

Taggart nodded as if this was a question he relished answering. "An armpit of hell. Between two buildings off Wheeler. Narrow, maybe thirty feet long, dead end, black walls, dark even in daylight. At night I check it every shift with the spotlight. Spikers go in there, real desperadoes. I pull ODs out all the time, found a DB this Christmas. It's a dumping spot too—a couple of Latinos last year, probably Mexican Mafia, so shot up they looked like target practice dummies. Three other guys beat into hamburger, a nineteen-year-old last month, he'll never know his dick from a cauliflower. It's a boneyard, you expect to see ghosts in there. Apparition Alley is a good name for it."

Impressed by his description, she reminded herself that one of those ghosts belonged to a dead man whom this cop sitting across from her was accused of shooting without justification.

"So what happened to the guy and the Indian woman?"

Taggart's mouth thinned to a straight line. "Beats the hell out of me."

She shook her head. Taggart looked, she thought, perfectly sane. But then so did a lot of citizens of the Planet Kookaburra—crazies that included some very bad or very lazy police officers who learned from testifying in court to be particularly adept at projecting credibility. "Let's back it up a little," she said. "So the man you're chasing, he drags an Indian woman into a dead-end alley. You're how far away at this point?"

"Half a block."

"You can tell from that distance he's the same guy you're chasing?"

"Sure. Same hooded sweatshirt, he's got the baggie in his hand."

"And you could see all that from half a block."

"Yeah. You don't believe me, I'll take an eye test."

"Did you see the subject's face?"

"Not much of it, with the hood."

"The hood didn't come off when he was running like Carl Lewis?"

"Nope. It was one of those drawstring types. I saw he had a mustache."

"What race was he?"

"Mostly white boys deal on Hollywood Boulevard."

Kate said doggedly, "So you're saying he was white—"

"I'm making this up? He was white."

"Cool down, Taggart. I'm just trying to get things clear here. I thought you said you pulled Latinos out of Apparition Alley."

"What I said was, it's a dumping ground for them."

"So this white male is dragging the Indian woman, he's now got a gun. Where's the baggie?"

"Still in his hand. He's got his arm around the woman's throat—" Taggart demonstrated, holding his right arm bent in front of him. "He's dragging her backwards, the baggie's in the same hand."

"So we're talking about a left-hander."

He looked at her.

"If his gun's in his left hand—"

"I see what you're saying. Yeah, I guess you're right."

"We're talking about how big a man?"

"Tall, maybe six feet, and stringy."

"And the woman?"

"Five-four or -five."

"Build?"

"Medium."

"Not exactly a midget."

"Yeah. But if the guy's speeding—"

She nodded. Speed, crack, smack—the streets in this town had come to resemble the war she had witnessed more than two decades ago as a Marine Corps officer in Vietnam. The combatants today had the same access to firepower and to potent drugs that all but disintegrated inhibitions. "Okay, so you see this man drag the woman into Apparition Alley. Exactly what did you do then?"

"Yelled at him to drop his weapon, there was no way out."

"Any response?"

"Nope. So I draw my weapon and go in there."

She studied him, trying to calculate whether such an act had come out of a storehouse of courage or if the man was simply a reckless fool. She remembered former partner Ed Taylor grumbling, "We gotta have a screw loose to do this job. Soldiers gotta do what they're told to do, but stupid us, we walk right in where any sane civilian would run like hell." No way would she go solo into a dark alley after somebody with a gun. Somebody like that, you gave him no chances, you took no chances yourself, you called for backup and overwhelmed him with everything you had.

She asked, "Did you discharge your gun?"

"I did not."

"What does ballistics say?"

"That my gun was fired, and they dug two slugs out of the back wall that match my Beretta."

"Jesus, Taggart."

He said in a Bogart imitation, "Looks kinda bad, don't it, kid."

"GSR?"

"Negative. They didn't test me until several days later, but there was no gunshot residue on my uniform."

"How do you explain it?"

"I can only explain what I did and didn't do. My guess is, ballistics is wrong. Or fabricated."

She did not immediately reply. The rank incompetence of the LAPD lab had been common knowledge long before the Simpson trial had exposed it to public pillory, but to her knowledge, the firearms unit had never shared that reputation.

"Let's back up again. You went into the alley after the man in the hooded sweatshirt and the woman. What did you see?"

"A DB. Male."

"How did you know it was a dead body?"

"You couldn't miss it. Lying faceup, in a swimming pool. Shot in the neck, two through and throughs. One slug took out the jugular, the other one went through the spinal cord."

Even with all her experience, it was not a scene she would have wanted to witness. She offered, "Those kinds of wounds—sounds like a hit." And a cop would know as well as any surgeon where to place two bullets for maximum effect.

He shrugged. "Yeah. Maybe."

"You don't think so?"

"I think maybe." He shifted in his chair, his gaze drifting to a bearded wraith bundled in layers of clothing, laboriously pushing a shopping cart, hung with black plastic bags, along the sidewalk. Kate also watched the man, a too common sight, one of a bedraggled army of occupation on the streets of Los Angeles.

"Okay," she finally said, "so where were the two people you followed into Apparition Alley?"

"Nowhere."

She shook her head. "I'm confused. Didn't you say Apparition Alley is a dead end?"

"I did."

She said carefully, "Could there be some other interpretation for what you saw?"

"Thank you for your tact, Detective. No."

"Could the male have dragged the female into one of the buildings on either side of Apparition Alley? You were a distance away."

"Not that far away. They went into Apparition Alley. Besides, the two adjacent buildings were closed up—locked."

"Then how do you explain it?"

"I don't. I can't."

"Any sign of the baggie?"

"Nope."

"Any evidence at all, any trace of the people you followed into Apparition Alley?"

Again Taggart's face lightened in the suggestion of a smile. "Did the woman drop her veil? No." He held up a hand as their food arrived.

"For the gentleman," the waiter said, sweeping down in front of Taggart a plate with the largest hamburger patty Kate had ever seen; it rested on a huge sourdough roll surrounded by french fries. "A piece of meat appropriate for the gentleman."

"Just my size," Taggart said. The waiter arched both eyebrows and watched with interest as Taggart slid his napkin down onto his lap.

Amused, Kate occupied herself in clearing room on the small table as the waiter put down a set of condiments for Taggart's food, then served Kate with a flourish. "Quiche for my lady, and I'll be back with more iced tea."

"Make it coffee, black," she said. Taggart's story was taking on all the aspects of a case, and she needed her usual fuel. As the waiter moved away, she asked Taggart, "Any theories?" None of it made any sense to her.

"It's some kind of elaborate scam. I don't know how they did it, though." He upended the ketchup container over his hamburger.

Kate said, "Let's go through it, okay? What did you do after you saw the victim in the alley?"

"Called in."

"From the scene?"

Nodding, Taggart finished soaking his hamburger patty, then covered the red mass with the top of the sourdough roll. She knew he would have used his ROVER, not his patrol car radio.

"You didn't leave the scene?"

"I didn't leave."

"What do you know about the victim?"

Taggart picked up his hamburger; in his huge hands it became average size. "Male Latino, forty-seven, parolee, priors for possession six counts, three years all told, then he graduated—seven for dealing, just out after another nine.''

"His name?"

"Julio Mendez.''

"Did you know him?''

"Yeah. I knew him. When he wasn't dealing, he was an informant. When he wasn't an informant, he was an all-purpose scumbag.''

"Any witnesses to what happened in that alley?''

"Oh sure. Hollywood is just filled with civic-minded citizens eager to come forward and assist their fellow man, especially the cops.'' He bit deeply into his hamburger.

"It's a question I needed to ask, Taggart. Why do you think this is a setup?''

Taggart finished masticating, then said, "They got my partner, and then they figured out a way to get me.''

The waiter saved Kate from having to make a response to this claim. Arriving with a coffeepot and a coffee cup, he halted and gawked at the table. "Why don't you leave the pot," Kate said.

She followed the waiter's horrified stare to Taggart's plate, which looked as if it were covered with blood spots from his dripping hamburger. "Why don't I," the waiter said, and sprinted away.

Kate dug into her quiche, and then took a surreptitious glance at Taggart's grim, rugged face. Once again his story had veered off onto a bizarre tangent. Of all eighteen divisions in LAPD, she reflected, Hollywood was the one most cops considered as the dregs for its tawdry milieu of drugs and vice and human corruption. And Taggart had been there for years.

She wondered if he had succumbed to the temptation of one of the vices it was his sworn duty to exterminate: his story fit particularly well with the paranoid delusions of a habitual cocaine user.

"How's your food?'' he inquired.

She saw that Taggart had devoured half of his enormous sandwich in the time she had taken to eat three bites of quiche. "Really good," she said, and it was, fluffy and creamy with cheese. She hardly needed to ask about his meal—his eating habits had all the refinement of an alligator's. Pouring herself some coffee, she said, "Tell me about your partner."

His green-blue eyes narrowed. "You at his funeral?"

"Yes. I remember he was very young."

"Thirty-three. Eight years on the department. A real good cop. Ever lose a partner?"

"Not like that, thank God. From the time I made detective, I only had one partner before Torrie Holden. Ed Taylor. He pulled the pin a few years back—retired to grow avocados."

"Yeah, I remember. An old-timer—I heard he was a pretty decent guy."

"He was a lazy, bigoted son of a bitch."

Taggart's face registered no surprise. "I guess you should know," he said.

The words had been expelled from her. Astonished at herself, she took refuge in her food. Never had she made such a statement to anyone, not even Aimee. Never had she realized the depth of her resentment and animosity toward Ed Taylor. She muttered, "I guess one should speak well of the dead—so to speak. Sorry," she said hurriedly, "I didn't mean to be so insensitive."

"Forget it. Some of my partners were no bargain either. Till I got lucky."

She asked reluctantly, "What did you mean when you said they got him? Who's the 'they'?" She guessed he would tell her that Tony Ferrera had represented some sort of squaring of accounts, maybe a drug hit.

He nodded acceptance of the question, but asked, "What did you hear about him?"

"Only what they announced at roll call the morning after. And what I read in the papers. He was off duty, walked in on a two-eleven. Two men in ski masks at a liquor store. That's it."

"That's pretty much the official story. RHD picked up the investigation—"

She nodded. Robbery-Homicide at Parker Center always investigated police officer deaths.

"—But I did a little digging around on my own. He was hit outside the liquor store. Anything seem odd about that scenario right off the bat?"

"Like what?"

"Like the newspapers reporting he walked in on a robbery, and the IO's report saying the same thing. But he bought it before anybody even tried to rob the place."

Imprecise generalities in an Investigating Officer's Chronological Report were nothing new, and the newspapers got details wrong all the time. "There's more," she suggested.

"Yeah. He got out of his car to go into the liquor store, was shot outside the entrance to the store. Then one of the doers pops a shot into the liquor store and takes off. Does that look to you the way it looks to me?"

Kate took another bite of quiche. "Enlighten me."

Taggart put down his hamburger and leaned across the table. "So there was no robbery, Detective. Yet one of the shooters takes the time to poke his head in the door of the liquor store and squeeze off a shot."

"So?"

"So why fire a shot into a store you're not going to rob?"

"To buy more time to get away," she replied.

"Not in my lifetime," he said. "Unless it's a Bruce Willis movie. You don't draw more attention to yourself with a gunshot."

"There were gunshots already," she pointed out.

"Yeah, but why take the extra time to go into a store and fire at a man who's behind a counter and hasn't made a move to come out?"

The same answer applied: to discourage anyone from coming out, to buy time to get away. But she would not argue the issue further.

"Besides," he said, "they were in disguise. Masked."

"True."

"I'll tell you what happened," he said, jabbing a finger on the marble-granite surface of the tabletop. "The guy fires that shot so the store owner for sure sees the ski mask and for sure understands they really wanted to rob the store and somebody just got in the way. There's another reason they don't go in the store—the surveillance camera."

"A plausible theory, but still conjecture."

"I ask you: If this is really a robbery, and the doers see somebody walking up to that store, don't they let him get his business done and hit the place after he's gone?"

"Was Tony in uniform?"

"Jeans and a leather jacket."

"So maybe they're dopers, armed, disguised, ready to make their move, and they moved. Maybe they figured they'd rob him too, while they're at it. Maybe Tony sees the ski masks, figures out what's going on—Did he have his gun out?"

"Yeah."

"Did he fire?"

"No. And I think that's another reason for the shot into the store. So the other shooter can pull out the gun and put it in his hand."

"Look, Taggart, what are you trying to tell me? Who do you think killed Tony?"

"Cops."

The power of speech was shocked out of her, but only momentarily. "For God's sake, man. Why on earth would police officers—"

"Because two days before he died, he told me they would."

"Who—"

"He didn't say."

"Why?"

"He didn't say."

"And now they've set you up because—"

"Because I've been nosing around. Because they're not sure what I know."

"If what you say is true, why not take you out too? The same way as Tony?"

"Two good reasons. I've been watching out for myself. And say I get wasted in the same kind of botched robbery as my partner—who's *not* gonna think something smells? So they do this. So now anything I come up with—it's just the delusions of a disgraced and discredited cop."

A suspicion beginning to glimmer, she asked, "Tell me what you know about Tony. His personal situation."

"A real family man. Growing up was real, real tough on him. Came from a big Italian family, with a father who was a disgrace. The bastard sold insurance and pocketed the premiums and landed in the slammer, ended up dying there. His mother was left to face all the friends and neighbors he'd robbed, and with five little kids to raise all by herself. Ferdie could never repay his mother enough, took care of her big time. Helped out a sister with college tuition too."

Ferdie. She wondered when she would hear a nickname. She had never been given one—at least to her face—but most cops were like children on a playground in the way they assigned nicknames. Partners who established a special kinship were especially apt to do so as an almost ritual display of their bond.

"Ferdie was easy-going, though," Taggart said. "A real fun-loving guy. Last Halloween he picked out these crazy masks and we wore them on patrol right along with all the other nutballs on Hollywood Boulevard. Ferdie was a real cutup."

"Was he married? Divorced?"

Taggart shook his head. "Not Ferdie. Too smart to make the mistakes I made."

So Taggart had been married at least once. The suspicion became more than a glimmer. "I take it the two of you were close."

"Close? Closer than brothers." He pushed his plate away. "At least my brothers. He was the best friend I ever had."

"Where did he live?"

"Echo Park." Again Taggart's face lightened. "A single apartment too small for a pygmy, but with a very big deck and a very big view of downtown L.A."

She probed carefully. "I hear it's a pretty colorful part of town."

Taggart shrugged. "Not my style. Too close to Dodger Stadium, all that traffic. Not to mention the Police Academy's right there too. I like it where I am. Laurel Canyon."

So much for thinking maybe he and Ferrera had lived together. She returned to the main subject. "Give me one good reason why cops would want your partner out of the way bad enough to kill him."

"Something he uncovered. Like I did. Ferdie was privy to stuff."

She smothered a snort of impatience. What cop wasn't privy to stuff? Anybody who worked Hollywood would be privy to every kind of shakedown, every corruption from white slavery to child pornography.

"Remember the God Squad, all the Men Against Women crap?"

Surprised, she nodded. "Sure."

"Ferdie was at West L.A. He had a pipeline into that whole Mark Fuhrman wing of LAPD."

He refilled her coffee cup as she digested this statement. She had heard all the stories during the tumultuous and disastrous years when Daryl Gates was chief of police, about Men Against Women, and that West L.A. Division was the last place where any woman officer wanted to be because of the officers who had banded together in overt and covert opposition to women. And then there were the rumored Bible-study meetings on the eighth floor of Parker Center by the born-agains who had gathered under the conservative religious banner of Gates's assistant police chief, Robert Vernon.

Her own career had been a cautious traversing of roadblocks, some subtle, some not, thrown up by male officers who bitterly resented every mandated change, who remembered as glory days the era when Police Chief Bill Parker had taken an organization in disarray and molded it into an LAPD proud and incorruptible, a thin blue line firmly encircling and controlling a rambunctious city. Some officers, most of them veterans, many of them at senior levels of the hierarchy, still clung fiercely to that vision of LAPD, and still banded together in pockets of resistance extending, word had it, all the way to the current rumored cabal against African-American Police Chief Willie Williams.

From her observation, racism was no more or less prevalent in LAPD than it was in the rest of America, and the sewage that had spewed from the tape-recorded mouth of Mark Fuhrman at the O. J. Simpson trial had been the same sickening news to her, and to every police officer she knew, as it had been to the rest of the country.

She said, "Your partner was inside all that?"

"He wasn't inside. Took him six years, but he found a pipeline in."

"Were you in the same pipeline?"

"Hell no. No way." He raised a hand in further emphasis. "I was approached. Years ago. Blew it off. I'm no liberal, I got my own beefs about the level of crap we take, but I was born with a futility detector." He shrugged. "Besides, Ferdie and I were partners only a year, and by then I was totally buried with all the prostitute stuff."

She didn't know what he was talking about, but she did not want to sidetrack him.

"Ferdie went along with all of it like he believed it. He always had to know what was going on."

Kate wondered if Taggart's statements were an elaborate smoke screen. Whether the simple truth of this whole matter lay in the relationship between him and Tony Ferrera. Whether the death of his partner had plunged Taggart into paranoid fantasies, first about Ferrera, and now about himself.

She looked at him, at the steeliness in his face, the cool eyes that revealed only the outer limits of the man. She knew that if she pulled Taggart into an interview room and pummeled him for a week, he wouldn't reveal his sexuality if it was anything other than heterosexual and he had chosen to completely conceal it. Other police officers had come out of the closet in the five years since three lesbians and one gay man had so memorably followed Sergeant Mitchell Grobeson onto center stage at 1991's gay pride festival, but none of them were men.

A grudging, contemptuous sufferance of lesbian police officers had become the order of the day, just as it had when women had first fought their way onto street patrols and into the detective ranks in the early seventies, but for gay male police officers, absolutely nothing had changed. If loathing of gays was more selective in its context and expression, it was no less existent or vituperative. Gay officers were deeply hidden because the police hierarchy had made no genuine effort to eradicate from the ranks the conviction that fags did not and could not belong with the band of real men protecting the citizens of Los Angeles. San Francisco to the north, with its fully integrated police force, proved nothing; everybody knew it was a freakish, undisciplined city of fruitcakes and nutballs. To be an openly gay LAPD officer was to court a career of misery. Life as a cop was hard enough—she could attest to that—and few had the intestinal fortitude of a Mitch Grobeson, the first gay officer to pursue and win a sexual orientation suit against LAPD, and whose struggle continued to this very day against the cadre determined to make it abundantly clear that gays were not wanted.

A sudden gust of wind blew Kate's hair into her eyes, and even though she remembered to use her good arm as she brushed it aside, pulsing began again in her left shoulder. Apparently it was reflected in her face because Taggart asked, "Are you in pain?"

She conceded, "They tell me it will ache for a while."

"I know you're just out of the hospital. I appreciate you coming out to meet me."

She nodded, but he knew as well as she did that she had had no choice but to hear and consider his case. A police officer had the right to request any other officer to represent him or her at a Board of Rights hearing on officer misconduct.

She said, "You said something about 'all the prostitute stuff.' What was that about?"

"You heard about it, you must have. Hamilton and Avery?"

"Doesn't ring a bell."

"It was . . . God, I guess it's five years now. Not much wonder you don't remember. But some things never lose their odor. Avery . . ." His lips tightened. "Bud Avery was my first partner at Hollywood. His next partner was Jack Hamilton. They kept about a dozen hookers under wraps in return for pronging privileges."

Pronging, she thought, amused by the term. "I do remember something about that. I don't remember hearing you were involved."

"They got busted. And I broke the Code."

She looked at him. Not much wonder he was a pariah. Not much wonder she had heard only contempt expressed for him. The Code of Silence was alive and well and flourishing at LAPD; it still had the sanctity of the confessional. Chief Williams had proclaimed zero tolerance for any police officer who lied to protect another, but she knew that cops still covered for one another—at all cost.

"IAD came in, interrogated me about Avery and Hamilton. I told the truth. They were brought up on an association beef—"

"Association?"

"Yeah. The known criminal associates being pimps. If schtupping cops was okay by the hookers, it had to be okay by their pimps."

"Creative," she commented.

"Tacked onto CUBO . . ."

She nodded. Conduct unbecoming an officer seemed the likeliest of possible misconduct charges against Hamilton and Avery outside of criminal prosecution.

"Avery worked out a quiet little deal and resigned. Hamilton got a suspended sentence and community service. It made a medium splash in the papers. IAD never tells anybody diddly unless it suits their purpose, and what I'm saying is, I told the truth about those two guys, but I didn't turn them in to begin with. Avery and Hamilton accused me, and IAD didn't do one thing to cover my butt. Not that it mattered. I still broke the Code and everybody said it wasn't worth losing two good cops for what they did, and I've been a walking turd ever since."

"In your shoes," she told Taggart, "I'd have told the truth too."

"From what I hear, I think maybe you would. But the pressure . . . from both sides, not to mention your conscience and what you want from your career—you never know what you'll do till you're there."

She nodded. "You're right, of course. I'd have wanted to tell the truth. I like to think I would have."

"Nobody wanted to be partnered with me after that. Nobody till Tony." He looked at her levelly. "It's only my word on everything I'm telling you, and I'm sure no bargain to take on, so if you have a problem about being my defense rep . . ."

His retreat, however slight, from the demand that she represent him, thawed her resentment. And also the conviction that while she had covered for Ed Taylor's laziness and his incompetence, never would she have covered for his, or anyone's, criminality.

She asked, "Do you have a lawyer?"

"Not at the moment."

"You need one."

"I guess I do."

She said, "I wish you'd tell me honestly why you chose me in particular to be your defense rep."

He crossed his arms, leaned over the table; but his gaze moved away from her, up at the faded flags whipping on the flagpoles lining the grass median strip dividing the east and westbound traffic on Santa Monica Boulevard. "Because you don't know me. Word is, you're a straight shooter, a real good detective who comes into everything with a clean mind. Word is, if you were a token woman back in the seventies, nobody thinks it now." His gaze shifted back to her, met hers directly. "Talking to you, you look to have something I don't see very much of. Mettle."

She felt scalded by his praise, her skin burning under his stare. "Mettle?" she said lightly, considering the word. "I never did anything like pursue somebody with a gun into a place called Apparition Alley."

"Word is, you're not crazy, either." For the first time he smiled, revealing slightly buck teeth with the incisors angled toward their front neighbors.

Something about his misaligned teeth pulled something loose within her. Smiling back at him, she repeated his earlier jibe: "Insults will get you nowhere."

Maybe she would look into his story, preposterous as it appeared. If she couldn't go away for a vacation with Aimee, what else did she have to do at the moment? Who knew how long her shoulder, and Calla Dearborn, would keep her away from work? This chaotic city, with its tanglement of police work, seemed to mutate to a slightly different place every single day. Prolonged absence from her job would leave her disconnected and marooned unless she were a daily witness to the changes. Representing this man would give her continuity with her profession. Maybe even some fresh insights.

She asked Taggart, "Did you ever try to get out of Hollywood?"

"Nothing to be gained," Taggart said. "My rap would follow me anywhere I transferred to."

"Taggart, why did you want to be a cop?"

He shrugged his big shoulders. "It actually came out of wrestling—and college ROTC. I've been blessed with a real strong body, and what I got out of wrestling and out of the military is that the highest and best use of strength is with restraint. I think combining the strength of authority with restraint is the greatest challenge of police work."

She had never heard an answer like his. She liked the answer, but she still didn't trust him or the truth of anything he had told her. She said, "I can see why Ferdie took a chance on getting to know you. I'm sure he had a nickname for you too."

"Tag. He called me Tag. I'd like it if you would too."

"Please call me Kate," she said.

6

KATE answered Calla Dearborn's smile and greeting with a response in kind, then sat down in the wheeled armchair across the desk from her. Expecting a continuation of the previous intrusion into her personal life, she braced herself.

Dearborn's first question was innocuous enough: "How's the shoulder today, Kate?"

"Better. Better all the time."

Dearborn, today wearing a dark brown jacket over a pale lemon blouse, opened her leather binder and picked up her malachite pen, signaling that this was to be the extent of the pleasantries.

"We started to talk about your home situation before our last session was interrupted—"

"Personal matters—I expressed concern about confidentiality."

"And I promised you confidentiality."

Kate pointed to the yellow pad. "You're making notes."

"Purely for my benefit. My version of shorthand for my own thought process."

"I don't care if it's Sanskrit. Anything that gets written goes into a file. A file that goes—"

Calla Dearborn detached the top sheet of paper and closed the binder. She opened the top drawer of her desk and dropped in her pen and the binder. She took the page with the notes on it, ripped it in half and handed the halves to Kate. "I would hate to be one of your suspects, Kate. I don't have total recall in terms of what I need to put together for your benefit."

Mollified, Kate nodded, and stuffed the paper into her jacket pocket. "I appreciate it." Nevertheless, she knew that in this age of electronic wizardry, the Lucite card holder on Dearborn's desk could hold, along with Calla Dearborn's business cards, the transmitter for a tape recorder. Most dangerous of all was Calla Dearborn herself, who could possess God knew what personal prejudices that might begin a derailment of her career.

"In our last session," Dearborn said, "you mentioned that your domestic situation is a partnership with a significant other."

Kate could not help smiling at the tortured jargon, but she said, "I also said that I don't see why I should be required to answer questions I don't want to answer about my personal life."

Calla Dearborn removed her glasses, massaged the bridge of her nose. "Kate, next to simply taking down your name, rank, and serial number, I'm asking the most basic questions I possibly can to keep you from coming here any more often than you have to. Your personal life is integrated with your professional life, personal stresses are the ones that break down officers; all the studies show it, I know it too well from my own experience. What affects your emotional health is all that matters to me. I'm not the one who needs to know these answers—you are. In any psychological evaluation, any decent therapist would—"

"Okay." Kate held up a hand. "As I said last time, I have a significant other."

Watching with interest as Calla Dearborn put her glasses back on and then fussed with the collar of the blouse under her jacket, pulling and patting at it like a bird smoothing its feathers, Kate added conversationally, "Along with a significant other, I have a cat I love named Miss Marple. Miss Marple belonged to Vera Cowley, the woman hit and killed by the van." Kate's experience told her that this therapist was agitated for some reason, and she was trying to conceal and control her agitation. "The relatives were going to put Miss Marple to sleep, so I took her. How could I not take a cat named Miss Marple?"

Dearborn looked up and said in a cool, resonant voice, "How indeed. Of what duration is your current relationship?"

Kate looked at her with respect. "Six years."

"And how would you characterize it? In a word."

Kate reflected. She and Aimee both tended to prickliness, but overall . . . "Solid," she said.

"Your partner has no trouble with your profession?"

Kate watched her carefully as she enunciated, "Of course she does."

She. There it was. For Calla Dearborn to do with what she would.

"From what I hear in your voice," Dearborn said, "you suspect I'll assign less value to your lesbian relationship than to a conventional one."

"Millions do."

"You're right. So be grateful I've decided not to hate you. I deserve points for tolerating you. Most people agree that you're culturally and inherently inferior, that God doesn't like how you live your life."

Shaking her head, Kate said, "I guess a version of this happens to you too."

"You could safely guess that."

"I thought African-Americans resented gay people equating their struggle to their own experience."

"Of course we do. Whatever your blood and pain, it can't possibly equate to the the suffering people of color have endured."

Refusing to be disarmed, Kate conceded, "I guess we both have a few things we put up with from society."

"Have you ever thought about the idea that hatred is *always* based on difference? The amount of difference people are willing to tolerate, where those lines are drawn—that's the struggle for both our communities." As if realizing that she had talked more than she meant to, Dearborn said briskly, "Your partner—what's her name?"

"Aimee."

"Aimee. What does she have trouble with in your work?"

"My hours are crazy. When I'm on a case, I stay on it virtually around the clock till there's a clear direction one way or the other—as you know. Beyond that, when I make an arrest and a murder case isn't pleaded out, I have to prepare for court, and it takes a lot of work to assimilate the tons of detail that come out of an investigation. It's very tough to plan any time away because courts take everything into consideration except the convenience of the police officer. If we don't have a certified reason for not being in court to testify, you can bet your gavel on a defense motion to dismiss."

"I know that's a big problem. What else bothers your partner?" Dearborn smiled faintly. "Your personal safety, perhaps?"

"Admittedly, I've had a close call or two—"

"Admittedly."

"But detectives aren't in the line of fire nearly as much as patrol officers."

"So you said last time. But of course now you've been shot. How was she about that?"

"In one word?"

Dearborn smiled. "A woman of few words obviously prefers as few as possible. Take as many as you like."

Kate was remembering awakening in the recovery room, first to the round, blurry face of a large, white-clad attendant of indeterminate sex adjusting Kate's gown and pulling a blanket up to her neck. Then another face hovering over her, pale, with vivid violet-blue eyes wide with anxiety. Aimee had smoothed Kate's hair back, taken Kate's uninjured right hand, and squeezed it.

"Sorry to drag you away from work," Kate had managed through the aftereffects of the anesthesia. Even through painkillers she could feel a dull heaviness in her left shoulder.

"A police car brought me through town with the siren screaming like a bad television show." Aimee's voice was tremulous. "Are you okay? How do you feel?"

My police family, Kate thought, warm with the thought of Aimee being so well taken care of. "I'm okay. Don't worry."

"I didn't believe Torrie for a minute. I thought for sure you were dying, I almost had a heart attack. Kate . . . is this really worth it for a police pension?"

Even in her befuddled state, Kate wondered if Aimee actually thought she was doing this for the pension. "I'm okay," she said. "Really."

Then, drifting off to sleep with Aimee saying, *"I don't know how much more of this I can take . . ."*

But of course the next day Aimee was restored to her usual feisty, positive self. Kate said to Calla Dearborn, "The word would be . . . *perturbed.* Aimee was plenty perturbed."

"How is she about you returning to work?"

Kate shrugged. "She doesn't like the risks around my job, but she knows it's what I do."

"You told me last time that you don't talk about your work very much, to her or anybody else close to you."

"Yes. Which you perceive as a mistake."

"Not just a mistake," Dearborn said. "A very big mistake."

It's none of your damn business, Kate thought. She said, "I thought you therapists didn't voice opinions. I thought you always asked your patients what *they* thought."

"After five years of this, I follow a blueprint of what I've learned that working police officers need for self-examination. Believe it or not, Kate, everyone at some stage of their lives needs to do some self-examination."

" 'The unexamined life is not worth living'—that's one of my father's favorite quotes."

"You said he was deceased. Tell me about him."

Kate answered willingly. "A World War Two vet, fought in Europe. Came home and took a temporary job as a sanitation worker. His dream was to have a landscaping business. Never happened. The temporary job turned out to be the only one he ever had. He was a crew chief when he died."

Dearborn's physical stillness was the sign of a good listener, but it was quite remarkable, Kate decided. Aimee was a good listener too, but she could not sit for more than a minute without running her fingers through her hair or shifting position. Calla Dearborn had not touched a finger to her modified Afro during this entire session; she scarcely moved in her intensity of listening.

"Did you get on well with your father?"

"Very well. Really well."

"What about your mother?"

"I was a lot closer to my dad."

"What was she like?"

"She was sick a lot. Never very healthy at the best of times. There were some complications when I was born that apparently weakened her health. She pretty much played the role of housewife."

The psychologist flexed her fingers, then steepled them. Kate realized that Calla Dearborn greatly wanted to make a note of what had just been said. It must be like trying to conduct a homicide investigation without being able to take notes, Kate thought with sympathy and a trace of malice.

Dearborn asked, "Do you think she wanted to do something else with her life?"

Kate shrugged. "I don't know. I don't remember any

of the mothers and fathers I knew ever questioning the roles they played—"

Calla Dearborn looked as if she were about to comment, then closed her mouth firmly. She said, "Do you feel any sense of guilt about your birth being responsible for your mother's poor health?"

"An aunt used to throw it up to me all the time. But it hasn't bothered me for years." Feeling she was on safe territory, Kate continued with information about her mother and father, spinning out answers to Dearborn's questions until the psychologist changed the subject. "Your current partner—tell me about her."

"She's a paralegal. Young, thirty-four. She's very . . . spirited."

"Is she your first relationship of duration?"

Kate exhaled slowly. "No. I was with another partner for twelve years."

"Oh? Why did that end?"

"She burned to death in a freeway accident."

"Oh my dear, I am so sorry."

The anguish in Dearborn's eyes and in her voice was so spontaneous and palpable that it ambushed Kate; she found her own eyes tearing up.

"How long since you lost her?"

"Thirteen years."

Dearborn asked softly, "What was her name?"

"Anne. We met just after I got out of the Marine Corps. We had a house together in Glendale." Kate said thickly, "She was the best thing that ever happened to me."

Dearborn rose to her full, imposing height and turned to her credenza, poured two glasses of water, came out from behind her desk to hand one to Kate, then sat with a hip propped on the edge of her desk.

Both women were silent for some moments, sipping their water, then Kate said, "These sessions with you remind me of the time I brought a car in to be waxed and detailed, an old Nova I was really attached to. The guy told me I shouldn't take a chance on steam cleaning the engine and disturb components that were holding everything together, making everything run."

Dearborn nodded. "Old engines can indeed get choked with grime and pollution. Maybe steam cleaning might have exposed a problem that could have extended the service of a faithful and proven and cherished car."

Kate smiled and did not reply.

Dearborn returned to her desk chair. She said, "Tell me the worst thing you ever saw on your job."

"The worst thing I ever saw was years and years ago and I will never talk about it. Ever. To anyone."

Calla Dearborn crossed her arms. "Believe me, Kate, I'm the last one to welcome hearing about it. But tell me, tell Aimee, tell a priest, tell someone. You need to talk about it. Believe that. *Believe* it."

Kate did not, but she nodded. Whatever it took for this woman to let her go back to work. She said, "Can you give me some idea of how long you need before you issue a positive RTD?"

"I give my assurance I'll return you to duty as soon as possible. But I won't have any pressure put on me— not by you, not by anyone, despite the department insisting that you have a daily schedule of appointments with me."

Gloomily, Kate settled back in her chair. Dearborn said, "Yesterday you told me what happened in the hallway at Gramercy. I'd like you to tell me how you feel about it."

"I feel like shit about it. How else would I feel?"

She fought back her impulse to apologize for the snapping anger of her response. Who better to voice anger to than a professional who was being paid to hear it? "We shot a seventeen-year-old boy. For no good reason except he was a *stupid* seventeen-year-old boy."

"You're angry with Darian Crockett."

"Hell yes, I'm angry." Her voice rose sharply. "Who

wouldn't be angry with the stupid damn fool? Why did he have to come into that hallway with a gun? He had absolutely no chance. He had his whole *life* to get himself straightened out, but the stupid damn fool has to come into that hallway with a goddamn gun, he has to—'' Kate broke off, incoherent with her rage.

"You didn't shoot Darian Crockett," Calla Dearborn pointed out calmly.

"It doesn't matter." Kate took a deep breath, let it out slowly. "Damn it, it doesn't matter. It's academic. I would have shot him, had things come down a little differently." Tears beginning to well, she looked away. "I'd have had to."

"How do you feel about your partners shooting him?"

"They had no choice. He was involved in a robbery where a man was killed. But I feel very sorry for my team." Dry-eyed again, she looked back at Calla Dearborn. "I don't know Alicia Perez very well, but I know she has children. Fred Hansen has two sons. Mostly I feel bad for my partner. Torrie's daughter is thirteen . . ."

"Have you talked to any of your team about the shooting?"

"They visited the hospital." A brief visit, with awkwardly hearty and uneasy expressions of get well wishes.

"Did you talk about the fact that it was one of the three who shot you?"

"No."

"You do know that you need to," Dearborn said gently.

"I know." Kate sighed. "It's not over by a long shot. We still have the Administrative Shooting Review Board to go through."

"How do you feel about having to testify about the behavior of your fellow officers, and them about you?"

"It's a justified shooting. We were given no choice. We need to tell the truth and get it over with. But I'm hardly looking forward to it."

"Your mixed feelings of grief and anger over Darian Crockett are perfectly normal," Dearborn told her.

Thank you very much for your permission, Kate thought, irked by the remark.

"Does it bother you to have to draw your weapon, Kate?"

Kate shrugged. "It's a rare occasion that I have to do it."

Dearborn's dark eyes acquired a hint of amusement. "That's a nice answer to a question I didn't ask."

Irked again, Kate said, "Drawing my weapon if needed is part of my job."

"Another answer to an unasked question."

"If I draw my gun, then it's with the expectation that I'll have to use it," Kate answered in a tone edged with sarcasm. This woman had mastered a gift for aggravating her. "The idea that you might have to kill or wound another human being would bother anyone who's not a sociopath."

"How will you react the next time you're confronted by a Darian Crockett?"

"I'll do my job," Kate said. "The job I'm trained and paid and sworn to do."

Calla Dearborn's face was impassive as she said, "Tell me something about the death scenes you witness."

"I've already told you about one of them. What is it you want to know?"

"Anything you'd like to tell me."

Kate said in exasperation, "Look, I'm kind of lost here. I have no idea what you want from me."

Dearborn steepled her fingers, resting her chin lightly on the tips to gaze at Kate. "All I want is what you can tell me."

Kate drew a deep breath. "Okay." She would try. "To me, a death scene is like everything's frozen. Like a clock stopping—like time stopping. You come into a death scene, there's absolutely nothing you can change. I don't know how books and movies can make such light of murder—it's one of the greatest crimes. Somebody's ripped away all the potential things a person can ever be. Or do."

Gathering her thoughts, she rolled her armchair slightly sideways and stared out the window at the hazy morning sky. "As if murder isn't obscene enough, every victim is robbed as well as murdered. Robbed of dignity. Like Marla Johnson last month. Eighteen years old, a drive-by at a bus stop on Pico and Crenshaw. She had to lie exposed for hours in the gutter in the rain till every detail about her was photographed and everybody including me got their jobs done. Then she gets zipped into a bag and hauled off to a morgue and a freezer drawer, no identity except a tag on her toe. Three days later, she's stripped naked and photographed again and a pathologist slits her open like a sausage. On top of that, she's robbed of all privacy too, everything about her fair game for strangers like me to poke into." She turned back to the psychologist. "But then I guess you've heard all this before."

A shadow seemed to cross Calla Dearborn's face. "All of you have your own . . . take on it. You express yours very well. And you're right, books and movies don't give anything like the reality." She pushed her glasses up on her nose. "You say murder is *one* of the greatest crimes. What other crimes do you put in the same category?"

That answer was easy. "Crimes against children, of course."

"What drew you to take a job in homicide?"

Kate said uneasily, "It was another step along the way in my career."

"You must have reflected over it at some time or other. At least in the beginning, if not since. What drew you to police work?"

How could anyone with a dimple in her cheek ask such snakelike questions? No one asked her these kinds of questions. "I wanted to . . . do something I could believe in." Feeling like a pious fool, she said defensively,

"I guess that's what everybody wants from their lives."

"And do you believe in what you do?"

"Actually . . . in some ways . . . I suppose so. People close to a homicide victim, I'm the one who understands how hideous a crime it is for them. I'm the road to retribution for what's torn up their lives. If I can't find the doer, then it's bad. They won't have even the small consolation of justice being done."

Calla Dearborn nodded but remained expectantly silent, and Kate added, "Arrest and conviction can't bring back what's lost, that's true. But it's a squaring of accounts, theoretically, and a victim's family needs it. I do understand that part, but for me, an arrest and conviction is one less killer on the streets. I don't much differentiate between the drive-by shooter of Marla Johnson and the driver who killed Vera Cowley with his selfish stupidity."

"Reverence for human life . . ." Calla Dearborn mused, but did not voice the rest of her thought. "For somebody who claims she hasn't thought much about this, you've thought about it quite a lot."

Kate slowly nodded. "I guess maybe I have over the years, without realizing it. A murder investigation—you try not leave any stone unturned."

"But sometimes everything you do isn't good enough."

Kate smiled thinly. "One thing about murder—the case stays open till it's solved."

"And that's a comfort of sorts."

"For an unsolved murder, it's the only one."

"You've been at the detective-three classification for how long now?"

"Twelve years." Again Kate was irritated. This psychologist had accused her of giving answers to unasked questions, but Dearborn herself was asking questions to which she knew the answers.

"Have you ever tried for higher promotion?"

"No." The woman knew damn well she hadn't.

"Any particular reason?"

"The selection process for lieutenant favors patrol experience, and I joined the detective ranks out of Juvenile."

Dearborn said crisply, "That wouldn't stop you for a minute. Your records state that you're a college graduate with a military background. And with the demands today for talented women with your level of experience—"

Kate said tersely, "My ambitions don't necessarily have to match LAPD's needs." Did this woman have to challenge every statement she made?

"A moment ago you said you moved into homicide because it was another step along the way in your career. You know that many more women are needed in the ranks of lieutenant and captain—"

"Look. That doesn't mean I have to want either job." Kate shifted in her chair, but not out of physical discomfort; she felt more at ease than she had during the first session because of the jeans she wore under her dark blue suit jacket. She said, "One of the smartest things I ever did was take the advice of a woman officer in Juvenile years ago. Marion Jeffries told me never to think of myself as a woman police officer doing my job unless somebody forced me to."

Dearborn asked with interest, "Did that help with the way men treated you?"

Kate smiled. "Of course not. But I think it helped me keep my balance, and I do it to this day. I try not to factor my gender into the job."

Calla Dearborn's slight nod did not convey agreement. "Your sexual orientation—how do you handle that with your department?"

"I don't," Kate said. "I don't mix my personal and professional lives. I mind my own business, I get along with everybody just fine."

"But you pay a big price in isolation."

"Maybe I do. And maybe you don't approve. But it's a comfortable enough trade-off for me."

"Whatever you do has to be healthy as well as comfortable. Do you consider yourself a feminist?"

"Of course. Women had to fight like hell to get into police work. Feminism made my whole career as a detective possible."

"My career too."

Kate studied her, thinking she might be older than she looked. Judging anything from Calla Dearborn's face was like trying to learn what was in a book from its cover.

Dearborn said evenly, "You don't think you owe anything to the women coming along after you."

It sounded more like an accusation than a question, but Kate said without rancor, "I think being the best I can be at my job is the best thing I can do for anybody." She knew it was a simplistic comment if not pompous, and that the African-American woman across from her could have a vastly different opinion, based on the lessons of her own life. "What's your take on it? What do you think you owe?"

"We can perhaps get into that some other time, Kate. What are your drinking habits?"

Jesus. Forgive me for trying to be friendly and interested in another human being. She said, "Am I not allowed any questions?"

"Your question is a good question. What you say is far more important than what I think—and my talking is a good way of not listening to you. My area of expertise is in listening."

"Mine too," Kate said wryly.

"Yes. And my hope is to reawaken your disposition to talk." Calla Dearborn's dimple reappeared with her smile. "Look at it from my perspective. Answering questions is too chancy a proposition with a homicide detective. You're experts at turning conversation into a full-fledged interrogation that lasts until the end of the session."

Exactly what she had in mind. Kate said, "You've had a lot of us in here?"

Again a shadow crossed Dearborn's face. "Some of you."

Obviously she was not about to reveal their names, much less any detail, and Kate did not waste her time asking. "Sometime," she said, "I'd like to know more about your own background."

"Fair enough. I asked about your drinking habits."

"I don't have any problems around drinking."

"But you do drink."

"Do you know any police officer who doesn't?"

"I'm only interested in you. So you feel you have no problems about your drinking?"

"Correct."

"Does anyone in your life *not* share that opinion?"

"I don't think so." Aimee grumbled sometimes, so did Maggie when Kate tied one on a little too tight at the Nightwood Bar, but that hardly counted since none of it was even close to being serious.

"Ever drink on the job?"

"Never."

"What about afterward—ever go out after work, like with your partner or colleagues?"

"I never did with my former partner. Sometimes with colleagues, but rarely. Sometimes with Torrie Holden, if we have a really hideous day and we sort of need our own postmortem—"

A single musical chime sounded from the crystal clock on Dearborn's credenza. Dearborn glanced at her watch and nodded to Kate. "That's all for today."

7

THE damn parking lot matched Parker Center itself for inadequacy, Kate thought as she wound her way yet another time around the sun-baked concrete slab adjacent to LAPD headquarters. Finally, the backup lights of a squad car signaled that her search was over.

The day was again breezy, the sun a welcome, healing hotness on her body as she climbed awkwardly out of the Saturn. Once more she felt grateful that she hadn't been shot in the other shoulder; she would have been seriously inconvenienced, especially in her ability to drive a car.

She walked toward the glass house, as Parker Center was sometimes called, a graceless box of green panes striped with gray masonry, quickly passing the fountain memorial to officers killed in line of duty. Her fate could have been much worse than a bullet in the left shoulder.

She had not been down here in some time, but nothing ever changed. LAPD headquarters seemed as settled into its environment as an old church, and with at least as many footfalls along its worn walkways. Constructed in the mid-sixties, it had once been a prideful edifice named for LAPD's greatest police chief, William H. Parker. It had aged badly. Eighteen antiquated LAPD divisions were clogged arteries leading to a decaying heart.

The lobby area, a section of its floor striped in hospital fashion with colored tapes for visitors to follow to various departments, was its usual churning mass of traffic, most of it police, uniformed or in plainclothes; people wearing Visitor stickers moved in a different, more awkward gait, looking around in wide-eyed interest. Other public facilities, such as the Criminal Courts Building, had bowed to the realities of an era when lunatics could learn bomb making from the Internet or the public library, and screened their visitors with metal detector units. But LAPD had not conceded that its own police could not guard its own headquarters, even if the nuts' favored target these days seemed to be public servants, even in such bucolic places as Oklahoma City. But then, Kate speculated, it might be a simple matter of budget; a metal detector at Parker Center one more item judged to be nonessential because the city could not afford it.

The lobby activity was refereed by police officers stationed behind a large rectangular reception area, the roadblock that guarded the entrance to Parker Center's interior labyrinth. Their easy, casual chatter did not detract from their sharp-eyed vigilance. Kate displayed her badge and ID to an officer who waved her on through, his blank-faced courtesy attesting to her insignificance as compared with Chief Williams and the assistant chiefs and commanders who came in and out daily, along with the occasional city council member.

She had come here to visit the Officer Representation Unit, to educate herself about the resources available to her and what she might expect as a defense rep for Luke Taggart. All she knew was that it was a department staffed with about twenty police officers who represented any of the approximately eight thousand men and women of LAPD who came up on charges of misconduct.

She opened the door to an office that rivaled anything at Wilshire Division for functionality and for clutter. File cabinets with clipboards of bulletins hanging from their fronts, along with a patchwork of taped-on articles and cartoons, lined one wall and formed room partitions. Pine table-desks were stacked with files and wide loose-leaf manuals and notebooks; multitiered file trays overflowed with paper. Bookcases were stuffed with penal code books, manuals, and phone books. Red plastic baskets and cardboard boxes filled with files and records sat on or under desks.

Three people were in the department: two men in white shirts and gray pants, and a stocky brunette in black pants and a gray lapelless jacket over a white blouse. "I'm Officer Girardi," the woman greeted Kate.

"Detective Delafield."

Girardi nodded solemnly. "I heard about the shooting. How you doing? How's the shoulder?"

"Doing fine. I'll be back soon."

"I also hear you're the one who's got Luke Taggart."

One of the men, hunkered down to flip through files in the bottom drawer of a file cabinet, looked up at the mention of Taggart's name. The other, sitting at a desk talking on the phone, donned a pair of glasses to peer at her.

"Good news travels fast," Kate observed.

Girardi smiled, revealing a wide gap between her front teeth. "He's entitled to the best defense he can find."

Kate said, "I was hoping you'd show me some of the ropes."

"That's what we're here for. To give you all the help we can."

Girardi led Kate on a brief tour of the section, pointing out the location of manuals and reference information, indicating as well a small coffee room and a lunch/meeting area equipped with a table, blackboard, bookshelves, television, and VCR. "All the comforts," Girardi said wryly. "Anything you need that's not here, just ask." She was a police officer who obviously did not engage much in small talk, and Kate liked her for it.

Girardi said, "Let's get you a look at the arena."

Kate followed her into an elevator and then along a wide, anonymous corridor busy with personnel, some of whom called out greetings. She opened a door into a room with high windows framing three sides of an acoustic tile ceiling banded with fluorescent light.

The Board of Rights hearing room was a minicourt-room, cheaply done. On a plain beige floor was a section of connected wooden chairs, their seats folded upward in expectation of spectators, and two separate lecterns. A blackboard and a calendar hung on the wall on the right-hand side of the room; on the far left wall was a small screen for visual presentations.

"High-tech," Kate commented, her gesture taking in mundane office supplies including jars of pencils, and Kleenex and Dixie cups on Formica-topped metal tables.

A box fan on the floor was directed at the room's dominant feature: a long walnut-veneer dais at the front of the room on which were similar office supplies along with white paper cups and two upended carafes on a white cloth. Behind the dais, between two flags, the Stars and Stripes and the California state flag, were three high-backed, black leather chairs, the only costly looking objects in the room. Kate knew that when she next entered this room, two captains and a civilian observer would be in those three chairs, sitting in judgment of her and the accused police officer she would be defending.

Girardi had been standing off to the side, silent until Kate finished her scrutiny of the room. "I need a smoke," Girardi said. "Come up with me to the roof?"

Kate had been on the roof before, but she was newly impressed by the thousands of cigarette butts strewn over its crushed gravel and tar top, monument to the indestructibility of filter-tip cigarettes, not to mention the intractability of a habit she herself had once had and still missed. There was, of course, also the symbolism of the chief's sixth-floor office being under all those cigarettes ground underfoot.

Leaning on the railing, her gaze on the hazy downtown buildings, Girardi inhaled her Kool. "You're in tough," she told Kate. "You've drawn Rodgers."

"A rough customer?"

"Pulling a badge is her life. Making it permanent is orgasm."

A woman. "Do you know Luke Taggart?"

"I know they hate him at IAD."

She was surprised. "A case years ago—he cooperated with them."

"Yeah, Avery and Hamilton."

Kate was interested that she knew about the case, and she waited for Girardi to continue.

Girardi drew deeply, blew out the smoke with the same deliberation. "I was in Hollywood back then, in Vice."

"Why does IAD—"

"The old story, Detective. They got him into their interrogation room, danced him till he gave them what they wanted. After they got it, they despised him for giving it to them."

Kate nodded. What Girardi had just described was hardly strange to her. Among the complexity of feelings she had felt toward certain of her interview subjects was pure fervent connection—a form of symbiosis—while she worked a confession from them. Sometimes afterward, when the tension of the situation drained out of her, she was left with a vein of pure, luminous contempt.

She said, "Tell me about Rodgers."

"Gates brought her in from Foothill. Back then she was a golden girl."

An odd route for someone on the fast track, but it still was a career path of sorts if you'd been hand-picked by a chief of police. Bad luck for Rodgers that Gates had been swept out on the Rodney King tide.

"I've heard she's gay."

Now this was news. "You're kidding."

Girardi chuckled. "I doubt Gates knew it. But then again, maybe he did."

"There's actually somebody gay handling this?"

Girardi flicked ash from her Kool. "Don't you know? We're a regular bastion of equal opportunity terminations these days. Real libertarians." Girardi's tone was withering. "It's the newest wrinkle. An African-American investigates a beef against an African-American cop, a woman investigates a woman cop, a gay cop takes on the gays."

Girardi's casual outing of Rodgers and her use of the word *gay* to describe a lesbian indicated to Kate that Girardi was straight. Was Girardi signaling that the department believed Taggart was gay? She said, "I take it this doesn't mean it's a brave new way of trying to make the world a fairer place."

Girardi's chuckle was low and mirthless. "If the brass want a certain outcome from a particular case, you can bet your badge they'll get it. It's no different from how it's always been, except it takes the starch out of any claim of bias from the officer in trouble. If you're a dumb enough asshole to get into trouble in the first place, no division's going to welcome you with open arms. You depend on the brass to get you kicked upstairs."

Kate knew there was no point in challenging or arguing with Girardi. The Internal Affairs Division and the Officer Representation Unit were natural enemies. She had had her own personal experience to show her why IAD was universally feared and despised. They were the antifamily part of the family whose role it was to put the bad paper in your file that closed off promotion opportunities, ousted you, or even put you in jail. A cop's worst nightmare was having your own family come in and interrogate you like you were the criminal. IAD could cripple you, professionally and emotionally.

Kate sighed. The political intrigue and pressure that Girardi had described were some of the reasons why

Kate had not wanted to advance beyond detective-three. And the cynicism in Girardi was symptomatic of the worst damage that had been done to the morale of the rank-and-file officers of LAPD.

"The civilian member of the Rights Board is your best chance," Girardi told her. "You might want to invite some sharks in with the barracuda. If you think you can get the press interested. Pretty easy to do these days with all the blood in the water."

Not on your life, Kate thought. "It all sounds wonderful. I can hardly wait."

Girardi shrugged. "I wish you luck, Detective. You'll need it." She tossed her cigarette down and crushed it underfoot, adding its corpse to the thousands of others.

8

AIMEE was again working from home, sitting cross-legged on a stool at the breakfast bar in a stream of sunlight slanting in from the balcony door.

"How goes the war?" Kate inquired perfunctorily, eyeing without a scintilla of interest the sprawling chaos of law briefs, files, and splayed-open law books that surrounded Aimee.

"Losing," Aimee muttered, squinting at her computer screen as she finished something in a staccato of typing. Her eyes darted to Kate's face and then down her as if in a quick checklist. "How goes your own war?"

"Losing," Kate said. "Any calls?"

Once again fixated on her computer screen, Aimee patted the counter, finally pulling up a Post-it, which she handed to Kate. "Louisa from the insurance company again. And some guy, he wouldn't leave his name but said he'd call back."

"Anything from Torrie?"

Aimee shook her head once, then again to toss dark hair away from her eyes. "Why don't you call her?"

"She'll call me when she's ready." Kate was not prepared to admit or discuss how perturbed she was that Torrie had made no effort to call.

As if in response to Kate's thought, the phone rang. She deftly plucked away the law book that leaned against it, careful to preserve the open page, and picked up the receiver. "Kate Delafield."

"It's Matt Brazelton from the *Advocate*. How are you?"

She quickly recovered from her shock. "How did you get this number?"

"That doesn't matter, Detective Del—"

"Wait. *Wait,*" Kate commanded as he continued to talk over her. "It matters. You're calling me at my home. It *matters.*"

"Look, it's no big deal—"

"It *is* a big deal. Put me through to your editor." The *Advocate* was a gay and lesbian magazine she subscribed to; she would get the goddamn editor's name off the magazine's masthead if necessary.

"Okay, I got your number from a source."

"What source?"

"You know I won't reveal—"

"Then put me through to your editor."

"He doesn't have a clue about any of my sources." Brazelton's voice was a confident, resonant baritone. "It's about Tony—"

Kate cut him off. "I have nothing to say to you. It's a misdemeanor to invade the privacy of—"

"Tony Ferrera. It's about Tony Ferrera."

Taggart's ex-partner. Get a grip, she told herself. She asked with no less hostility, "What possible interest does the *Advocate* have in a deceased police officer?"

"Can we meet?"

"For what possible reason?"

"For a mutually beneficial exchange of information."

Experience told her that a reporter offering "a mutually beneficial exchange of information" meant a one-way street that led straight into that reporter's agenda.

"It doesn't work that way, Mr. Brazelton. I have no information to give you. And we have people who deal with the press, as you know. If you have some fact or question about Officer Ferrera, then your responsibility is not to call me at my home but to contact the detective in charge—"

"Let's talk intelligently here." He met her coldness

with an icy anger of his own. "You think anybody at LAPD's willing to deal with the queer press?"

Nobody she knew liked dealing with any variety of press; she herself would rather put her hand in a basket of snakes. But still—why was he calling her? She answered, "LAPD will certainly deal with you depending on the uh . . ." She paused to add the heaviest possible intonation of sarcasm. ". . . *relevance* of your information."

Aimee had stopped typing to stare up at Kate in rapt interest.

Brazelton said, "Do you think LAPD cops should be able to come out of the closet?"

So that's what this was all about. "I have no comment to give you about this or anything else."

"Please listen to me," he said as she was about to put down the receiver. "We need to meet." His voice was husky with sincerity. "LAPD's done nothing—"

"Mr. Brazelton, there's no way on earth we're going to meet."

"Look, Detective—"

"You look. And hear. I have *nothing* to say to you."

He sighed. "Ask around about the death of Tony Ferrera. And please take my number. For when you change your mind."

She did not respond as he rattled off a phone number, but she reached for a pad and took it down.

"If I'm not here," he concluded, "I have voice mail."

"Mr. Brazelton, listen to me. Tear up my phone number right now, or you are going to be one sorry reporter. Don't call here again. Ever."

"I'll be in touch," he said and hung up.

Grinning at her, Aimee said, "You really took care of whoever that was."

Didn't I ever, she thought dourly.

"You're getting more like Jane Tennison every day, honey," Aimee said, returning to her work.

Was she indeed getting to be as antagonistic, cynical,

driven, paranoid, alcoholic, and generally beaten up by life as Aimee's favorite female TV detective character? Kate looked at Aimee without replying.

Aimee asked absently, "How did the session go with Dr. Dearborn?"

Kate tore off the sheet of paper with Brazelton's number on it and dropped it into her shoulder bag. "Only a few drops of blood on the floor today."

"Yours, or hers?"

"Are you kidding? Mine."

"Any indication when she might release you?"

"When I give the right answers to her questions."

"So you'll be off work a long time, then."

"What do you mean by that?"

Aimee looked up. "Joke, honey, it's a joke. You know damn well answering questions is not your strong suit."

"Dearborn's very good at asking them, I'll give her that."

"Is she," Aimee said with a darkening in her eyes Kate could not read. "What did she think about Luke Taggart?"

Kate shrugged. "I didn't mention him."

"Why not? Think she might be pissed?"

"I don't care if she's pissed or not. I think she's enough in my face as it is." She didn't know how Calla Dearborn might react to learning about Kate's new assignment. She didn't think Dearborn had the power to do anything about it, but she might.

"See you later," Kate said and kissed Aimee's forehead. "I have things to do."

"Right. Good," Aimee said distractedly, reaching for one of her law briefs.

Within the boundaries of her own Division, Kate was alert to the subtle changes within it, and Aimee often commented on her powers of observation whenever they traveled together through the city by car. But Kate knew that her trained police officer's mentality had narrowed down her view of the larger dimensions of the city she lived in. Driving down Santa Monica Boulevard toward Hollywood, passing the Sports Connection on the corner of Westbourne Avenue and then the cheerful pink-icing facade of the Ramada Inn, she found herself looking around as if she were a tourist.

This very street that she traveled the most often, Santa Monica Boulevard, reflected the breadth of L.A.'s economic layers to her like no other. That other boulevard two dozen blocks away, for which her Wilshire police division had been named, was one of the most elegant thoroughfares anywhere in the world, marching from the Pacific Ocean to downtown Los Angeles along fifteen or so miles of luxury high-rise apartment-hotels, smart office buildings, deluxe department stores, resplendent churches, sumptuous hotels. The other two boulevards, Olympic and Pico, were laid out in their own particular sprawl of business parks, furniture stores, modest motels, houses of varying costs, generic office buildings, and, toward the heart of the city, distinct neighborhoods of Hispanics, African-Americans, and Asians.

But Santa Monica Boulevard unfolded from the ocean like a ribbon, mutating from chic and trendy in the namesake city for which it was the main thoroughfare into the wealth of Westwood and Century City and Beverly Hills, altering into the decidedly rainbow texture of West Hollywood, then fraying altogether in a mean street of dilapidated minimalls and repair garages and nondescript stores and dingy buildings before it finally expired at Sunset Boulevard.

She passed through the busy intersection at Crescent Heights. Luke Taggart lived off somewhere to her left, where Crescent Heights became Laurel Canyon as it cut through the Hollywood Hills to North Hollywood and the San Fernando Valley.

She passed the eastern edge of West Hollywood, pawn and porn shop territory, minimalls with Fatburgers and

Burger Kings and one-hour photo stores, and entered a stretch of barnlike motion picture processing labs and production stages and equipment suppliers that had been serving the entertainment industry since the thirties and forties. She was in Hollywood.

Pulling into a parking place on Wilcox Street, she sat in her car to look across the street at the Hollywood Division station.

She had been here years ago, and she gazed with renewed pleasure at the handsome old fire engine company behind the station, its yellowish beige bricks and Spanish tile roof a contrast to the squat police stationhouse, which could have been built from the same lot of reddish bricks as Wilshire. Surely it was stamped out of the same design mold: a neat, solid construction on a granite foundation. The bail bonds company across from it could have been a franchise branch of the one across from Wilshire Division on Venice Boulevard.

Invariably, Kate went into the Wilshire Division station from the parking lot, seeing the front entrance lobby only when she met relatives of a victim or the occasional witness came in for an interview or to give a statement. The Hollywood Division station lobby was a clone of Wilshire: same reception counter, same wooden bench against the wall, same bulletin board filled with community relations flyers. And the same gold-framed photo of the division's police officers killed in the line of duty—Tony Ferrera the latest of eight officers portrayed in poignant, fresh-faced youth that brought back to Kate her time in Vietnam.

The jowly desk officer was in his fifties, his face so deeply hung with worry lines that Kate thought of an English bulldog. The four hash marks on his sleeve signifying twenty years of service gave her hope that loyalty to the profession would take him to his thirty-year pin instead of into the swelling ranks of officers choosing retirement. Smiling at him, she displayed her badge and ID card.

"So ya wanna go back to the squad room?"

Her smile widened. At least twenty years in Los Angeles, and he had not lost a fraction of his Bronx accent. "I do."

"Ya want I should call somebody? Ya wanna escort?"

"I'll find my way," she said, "thanks." She did not know what reception she would receive as Luke Taggart's defense rep; it seemed better strategy not to announce herself and put anyone on guard.

As she went through the side entrance, a heavyset uniformed female sergeant halted on her way past Kate, peering at her with a half-smile as if she had sized her up as a cop and was not quite sure whether she should recognize her. "Help you?"

"Homicide," Kate said.

The sergeant pointed, then went on her way.

The detectives squad room was a thrum of activity, its personnel working at the tables on telephones or tapping away at typewriters and a computer. Only two detectives sat at the homicide table, both male, one slouched in his chair with a shoulder holding a phone to his ear as he took notes, the other hunched over a blue loose-leaf murder book. She introduced herself to the latter detective.

He rose, leaned across the table. "Jack Frasier," he said, shaking her hand. Indicating with an inclination of his head the man on the phone, he added, "Max Mussino."

Mussino glanced up, lifted his left hand and dropped it as if it had a weight attached, and resumed his low-toned phone conversation. Kate continued to look at him, amused by the name Mussino combined with his large ears, small nose, and bristling white mustache. Undoubtedly his partner and colleagues called him Mouse.

"Pull up a chair." Frasier pointed at her damaged shoulder. "Heard about that. Bad luck. You doing okay?"

She lowered her shoulder bag and sat down across

from the two detectives, careful not to disturb anything around her; this was someone else's chair and turf. "I'm well on the mend, thanks."

"At least you got the piece of shit. A good shooting, I hear."

We killed a seventeen-year-old boy. "It came down to no choice," she said, studying him. Dark hair that had survived a wholesale retreat from his forehead was closely trimmed. Rimless glasses perched halfway down his nose. His tie, tiny white polka dots on dark blue, was pulled away from the unbuttoned neck of his white shirt.

"I worked Wilshire," he told her in a gravelly voice. "Long time ago."

Searching for a polite rejoinder, she offered, "The name sounds familiar." Her career had had an unusually high degree of geographic stability; most cops, at least early in their careers, worked in many divisions of the city.

"Then you have a hell of a good memory," Frasier said, looking at her owlishly over the top of his glasses. "It was maybe two weeks back in the early eighties. I was on loan from Pacific."

So much for trying to establish rapport. "Must have been a different Frasier," she said wryly.

"What can we do for you?"

She made her answer succinct. "I'm Luke Taggart's defense rep."

Looking not in the least surprised, Frasier cast a glance at Mussino as if his phone conversation were a deliberate ploy to leave Frasier to handle this.

Kate said, "The dead man in Apparition Alley—Julio Mendez. Who was the catching detective?"

He looked again at Mussino. "It went downtown. You know the guys in Robbery-Homicide at Parker? I think it was Moynihan and Oliver down there."

She waited until her silence drew his gaze back to her. "Someone here was on call. Someone here initially went to the scene and took charge."

Again Frasier looked to Mussino. "Why don't you wait and talk to Max."

"This is no big deal, Detective. Why don't you just pull the file—"

Mussino covered the phone receiver. "Be right with you." Frasier sat back and ignored Kate; he continued to leaf through his murder book.

A scant minute later, Mussino hung up and leaned across the desk to take Kate's hand in a grip that she endured in a determination to not allow her discomfort to show. A bone-crushing handshake, she believed, was neither a sign of sincerity nor an assertion of power but simply an excuse to inflict pain.

"Detective Delafield," Frasier was saying to Mussino. "She wants to know about Mendez."

Mussino leaned back in his chair. Unlike Frasier's neckwear, his brown-and-yellow tie was cinched neatly up on the collar of his beige shirt, but his sleeves were rolled up on his spindly arms. "Jack, why don't you get that stuff from R and I and I'll talk to the detective."

Phrased in the form of a suggestion, it was clearly an order. Frasier got up from his desk with alacrity, hitching the gun on his hip. "You got it, Mouse."

Mussino sat back in his chair and folded his arms. "So how long you been a three?"

"Twelve years."

"That so. Only a year for me. Feels like twelve."

She recognized this as his declaration of equal status with her in the detective ranks regardless of her years of seniority. He said, "Taggart went off the planet for a defense rep."

She smiled thinly. "Yes, well . . . here I am, my spaceship on your doorstep. Were you the case detective?"

"Yep, for the fifteen seconds before it went downtown. Ken Morales and me. Yesterday we found a DB out at the reservoir, Mexican hooker. Kenny's still up there fucking around."

She had read about the murder in the paper this morning. "Identify her yet?"

"Nope. We're doing the useless usual. Canvass of her street sisters and all the beaner organizations. But a dead wetback—much less a hooker—that makes everybody's so-what list."

Mouse Mussino was going out of his way to treat her as he would a male colleague. Obscenity- and bigotry-laced talk from male officers had happened to her before, but mostly in her early career, inflicted as a challenge. Kate knew better than to react.

He shrugged. "Some john took a taco belle up there and fucked her every way she didn't want him to." The white bristle of his mustache twitched. "Opened up a few new holes in her."

Again she remained silent. Ed Taylor at his worst had not been as bad as Mouse Mussino.

"Speaking of useless beaners, what do you need to know about this Julio Mendez?" He pronounced Julio contemptuously, with the hard English *J* instead of the Spanish *H* sound.

"I'd like to see whatever you have. The fifty-one, crime scene attendance log, preliminary report, autopsy protocol. Investigator's summary, summary reports of the interviews, evidence inventory list—"

"How about my jockey shorts too?"

"Fine, if they're on the evidence list. Look, I'm the defense representative—"

"Which puts you right in with the bottom-feeding lawyers." He took a shiny red McIntosh apple from his desk drawer and took a bite out of it.

She said quietly, "I'm representing a fellow officer. You may not like it, I might not like it, but it's not my choice in the matter."

"Correction," he said through his mouthful of apple. "You're representing a piece of shit. It's not your choice—so go through the motions. He isn't worth anybody's time of day."

"I may very well come to agree with you. But I still need to—"

"Hey, do whatever you think you need to do. But not here. Take your questions downtown."

With effort, she checked her anger. "I'll do that at some point, but I'm taking my own look into things. Which means starting at the beginning."

"Don't expect me or anybody here to waste two seconds helping you help that asshole."

"At least answer me this, Detective. Why all the animosity?"

"You heard what he did with IAD?"

"I heard about Avery and Hamilton."

"Lucy Taggart got down on his knees and sucked IAD cock. Took out two good cops doing it. And one of them was his *partner.*" He took another bite from his apple.

"The two officers did break the law," Kate reminded him. "You know the Chief's current policy. Zero tolerance. We don't protect bad cops anymore."

"Bad cops? What the hell did they do? Screwed a coupla whores?" Bits of saliva spewed out from his chomping of the apple. "So what? What difference did it make? You think two cops fucking a few whores made some kind of big difference in the lives of those losers? Two good cops go down for no reason, and we got yellow belly Lucy Taggart swaggering around."

Mussino tore another bite out of his apple. "As for our beloved spade police chief, one more year and he's history. Anything coming out of his fat black ass these days doesn't even smell."

Kate knew without looking around that she and Mussino were alone. That every word coming out of his mouth was deniable, and he knew he was invincible and he was enjoying it. An echo from her past sounded from deep inside her, and she sent a curse in the direction of Calla Dearborn for dredging it up.

She said, "Avery and Hamilton were a long time ago."

"Not long enough." He spat an apple seed into his

wastebasket. "Lucy Taggart fucked up the only two partners who ever felt okay about working with him." He
held up a hand. "Okay, Lucy didn't pull the trigger on
Tony Ferrera. But Lucy's such bad luck I gotta figure
it's Lucy's fault Tony's at that liquor store to take a bullet. Did he tell you all his shit about cops blowing away
Tony?"

She said carefully, "I heard about it."

"Yeah, well here we all are, all of us feeling like shit
over Tony, and Robbery-Homicide comes busting in
here and makes everybody give up their service revolver
for fucking *testing* because they need to check out what
Lucy Taggart told them." Red was beginning to creep
over Mussino's face as he strained to keep his voice from
rising. "Can you fucking *believe* that shit? Can you fucking *believe* one cop fucking accusing his fellow cops of
blowing away one of our own? Can you fucking *believe*
it?"

She did not reply, but she could believe it. Hadn't
Taggart suggested that the same thing had happened to
her when she had been shot?

"And as for Bud Avery . . . anybody that brushes up
against Lucy Taggart sooner or later turns into a pile of
shit. Two cops dead because of him. I tried to tell
Tony—"

"*Two?* Two cops dead?"

"Yeah. You said you knew about Avery."

"I knew he'd taken a deal and resigned."

"And then he ate his gun."

Kate was silent at this police jargon for a cop killing
himself. Taggart had not mentioned Avery's suicide.
What else had Taggart not mentioned to her?

Mussino said, "I'm telling you now—it'll happen to
you too. If Lucy Taggart did Avery, he could do any
cop—none of us are saints. Avery was a good guy, he
should never have had to swallow his gun. Tony Ferrera
was a good guy too. Good to his family, a real good cop.
Lucy Taggart's a barf bag."

Mindful of her rule that she would not out gay people to nongays, she said carefully, "You call him Lucy. Do you think he's gay?"

"There's gays and then there's faggots. Anybody that sucks IAD cock is a faggot in my book."

She interpreted this to mean that he did not think Taggart was gay. "When Tony Ferrera was killed, were you the case detective before it went downtown?"

Mussino flung the remains of his apple into the wastebasket and leaned toward Kate. "Tony Ferrera's off limits. You asked why I hate Taggart's yellow guts, and I answered the question. Otherwise, Tony Ferrara's none of your fucking business. I'm not answering one fucking question about him. He's got nothing to do with the guy Taggart took out." He reached into a tier of file trays and yanked out a gray interoffice mail envelope in clear dismissal of her. "You go dig up your own information about Julio Mendez." Again the derisive pronunciation of the name.

She said, "Whatever you think of Luke Taggart, he has a right under the Police Officer's Bill of Rights to discovery privileges—"

"Fuck that for a joke." He ripped open the interoffice envelope.

"It's no joke, and you know it. Look, Detective Mussino—let's get this conversation onto a useful track. I understand there was no GSR test on Taggart."

"So what? We didn't know to test him till three days later."

"Did you test his uniform?"

"Yeah, we did. So what?"

"So a case was just dismissed because lack of gunshot residue on a suspect was ruled reasonable doubt that he had fired a weapon."

"It sure as fuck wasn't a case where they found bullets that matched the doer's gun. If I find some asshole's fingerprint at a crime scene, you're gonna tell me he wasn't there? This is the same fucking thing."

"How do you explain the absence of GSR on Taggart—not testing for it?"

Mussino chuckled. "You think any jury's gonna believe or care about a GSR test? When we can carry the fucking bullets from Lucy Taggart's fucking gun into court?"

Kate asked with interest, "Has the DA decided on what they'll go for?"

"The DA's got a little problem with this case." He waved a hand scornfully. "Number one, they hardly give a fuck since they lost their own roll-out team investigators to budget cuts. Number two, Taggart's too smart to plead this one out, he knows they got a problem finding a jury that thinks a cop blowing away a two-time loser piece-of-shit drug dealer is a real bad idea."

Kate leaned on the table, further closing up the space between herself and Mussino. She held his stare. "Detective, are you going to cooperate with my legitimate requirements, or do I actually have to waste your time and mine by going to your captain?"

Mussino held her stare, then leaned back in his chair and looked up at the ceiling as if to say, *Okay, I tried.* He said, "I suppose you and I both should see Captain Thomason for a way to go on this." He blew air out through his mustache in a protracted sigh, tossed the unread contents of the interoffice envelope back into the file tray. "But he's downtown today. Let's go one step at a time . . . and see what we can get done."

Kate pulled out her notebook.

9

DRIVING around Hollywood, Kate stayed close by the station, as if leaving its proximity would fracture her thought process. Vaguely, she noticed her surroundings: dilapidated houses with peeling paint and rusted cars parked in slovenly front yards enclosed by wire-mesh fencing. A cluster of teenage gang bangers, with identical side-shaven heads, sloppy Lakers shirts, oversize pants, and elaborate jogging shoes, leaned against a dented, corroded Pontiac Firebird. Delongpre, she picked up from a street sign.

She was sifting through her impressions of the paperwork on the Mendez shooting. The original file had been forwarded to Robbery-Homicide and Internal Affairs at Parker Center, but Mouse Mussino had allowed her to see the division's records. If he had his reasons to exercise his own judgment and authority as a D-3, she was happy not to risk interference from a member of the brass whose reading of the political waters might raise bureaucratic hoops that could cost her considerable time and energy to leap through. But Mussino's decision was in itself a matter to ponder. Had she been in his position, she would not for a moment have acted autonomously; she would have brought the matter before Lieutenant Bodwin to assure compliance with police regulations that had only erratic relationship with civilian law—and undoubtedly Bodwin would have kicked it up to Captain Delano.

While Mussino had allowed her to look at the file, he had not, however, allowed her to make copies except of the autopsy report, which was a public record; she had been reduced to taking notes as efficiently as possible. And there was a lot of paper to review, since the case had not immediately been classified as an officer-involved shooting and thus had not gone immediately downtown.

Kate found another street sign to orient herself, and then drove toward Hollywood Boulevard. This division of LAPD might not be as big as West L.A.—which covered an immense sixty square miles—but it was enormous, she reflected, extending as it did all the way up to Mulholland Drive; and with the town's status as a tourist mecca, its several major motion picture studios and numerous independents, its television networks and famous landmarks, Hollywood Division had distinct policing problems. There were big dance clubs here, with Fridays and Saturdays major cruising nights, Latino kids by the thousands out in their cars. LAPD's solution to handling the problem had been to close down Hollywood Boulevard on weekend nights just as it closed down Westwood, and to hassle cruisers with traffic tickets. The better solution, in Kate's mind, would be to redirect them into an area where they could feel unobstructed, yet where LAPD could adequately supervise them. Easier said than done, with so few police to cover so many people and so much territory.

She returned to her assessment of the Mendez shooting. Sequestered in an interview room, breathing air putrid with stale cigar smoke, she had pored over the crime scene attendance log, taking down the name of every officer responding to the scene. Next she studied the photographs, first the long shots of Apparition Alley and then the victim in context with the scene; she spread out and arranged the close-up photos of the body into the angles from which they had been taken, so that she could look at the dead Julio Mendez in full perspective. Next, she examined the summary reports.

According to the responding officers, Pedro Fernandez and Paul Curtiss—Fernandez authoring the report— they had entered the scene at approximately 10:25 p.m. with Officer Luke Taggart to confirm that the victim had expired, a fact evident from the fatal nature of the wounds. Fresh blood at the scene and the still-warm body temperature of the victim indicated recent demise. According to the lucidly written report of Sergeant Antonio Lopez who had taken charge of the scene, Taggart had explained his presence by recounting the pursuit of an armed male drug suspect holding a female hostage into the locale commonly known as Apparition Alley, and that both subjects had then disappeared. Taggart's version of events appeared to be at complete variance with the layout of the scene, which was a dead-end alley, but he held fast to his account. Obeying the instructions of Sergeant Lopez, Taggart had remained at the scene pending the arrival of the investigating detectives.

Mussino and Morales's report—Morales the author— contained a repetition of Taggart's story. Taggart accompanied Mussino and Morales to the Hollywood Division station where he once more related his account of events on audiotape and made out his own written report.

She had carefully gone over Taggart's report of events, which did not deviate in any major or minor point from what he had told other officers—or her, during her meeting with him.

An immediate canvass of the area had produced no witnesses; and because Taggart's account was in contradiction with evidence at the scene, the investigating detectives impounded Taggart's service revolver, and Divisional Captain Seymour Thomason then assigned Taggart to desk duty pending further investigation.

As she drove up Gower toward Hollywood Boulevard, Kate's gaze was drawn upward to one of L.A.'s most famous landmarks, the Hollywood sign, its irregularly spaced letters milky in a mist that lay against an untidy brownish green hillside. The turntable-shaped Capital Record Building came into view, and as she turned down Hollywood Boulevard and headed toward the intersection of Hollywood and Vine, the Pantages Theater. A Broadway department store had once been on the corner of Hollywood and Vine—she had shopped there years ago with Anne. Now it was the American Business Institute.

She returned to her review of what she had discerned in the interview room from the files. Among the items on the evidence list, of greatest interest to her had been the two bullets extracted from the rear wall of Apparition Alley—and sixteen baggies of crack. Discovered in a belt pouch on Julio Mendez by the medical examiner, the crack had been bagged by the crime lab technicians and immediately logged in as evidence. Indication of bullet holes had been found by investigating detectives Mussino and Morales in the rear wall of the crime scene and the extracted bullets were consequently bagged and tagged. Chain of custody on both of these crucial items of evidence appeared to be ironclad.

In a report dated three days after the shooting, ballistics tests declared a match between Taggart's gun and the bullets from the wall. Robbery-Homicide was notified. Taggart was taken into custody and questioned by Detectives Roy Moynihan and Robert Oliver, then placed under arrest, advised of his rights, and booked. With the case transferred to Robbery-Homicide, the file record ended. Kate knew from newspaper stories that Taggart had been arraigned the following day and released on a quarter of a million dollars bail.

The two dozen or so field interview cards filled out by Mussino and Morales from the follow-up area canvass produced no corroborating witnesses, no cooperating witnesses. The FI's were interesting to Kate—because they were too much the same and had too much the same phrasing. They looked like filler to her, and she knew filler when she saw it from working with Ed Taylor, who had not taken one step more than he needed to during his entire final decade of police work.

Glancing at the pedestrians on Hollywood Boulevard as she drove, Kate decided that except for the occasional purple head of spiky hair or a leather man, everyone looked reasonably normal today. Maybe because the rest of the world had caught up with the zaniness that had once been the hallmark of this street. As usual, it was easy to spot the tourists: they were the ones peering down at the names of entertainment luminaries embedded in large metallic stars in the sidewalk.

No one would ever confuse Hollywood Boulevard with any other street in any other city—and maybe there can never be a cleanup here, she thought, passing the fabled Musso & Frank Grill where Industry power players still lunched. Maybe there had to be a place in L.A. exactly like the Boulevard, gaudy and bawdy, with dreams and mythology brought together in a jumble of an Egyptian Theater and a Scientology Building, a Frederick's of Hollywood and a Guiness World of Records Museum, and wig shops and junky jewelry emporiums and stores with tawdry souvenirs of the movies—and most of all, Mann's Chinese Theater, crowded as always with visitors of all ages and nationalities hunkered down beside the famous footprints to photograph them and to be themselves photographed. Somehow all of it came together in an alchemy of magic. It had been magic when she had first seen it years ago as an émigré from Michigan, and it was magic now.

Turning left on La Brea, she came back down Sunset to Stewart and parked north of Hollywood Boulevard, then set off on foot. She entered the Burger King that Taggart claimed he had come out of on the night of the shooting. Notebook in hand, ignoring the patrons, focused entirely on her memory of events as Luke Taggart had related them, she stood gazing out the front window, then left the restaurant. Where had Taggart's patrol car been parked, she wondered, and made a note to ask. She watched a black-and-white drift by, the driver's window open to the day, the blond driver wearing sergeant's stripes on the arm she rested on the window's edge.

Hard to imagine a large, clear plastic baggie of drugs being openly exchanged on this street, right here on the Walk of Stars, Kate mused, even under the cover of darkness. Not with patrol cars constantly traveling a beat along this street. The desperation of drug users and the stupidity of drug suppliers could hardly be underestimated, but still . . .

She moved on down the street, the pavement slick under the smooth soles of her shoes. She remembered trying to walk on this surface at the beginning of a rainstorm, the pavement such a skating rink that she wondered how the district of Hollywood could not be inundated with lawsuits from people with broken hips.

At the corner she made her way down Stewart, concentrating on the terrain, and on a group of deteriorating eight- to twelve-unit apartment buildings with stucco facades sunbaked into pallid suggestions of their original colors and ribboned with streaks from winter rains. They were buildings whose survival rested solely on the pedigree of their construction—upkeep had been of no obvious concern to anyone for years. Foliage, however, had thrived independent of human care: luxuriant bougainvillea climbing up over fences and trellises and roofs in brilliant blossoms of scarlet and orange, full-headed emperor palms waving imperiously in the Santa Ana winds, several of their dry, brown, discarded fronds scudding and tumbling along the street. She walked slowly down Wheeler Avenue, stopping briefly to survey the apartment buildings whose windows faced out onto the street.

Had she not had Luke Taggart's description of Apparition Alley, she could have identified it by its smell:

the sour stench of garbage, urine, alcohol, and vomit assailed her before she reached the opening to the alley. In its dank, shadowy depths, the figure of a woman was discernible, lying back against the far wall beside her loaded shopping cart, legs splayed out, motionless. Approaching carefully, remembering Taggart's description of the DBs and ODs he had pulled out of Apparition Alley, Kate saw that the woman's eyes were closed and that there were no signs of breathing; but the rise and fall of her chest could be concealed by the layers of clothing she wore even in this mid-eighty-degree heat. Aware that many homeless people were diseased and covered with contagious lice and crabs, Kate was annoyed that she did not have a set of plastic gloves with her. But she had to to check for signs of a pulse, and so she leaned forward.

The woman shocked her by suddenly sitting up on the paved alley, eyes popping open like a doll that had been picked up.

Recovering, Kate peered at her. She looked to be in her fifties, and she reeked of body odor, her matted hair tied back by a wide, filthy velvet ribbon. She was either intoxicated or ill, and Kate needed to know whether she should call immediately to have her picked up. She asked, "What's your name?"

"Whassit to you." The voice was reedy and wheezy.

"Making conversation, that's all," Kate said, hunkering down beside her. "My name's Kate Delafield. What's yours?"

"Roshie."

"Rosie—what's your last name?"

"Roshie."

"Rosie, is this your territory?"

"Naw. Over there." She waved a hand weakly in a vague direction. " 'S my birthday," she mumbled. "Thirty-sixsh. Hap' birthday to me ... Come here to shelebrate."

"Is this where you always come to celebrate?"

"Whassit to you?"

"When were you here last, Rosie?"

"Whassit to you?"

"Last week? Last month?"

"Got'ny shpare shange?"

Kate fished a five-dollar bill from her wallet and handed it to her, holding firmly onto it as Rosie seized it. "For food. Buy food, okay?"

"Sure."

Kate released the bill. Folding it into the smallest possible area, Rosie pulled her lips up in a smile. Her front teeth were missing. Kate wondered if they had been knocked out in an assault or a rape.

Kate rose to her feet. "You take care of yourself, Rosie."

Rosie lay back again and closed her eyes, tucking the folded five-dollar bill into what she obviously felt was her safest hiding place—under the filthy ribbon holding her hair.

Kate gazed at her surroundings. Battered and misshapen garbage cans, belonging presumably to adjacent buildings, were arrayed at the entrance to this rank-smelling place. Two ancient, dented Dumpsters sagged against graffiti-sprayed black walls that were gouged in places to their gray brick origins and coated with dried vomit.

Portions of a taped outline had been pulled away from the pavement, but the silhouette was still clearly that of a body. She knelt beside it and studied the distance from the outline where the dead Julio Mendez had lain to the entrance to the alley. Pulling a penlight from her shoulder bag, she shone it to the back wall of the alley. Its beam illuminated gouge marks.

She got up and moved to the wall, seeing from the splinters around the dug-out bullet holes that it was made of wood. At eye level and approximately six inches apart, the holes looked freshly made and were easy to spot even without the use of her penlight. Thoughtfully, she looked at the angle from the bullets back to the outline; the bullet holes were in direct, perfect line with where Julio Mendez's head would have been before he fell.

A clink drew Kate's attention back to Rosie. She had pulled a pint bottle from the folds of her voluminous clothing. She raised it to Kate in salute.

10

KATE drove down Hollywood Boulevard, following it off to the right as it turned into Laurel Canyon. Winding in two narrow lanes up into the Santa Monica Mountains, the road would come out as four lanes in the San Fernando Valley, a daily commute for thousands of Valley dwellers and one that Kate was happy she had never had to make in all the years she'd lived in Los Angeles. But she enjoyed driving the road in nonrush-hour traffic, especially on this, the L.A. side, with its eclectic mixture of rawly new contemporary homes cut into the hillsides and vine-covered cottages that looked as if they had virtually taken root on their sites. Byways, many of them dead ends, led off Laurel Canyon above the semiarid landscape of the Los Angeles basin and into a rustic paradise of houses on stilts overlooking steeply canted, forested hillsides and glens and box canyons.

Kate took Willow Glen to Fernleaf, its identifying sign barely visible in a cluster of bush and trees and mailboxes, then followed hairpin turns along a narrow, raggedly tarred road thickly lined with foliage, passing gravel driveways that vanished into thickets of trees. In a trash-strewn clearing on her right, a battered sixties-vintage Volkswagon van shared turf with a rickety, falling-down shack. Four Dobermans flung themselves at Kate's car and chased it down the road in slathering ferocity; all the while an immensely fat woman in a bright yellow housecoat placidly hung clothes on a line strung between two pine trees without so much as a glance at Kate.

The house was identified by LUKE TAGGART neatly painted on a redwood post, under another name: LINDY DAVIS 1963–1993. Situated at the end of the road, the house was tucked against a grouping of elm and pine trees where it would receive afternoon sun. The Dobermans had given up their pursuit, but now Kate's car was circled by a German shepherd and a golden retriever, the retriever wagging its tail and barking, the shepherd growling deep in its throat.

She could hear music faintly, an aria sung by a soprano, and she lowered her window. She knew nothing about opera, but the song seemed to soar in ethereal beauty into the trees and sky. She sat in the car, absorbed in the music, looking at a house of faded gray timber, not large, but clearly designed by an architect, the framework and the oversized doors and sculpted, high windows rising in a vaulted peak. A gray Range Rover was parked on a gravel drive by the side of the house.

Not much wonder Taggart was able to raise bail, she thought. There was a lot of money here, too much for a city patrol officer with ten years of service.

Taggart came out of the house barefoot, in dark gray shorts, the tight gray T-shirt stretched across his chest stating Prisoner of Alcatraz. His dark gold stubble had thickened in the day or so since she had seen him. He called to his dogs: "Turk! Dreamer!"

She eased herself out of the car and held the back of her hand to the dogs to let them sniff her, then knelt to stroke first the retriever and then the shepherd. Her living circumstances in the years since she had been with Anne had prevented her from sharing her home with any pet larger than a cat, and she still missed Barney, the gentle collie who had loved and protected Anne. "They're beautiful," she told Taggart.

He ruffled the fur of the retriever. "They're pretty good guys."

Birds chittered from all around her; the smell of pine trees and leaves and earth was vivid and intoxicating. She accepted the hand Taggart extended to pull her to her feet, then gestured toward the house. "This is wonderful."

"Glad you like it. First time in my life I've had something that suits me. Come on in."

She only vaguely noticed pine floors with scattered cotton rugs and scant pieces of simple furniture, so stunned was she by the rear of Taggart's house: several vast sheets of glass opening out to a vista of the forest beyond. "Sit outside?" he inquired, turning down the volume on the CD player.

She nodded. A raw cedar deck off to one side held a table and chairs, and Kate wondered if Taggart took his meals out there. God knows she would be out there every possible moment if she owned a place like this, especially with a set of exterior speakers that took the exquisite operatic aria outdoors with her.

"Make yourself comfortable," Taggart called. "Be right there."

She lowered her shoulder bag, eased herself out of her jacket, and took a chair that allowed sun on her back and sore shoulder. She sat looking peacefully off into the depths of the forest, the shepherd hunkering down beside her. This, she thought, would rank very high on my list of possible heavens.

"If it weren't for the dogs, deer would come down here," Taggart said, putting down two glasses of lemonade and sitting opposite her. "We get raccoons, squirrels, rabbits, chipmunks . . ."

Kate asked enviously, "How long have you lived here?"

"A couple of years."

"How did you ever manage to get this?"

"My ex-wife."

Something about his tone drew her gaze away from the woods and to him.

But Taggart's face was expressionless as he continued, "Divorced five years. Could have blown me over with a feather. I walked out on her—and she leaves me a portfolio of stocks and bonds. I figure Lindy flat forgot to change her will, or thought she had to make amends, or maybe it was just her idea of a joke."

"She died young," Kate said, remembering the name Lindy Davis and the dates 1963–1993 on the sign in front of the house.

He nodded. "From AIDS."

"Did you know about it?"

Taggart said, "She didn't get it from me."

"That's not what I asked," Kate said.

"I could see the question in your face."

"No, you didn't. Because it wasn't there."

The retriever climbed up onto the deck and padded over to Taggart. "Okay. Maybe it's my own guilt." Taking a drink of his lemonade, he fondled the dog's head. "I didn't know she had AIDS. I had shit for brains about her. I was number two in her life by a New York mile. Her one true love was cocaine. When Jamison called me about the will, he told me how she got all this money. She was into hooking big time—like, Heidi Fleiss big time. Cocaine wiped out her immune system, pneumonia did the rest."

The aria softening to its final sweet notes, Taggart jerked a thumb back toward the house. "I didn't know what the hell to do with her money. So I did this."

He bought the peace she couldn't find, Kate thought. Feeling inexplicably grieved as the aria died away, she asked, "What's the piece that just played?"

" 'Addio del passato,' *La Traviata*. The singer's Montserrat Caballé."

"Would you write that down for me? I want to get it."

"It's yours. The CD's yours. Least I can do."

That's the truth, Kate thought. You've added nothing

but mess to my life. "Thank you," she said. "I dropped in because I have a few questions."

"And here I thought this was a social call," Taggart said dryly.

She managed a smile. "Just trying to put a complete picture together. The night of the shooting, where did you park your patrol car?"

"Does that have some significance?"

Was this an evasive tactic? But why would he want to evade so simple a question? She noticed that Taggart had dropped his macho posture, as if her invasion of his personal space had blown his cover as the tough and ready street cop. She said, "It wasn't in any of the reports."

He looked surprised. "You've seen the reports?"

She nodded. "I went to Hollywood Division and saw Max Mussino."

"No kidding," he marveled. "Mouse and Moron actually cooperated with you."

She smiled at Ken Morales's nickname. "Mussino did. What was on file at the station."

He shook his head. "Mouse and Moron are to homicide detectives what an anthill is to space travel. I'm sure they did damn little investigating—in case they found something that didn't fit their scenario of what they think I did."

"There wasn't anything in your own report about where your patrol car was parked," Kate pointed out.

He shrugged. "I parked it on Stewart, about three houses down from the Boulevard. I'm not a detective, I didn't know it was important."

"Every detail needs to be in place. Did you find anything during your own investigation?"

"No."

But there had been the barest hesitation before Taggart answered. She said, "You did investigate."

Again he shrugged. "I looked into it."

She looked at him in exasperation. He had investigated in thorough detail his partner Tony Ferrara's death, but he had only "looked into" the killing he had been accused of committing. She asked rhetorically, "Why do I have this feeling that key information is being kept from me?"

"I don't know," Taggart said calmly. "Such as what?"

"Such as the fact that you didn't tell me everything about Bud Avery."

Taggart's face froze; then he rubbed his stubbly chin, his hands moving back over his buzz-cut hair. "I don't think that's much of a mystery. If somebody swallowed his gun because of something you did, you'd hardly go around talking about it."

"I would if it went directly to the prejudice cops in my station house felt about me."

"You sound like a lawyer."

"Insults will get you nowhere," Kate reminded him, and Taggart smiled. "Tell me about Bud Avery."

Hunching over in his chair, he said somberly, "We were in the same class in the academy. He was really gung-ho, bought the whole rah rah rah—being a cop was his call to the priesthood. He got sent to Newton and I got Central, and then we moved around some more till we both ended up in Hollywood. I was glad to be partnered with him, I expected he'd developed into a good cop. I did hear he'd blown a guy away at Newton, but I didn't have the brains in those days to think that much about it."

Taggart leaned forward, rolling his glass of lemonade between his huge hands. "The shooting . . . it turned him into a fucking John Wayne. I mean, he could've been wearing a cowboy hat and boots and chaps. He'd talk to me like this: 'The world's fulla scum, Tag, and a man's gotta do what a man's gotta do,' " he mimicked in a low, chesty voice. "When he started plonking hookers, he thought he was this macho protective hero the hookers all worshiped. He couldn't see these were working women doing what they had to do to keep themselves and their pimps out of jail. I couldn't figure out what'd happened to the guy. I told him he was a sap, I told him he'd turned into a piece of stupid shit. He called me a faggot—and got a new partner. Then IAD comes down on him, and the next minute he's on the rubber gun squad."

Kate nodded at this parlance for officers whose service revolvers have been taken away because of an internal investigation or psychological danger signs.

"He'd just got married. To Jack's sister—Jack Hamilton, that's his dimwit new partner who thinks if a veteran cop has screwing privileges, it's okay for him to screw around too, and steal a little drug money while he's at it. Avery'd bought a new house, he's got all this financial pressure and IAD is up his ass. So the next thing, he comes to work drunk. Now he's relieved of duty and for total humiliation they frog-march him to one of the shrinks. He's in deep shit with his wife, the press is all over him. Then comes his hearing. They strip his badge, gun, uniform. He's John Wayne with his gun taken away, kicked off the range. It was like they'd busted all his bones. He didn't have a clue how to drop the macho crap and become the guy he'd once been."

Kate had listened intently to Taggart's story. "How do you know all this?"

"Common knowledge, most of it." His eyes narrowed. "I got a phone call from Avery's wife I'll never forget. Mostly she screamed 'Murderer' over and over again. Mouse Mussino, he'd say things to me like, 'Hey, is that a piece of Bud Avery's brain on your uniform?' He made sure everybody knew Avery eating his gun was the same as if I blew him away."

Kate shook her head. "He blew himself away. He betrayed his oath as a police officer."

Taggart raised a hand. "Yeah, so I told myself. But I've seen some of my fellow officers get clean away with one hell of a lot worse than anything Bud Avery ever did."

"You're talking now about what you think happened to Tony Fererra."

"Yeah, I'm talking about Ferdie. You find out anything about Ferdie's death?"

She said with ill-concealed impatience, "It's none of my business."

"It is. I tell you, it's connected."

"In your opinion."

Taggart rattled the ice cubes in his lemonade, staring at them as if they were tea leaves he was trying to decipher. "When we met at that restaurant, you asked why I wanted you as my defense rep. Everybody knows you're one of the best detectives in LAPD. I was hoping you'd help me find out what happened to Ferdie."

She said in exasperation, "What the hell's going on here? Are you telling me to forget about representing you over the shooting of Julio Mendez? Are you trying to tell me you actually did shoot that man in Apparition Alley?"

"No, I'm not trying to tell you that," Taggart said heatedly. "No way am I telling you that."

"Do you swear the story you told me about him is the truth?"

He raised his right hand and said slowly, emphasizing each word, "I absolutely positively did not shoot Julio Mendez. I had nothing to do with his death."

"Then I'm telling you that the case I have to investigate is Julio Mendez. He's the one who's put your career at risk."

"Kate, listen to me. This is God's truth. I'm a dead man walking. It doesn't matter. I'm history at LAPD."

She remained silent. Whatever came down at the Board of Rights hearing, if he were exonerated on reasonable doubt, he would remain tainted beyond redemption, like an acquitted child molester. As a police officer, he would be an outcast. No cop would ever trust him. She could not imagine being in his position, painted into so dead-end a corner. Just like Bud Avery...

"Tag, they can prosecute you."

"If they do, I like my chances with a jury."

Shaking her head, she elected to abandon the subject for now. "Do you know anything about an *Advocate* reporter named..." She fished in her shoulder bag, pulled out a piece of paper. "Matt Brazelton?"

"An *Advocate* reporter?" he said incredulously.

Obviously he recognized the publication; and his reaction seemed odd for its vehemence. What else was he concealing? "That's what he said." Her tone was short, her patience suddenly shredding. What's the matter with me, she wondered. Why is my fuse so short these days? It's Calla Dearborn, she thought bitterly. The woman isn't helping me, she's messing up my head.

Taggart said, "I don't know anything about an *Advocate* reporter. I do know about an *L.A. Times* reporter. Has Corey Lanier contacted you?"

"I never have anything to do with the press."

"You can forget that. If she wants to talk to you, she's a heat-seeking missile."

"Maybe I'll stay here," Kate muttered. "Nobody could find me here."

"Don't be so sure."

"What do you mean?"

"I'll show you," he said cryptically. He gestured to the forest. "You're the first person who hasn't asked how I manage up here in the winter rain and mud."

"If I lived here, it wouldn't matter," Kate said.

Taggart got up from the table and told the golden retriever who climbed eagerly to her feet, "Dreamer, you stay."

Kate smiled; she had guessed that the German shepherd, which continued to snooze on the deck, would be the one named Turk.

She picked up her shoulder bag and followed Taggart back through the house, this time looking around her at expressionist prints on the walls, at overflowing book-cases. While Taggart removed the opera CD from the player, she stopped briefly to look at a bookcase filled entirely with texts on the minutia of police work, re-search literature on everything from crime scene tech-nique to DNA typing to mass spectrometry to ballistics and firearms. Her work was far more technically ori-ented than his, but standard police and FBI periodicals were the extent of her extracurricular reading.

"Pretty fancy computer," she said, indicating a sleek laptop sitting on a walnut desk, a game of solitaire laid out in bright colors on its screen.

"Ferdie's," he said, handing Kate the CD. "Ferdie was a real computer geek. The Internet and all that shit. All I ever do with it is play games."

Kate nodded. Aimee was highly computer literate, not only assisting Kate but often offering technical advice over the phone to friends suffering what Aimee called "computer distress." Kate said, "I'm pretty much a dunce myself, but not having access to one for all my notes makes me realize they're indispensable."

"Borrow this one," Taggart said.

"No, it means too much to you."

"Take it. It's just a machine."

She hesitated. Aimee was working on their home com-puter her every waking hour, and going into Wilshire Division while on leave was not a viable alternative.

"I insist," he said, and grinned. "It's the least I can do."

"Thank you," she said, "I appreciate it." The forms and reports that needed to be filled out on a case might be maddening, but they did end up as a comprehensive history, and she felt clumsy without the discipline of any record other than her notebook.

He turned the computer off, yanked out the plug, and quickly found the Compaq's carrying case.

Then he went out the front door, Kate following, and halted to point up at one of the high, curved windows.

"My bedroom," he said. "See that network of cracks there on the left side?"

"A bullet hole," Kate said.

"I leaned over to tie my shoes, it went past where my head just was. I don't get dressed or undressed in front of a window anymore."

"When was this?"

"Week ago."

"Did you report it?"

"In my shoes, would you?"

"Of course I would," Kate said. "Did you find anything? What about Dreamer and Turk—did they bark?"

"The guys didn't let out a peep. The shot came from the trees, outside the property. A real marksman."

"Did you find a casing? The slug?"

"No casing, not much chance in these woods, but the slug was your standard cop-issue nine millimeter."

"Do you still have it?" She added acidly, "Even though it's now useless as evidence?"

Hands on his hips, he confronted her. "I ask you: if cops are shooting at you, what's the point in calling the cops?" He pointed to her left arm. "You decide to let them get away with pinging you too?"

"It was an *accident,*" she stated, turning away from him. "Thanks for the lemonade. I have to get back."

Wordless, she went to her car. She placed the computer in the backseat, resisting the impulse to hurl it there just because it was Taggart's. God damn him for continuing with his insinuations. God damn him for trying to shatter her confidence, to foul her faith in her team. Not much wonder everybody despised this shit bird.

11

HALF an hour later, Kate was again parked on Stewart Street and making her way up to Wheeler Avenue.

The depths of Apparition Alley seemed possessed now only of murky shadows, the tattered tape outline of Julio Mendez's corpse, and the same pervasive, nauseating stench as earlier. But she searched the place, including the Dumpsters, to verify that it was clear of human presence.

Once again she went to the back wall and examined the entire expanse of it minutely with her penlight, including the dug-out bullet holes.

Crossing the street to assess adjacent buildings for a canvass, she was aware of a lightness invading her mood. Under most circumstances she did not conduct field interviews but analyzed them for possible follow-up investigation; it felt good to sink her teeth into basic police work, even something so nitty-gritty as canvassing.

The two-story faded beige stucco apartment buildings flanking Apparition Alley were similar in design, presenting solid facing walls on their alley side; foliage blocked direct view from either behind or in front of the alley.

A sign on the mailboxes in the tiny lobby of the building east of Apparition Alley directed her to the manager's office in the building on the other side of the alley. Kate made her way over there and buzzed the office.

"Yes," wheezed a voice over the scratchy intercom. Kate announced herself and the voice responded resignedly, "I'll come out."

An old man with a shiny bald pate, his baggy pants held up by suspenders, shuffled on slippered feet into the lobby. Ignoring her offer of identification, he said, "I live all the way in the back. I don't know nothing about what happened with that dead fellow."

"Other officers have been here, then."

"Came in here that night and one other time."

But detectives could have been here other times, she surmised. They could have been admitted by tenants in either of the buildings. "I need to talk to all your tenants," she said.

"I figured." He pulled a key on a rabbit's foot key chain from a pocket of his baggy pants. "Opens the other building. Bring it back when you're done." He shuffled off.

She returned to the other building, deciding to start with the one least likely to produce witnesses, since the events of that night, according to Luke Taggart, had unfolded from the direction of Stewart Street, on the west side of Apparition Alley.

The lobby of the east building opened onto fourteen units of small, single apartments with windows shrouded by dark curtains, arranged along two exterior corridors surrounding a courtyard of cracked, weed-clotted concrete. It was not at all reminiscent of the apartment building where Kate had been shot, and she was grateful. Mindful of the manager's indifference and of Taggart's sarcastic remark that "Hollywood is just filled with civic-minded citizens eager to come forward and assist their fellow man, especially the cops," she checked that her gun was clear and quickly available in her shoulder bag, and began her canvass.

Of the fourteen units, nine, including several whose curtains parted slightly, produced no response to Kate's knock and loud announcement that she was a police

officer. To Kate's regret, the two apartments overlooking the street appeared absent of occupants. The
other five residents, all of them old Russian women in
somber, dark-colored dress, strained to understand her
questions, repeating them back to her in heavily ac-
cented English, but had no information to offer. They
had not, they claimed, been questioned by anyone else,
but their equivocal answers as to whether they had even
answered their doors to other officers undercut their
claims and reconfirmed what Kate had learned at the
very beginning of her career—that as a woman she
could gain entry through doors opened with reluctance
and suspicion to male officers.

In the other building, four old men on the first floor
invited her in and offered no information but issued
variations of finger-shaking complaints that the police
should only be so diligent in taking all the drug addicts
out of the neighborhood. On the second floor, a woman
called "No" to her every question through her closed
door. A middle-aged blonde reeking of gin slumped
against her doorjamb and offered a blank memory of
the night of January third, including whether she had
ever been questioned about it.

Kate had left the two second-floor front apartments
for last. The first one did not respond to Kate's knock.
The lightness having all but evaporated from her spirits,
she tried the second apartment.

Her knock and call of "Police officer" was answered
by a faint, querulous, "Take me a minute or two to get
there." The voice held a slight southern inflection.

As she heard a fumbling at the door, Kate stood to
the side and reached her good arm across the door,
holding up her ID case as she had at every apartment.
"If you'll look through your peephole, you'll see my
identification."

The door opened to a white-haired, stoop-shouldered
old woman leaning on a walker. "Saw you out the window across the street, looking at the place. Figured you

were police. Either that or up to no good."

Smiling, Kate introduced herself and added, "I appreciate your trouble. May I know your name?"

"Ida Wilson. There's coffee makings over there." She gestured with her head. "Go help yourself. I'll catch up with you in my own good time."

Kate made her way into a room with scant furniture, a shabby gray carpet, and a view directly out onto Wheeler Avenue. Ida Wilson was an old woman, in her late seventies if not her eighties. Would she have been awake at 10:30 at night, much less looking out into the street?

A plugged-in electric teakettle, a jar of instant coffee, a bowl of sugar, and several mugs sat on a plastic TV tray. Kate helped herself to the coffee, surveying the room as she did so. Its distinguishing feature was a worn corduroy recliner placed sideways against the window, another TV tray beside it holding an array of nearly a dozen prescription medications. Other furniture included a small television, an office-size refrigerator, a hot plate, a flimsy cupboard, a pine rocker, and a few well-used books in a pine bookcase. An afghan-covered daybed served as Ida Wilson's bed. The Oriental carpet of obvious quality under the recliner hinted at more affluent days.

As Ida Wilson moved her walker at a snail's pace over to the window, Kate discerned that it was arthritis that had crippled her, had deformed her spine to bend her forward and twisted her fingers into abnormal shapes. Obviously, the old woman could not wear rings, so Kate guessed that she would be a widow and asked, "May I fix you some of this coffee, Mrs. Wilson?"

"Call me Ida. Be glad to have you do that. Take a pinch of sugar in it." Clinging to her walker, Ida eased herself slowly back into her recliner. Kate prepared the coffee, sensing that she should not otherwise offer to help.

Ida accepted the mug between her crippled hands. "What's happened to your shoulder?"

"A work-related injury," Kate said, taking a seat in the rocker. "It's almost healed."

"Ah, good."

The comment seemed more than perfunctory to Kate. This pain-ridden woman was probably glad to be reminded that some ailments healed and that suffering did end. Taking her notebook from her shoulder bag, Kate said, "I have some questions about the night of January third."

"Guessed as much. Another detective was here a few days after. Tall, very nice-looking young man."

"Did anyone else talk to you?"

"Somebody knocked on my door real late that night, but I'd gone to bed by then, would've taken all of ten minutes to get myself together to go to that door, and I didn't try."

So in the three days before the murder of Julio Mendez had gone downtown for investigation by Robbery-Homicide, neither Mussino nor Morales had designated an officer for a follow-up interview of a woman with a crystal-clear view of the street, nor had the two detectives bothered to follow up themselves.

Writing anything down proved to be an awkward business with her left arm out of commission, but Kate propped her notebook on her raised thigh and recorded Ida Wilson's exact response. She asked, "Would you tell me what you remember about that night?"

"It was a Wednesday. I was sitting here in my chair watching *Dateline NBC* like I always do on Wednesdays. I heard a car come up and stop awhile by the alley, you know, with the engine going. Then I heard a backfire— well, I hoped it was a backfire. And then the car came on past."

Her mind igniting with what she had just heard, Kate decided to interrupt and take the old woman through her story detail by detail. "What direction was the car traveling?"

"That way, of course." Ida gestured in front of her, toward Stewart; from where she sat sideways in the window, the car had come from behind her.

"Could you see who was in the car?"

"Went by way too fast."

"Ida, when you heard the car stop and idle in front of the alley, did you hear a car door open?"

"I did. People stop and use that alley to dump their trash, Mrs. Christie tells me. That's what I thought it was."

And that's what it very well might have been, Kate reminded herself. "Tell me exactly what you remember hearing."

"Heard the car stop, the door open. A short bit later heard the backfire, then pretty quick the door closing again. Then it came on past me."

"When it was stopped by the alley, did the engine stop too?"

"Don't remember that it did."

"When the car came past, do you remember anything about it?"

Ida shrugged her rounded shoulders. "Just a big old car."

"Do you remember the color?"

"Hard to say. Dark, I'd say."

"Could you see it clearly that time of night?"

"I could. Light falls out there real good from the lamppost."

Lamppost. An old-fashioned word Kate had not heard in years. Looking at the seams and layers of age in Ida Wilson's face and crepey neck, the faded blue eyes, Kate thought she could be anywhere from seventy to ninety years old. "Station wagon? A van maybe?"

"No. You ask better questions than that young fellow did," Ida said. "More like the Oldsmobile Ninety-eight my husband drove back in the fifties."

So this old woman had indeed been more comfortably off than she was today in this birdcage of an apartment. "Then what happened, Ida?"

"A few minutes after the backfire, I heard another car stop at the alley. Then it came on past too. A police car."

Kate looked up sharply from her notes. "A police car?"

The old woman's face broke into a new network of wrinkles as she smiled. "There's no confusing them with other cars, you know."

Kate smiled back at her. "You're right."

"One comes along this street most nights. Mrs. Christie—she's my neighbor in number twelve, she's a little more spry than me, she gets out every day unless the weather's bad. Claims you police keep a close eye at night on that awful alley down the way. You people should be here during the day too. Worries me when my daughter doesn't get here the minute she says she will."

With all the drug addicts and the occasional dead body pulled from Apparition Alley, Kate could well imagine the dangers on this street. "I'll do what I can, I promise you." She would discreetly request through channels an extra patrol for the basic car assigned here. "Ida, what time was this?"

"Quarter to ten."

"Are you sure?"

"They were doing the quarter-hour commercial on *Dateline NBC.*" She nodded toward the TV. "Clock's right there next to the TV."

The clock was a small box with large numbers, the kind sold in drug stores. Kate wrote down the time Ida Wilson had given her, nine forty-five. Taggart, and all the police reports, had stated that all police activity had occurred between ten-fifteen and ten-thirty.

"Ida, there's no doubt in your mind about the time?"

The folds in Ida's neck quivered. "That's what the

young detective asked too. Treated me like I was some old bat he'd found in his attic.''

Kate shook her head. "I'm sure he meant no disrespect. Nor do I. Matching up all the facts in a case can be difficult at times.''

She did not doubt that the Robbery-Homicide detective probably had been rude, however unintentionally. Younger detectives characteristically judged people fragile with age as dotty. She herself had little reason to feel holier-than-thou. At a felony accident scene she had investigated several months back, when paramedics attending to three badly injured victims had ministered to the two teenagers first and then the elderly victim, Kate had realized her unthinking acceptance of this prioritizing of lives by age throughout her years of police work.

"You say that a police car came by. What direction was it traveling?''

"Same as the other car.''

"You said it stopped at the alley before it came by your window. How long was it stopped?''

"Not too long as I recall. A minute or two.''

"Then what happened?''

"Nothing, for a time.''

"Nothing?''

"Not another thing. The ten o'clock news came on channel five, and a good fifteen minutes later, I saw a policeman come running past.'' Ida indicated with a liver-spotted hand so distorted with arthritis that her fingers were angled sideways. "From that direction, toward me. From Stewart.''

This was the first statement that matched Taggart's story. "So this would have been about ten-fifteen.''

"Ten-fifteen, that's right. Then I heard shots. With the policeman running and all, I didn't imagine it was another backfire.''

"Ida, this is important. Did you see anyone else come up the street before the policeman?''

"Young couple, maybe fifteen minutes before, just as

132   KATHERINE V. FORREST

the news came on. Strolling along. Don't have too many young folks on this street. They live in that building 'cross the way." Again she pointed with her crippled hand at a building screened from the street by foliage.

"Would you tell me what they looked like? What they wore?"

"Raggedy jeans. Like all the young people do. Blond, the two of them, and all foolish and cuddly with each other."

"Did you see anyone else?"

"Before the police cars came, you mean? Not another soul."

So what about the man Taggart claimed he had chased, the one in the hooded sweatshirt with the baggie of drugs? What about the Indian woman in the veil that the man had taken hostage? Kate asked, "Did you leave the window between a quarter to ten and ten-fifteen? Could you have missed someone?"

"Sat here the whole time. Didn't see anybody else, and I don't miss a thing out there. I watch the television, but I catch anything that moves out of the corner of my eye. All told, I've sat in this window thirteen years now."

"May I ask how old you are, Ida?"

Ida looked at her coyly. "How old do you think I am?"

"I'd say . . ." Kate paused and looked at her as if in appraisal. She knew how to play this game; people who asked such a question always believed that they looked much younger than they were. "I'd say maybe early seventies."

"Ninety-two," the old woman said proudly.

"That's amazing, Ida." Kate hoped her enthusiasm concealed her sadness for this old woman and this tiny room where she passed her days. She hoped she had friends in this building, that Ida's family did more than deliver food and medication, that they took time out of their busy lives to relieve her isolation. She asked, "You

can see both sides of the street from there? Both side-
walks?''

"Come on over here and see for yourself," Ida said
tartly. "My eyesight's better'n people half my age. Hearing's just as sharp as it's ever been."

"I believe you, Ida." Putting her notebook aside, Kate
got to her feet, coffee mug in hand. "If you don't mind,
I'd like to get an idea of how far down the street you
can see from here."

"You just come right ahead."

Drinking her coffee, studying the street from beside
Ida, Kate saw that the old woman, her chair facing west,
would clearly see anyone coming along the sidewalk
from the direction of Stewart, unless someone skirted
very close to the buildings and shrubbery on this side of
the street.

"When you heard the shots the second time, how
many were there?"

"Two."

"And the first time, when you thought you heard a
car backfire—"

"The same. Two times then too."

"So all together that night you heard four sounds that
could have been shots."

"Four. That's right."

Chilled by what she had heard, Kate went back to the
rocker and sat for several minutes making careful notes
while Ida Wilson placidly gazed out at the street.

A car, two shots—and they were shots, not backfire,
she was certain—then a police car coming along this
street and stopping at the alley well before Luke Taggart
claimed he had arrived on the scene. Then Taggart arriving, and two more shots, the shots Taggart claimed
he hadn't fired . . . This matter was more puzzling, and
more ominous, all the time.

Kate finally asked, "Did you see another car around
ten-fifteen, when you heard the shots?"

Ida thought for a moment, then shook her head.

"Could one have come up to the alley from the other direction, from behind you?"

"Maybe. Didn't hear one, though. I hear sounds from the street better than I want to up here."

Kate knew that she would. Uncushioned by foliage, sound echoes would bounce off the pavement.

Ida continued, "Wouldn't ever trade this place for downstairs. Addicts and crazy people rattle those windows looking to get in. They get themselves in the building too, try doorknobs to see if anybody's left a door open. Sitting here, I see who's coming along that might bring trouble."

"The policeman you saw running along the street, can you describe him for me?"

"Big fellow. Big shoulders, real short hair. Moved right along for the size of him."

The sketchy description fit Taggart well enough. "What did you see after the officer ran past?"

"A few minutes later, police cars, lots of them zooming up with their sirens making a horrible ruckus and their flashing lights making my eyes hurt. Neighbors out on the street. Lots of commotion."

"I want to back up a minute, Ida. The police car that came along at a quarter to ten, the first one you saw. Tell me what you remember about it."

"It was going pretty slow. Like it always does. That's all."

"How many officers were in the car?"

"I only saw a driver. Could be somebody was in the back."

"A man or a woman driver?"

"Man. But I couldn't tell you one other thing about him."

"Do you know if the tenant who lives in the apartment next to you was home that night?"

"Nettie? She's been gone visiting with her relatives in Phoenix these past three months. And she's useless anyway, never sees or hears a thing. Those old Russian men that live in the front of that other building, Mrs. Christie says one of 'em's half deaf and got cataracts, and the other one's in his bed watching the television the whole day.'' She added proudly, ''I'm the only one that ever sees what goes on.''

''I'm sure you are, Ida.''

Kate sat over her notes. She had finally located a witness to the events surrounding the murder of Julio Mendez. Yet how credible a witness was a woman ninety-two years of age, immobilized by arthritis, and under prescription medication?

Flipping back the pages of her notebook to take Ida Wilson through her story once more, Kate knew she had considerable work to do. Her natural allies had a vested interest in getting rid of a cop they despised, and so she must do the work alone. She was a member of a vast police fraternity, but for this case, she was on her own.

A canvass of the rest of this block might corroborate what Ida Wilson had seen on the street and the four shots she had heard. Or possibly contradict her. At this point, she hoped with all her soul for contradiction. The worst apparition to come out of Apparition Alley was the probability that police misconduct had indeed been committed. And perhaps by someone other than—or in addition to—Luke Taggart.

12

WITH her shoulder aching and tiredness invading every bone in her body, Kate drove up Kings Road toward the condo. Her attention was drawn to a shiny new white Mazda, still bearing its dealer plates, illegally parked beside the fire hydrant in front of her building. The woman behind the wheel started the engine as Kate slowed to pull into the garage under the condo; when Kate opened the electronic gate and drove in, the Mazda zipped in behind her before the gate could close.

Kate climbed gingerly out of her car, her eyes never leaving the Mazda as the driver pulled into the nearest parking spot and sprang from her vehicle. The shoulder bag she pulled out with her so closely resembled the one Kate carried that Kate immediately suspected that like hers, it too carried the tools of a trade—and she had already gloomily guessed the nature of the trade.

The woman, in her mid-thirties, wearing dark pants and an oversized candy-striped shirt, approached Kate. Hitching dark-rimmed glasses farther up on her nose, she said, "Detective Delafield." The voice, Demi Moore–throaty, matched the woman's audacity, as well as the feline femininity of her appearance. "Corey Lanier, *L.A. Times.*"

Jim Newton was the usual feature story writer for the *Times* on police issues, but Kate recognized the name from an account of the shooting of young Darian Crockett, which had run under Lanier's byline. A reporter coming to where Kate lived was a far different matter from covering a police-involved shooting. "How did you get my address?"

Corey Lanier's smile was amused and a little incredulous; she removed her glasses and propped them on top of honey-colored, shoulder-length hair, her gray-blue eyes coolly appraising Kate as she said, "You're actually asking a reporter that question? Next thing, you'll want to know if I can type and spell."

"Please leave my property, Ms. Lanier."

"The name's Corey, and that's crap, okay? This common area is not your property. I know you hate the press, but let's just put that aside—"

"I don't intend to put anything aside," Kate snapped, slamming her car door. "I have nothing to say to you."

"Look. I'm working on a story, and you're part of it."

"That's ridiculous. Not to mention impossible, without my cooperation."

"Your cooperation is what I'd like to discuss."

"Forget it. We have absolutely nothing to talk about." Kate headed for the stairway.

"I'm working with these facts, Detective Delafield." Corey Lanier trotted beside Kate to keep up with her. "I know you're the defense rep for an officer brought up on a bad shooting charge. The story I'm working on is a police conspiracy against gay officers. Officer Luke Taggart is right in the middle of it."

"I have no information to give you." But Kate involuntarily slowed her pace, shocked by Lanier's words.

"Look, I just want to talk, okay? Off the record. Why don't we take a walk, I'll tell you what I know. Everything completely off the record, okay?"

Kate looked at her, allowing the full dimension of her skepticism to show in her face. "Do you have a tape recorder?"

"I do." Corey reached into her shoulder bag and efficiently extracted it.

Kate took it and examined it to see that it was not

voice-activated, then dropped it into her own shoulder bag. "I'll return it when we're finished."

"You don't trust freedom of the press at all, do you?"

I don't trust freedom of anything very much, Kate thought. She could smell Corey Lanier's perfume, musky and sensuous; as she walked out through the lobby and onto the sidewalk, she felt as if she were in the web of a black widow spider.

Lanier waited until they were on the sidewalk, then said, "My information is, Luke Taggart broke LAPD's sanctified Code of Silence during the days when cops covered for each other and Chief Daryl Gates did it better than anybody. My information is, our new and highly unesteemed African-American police chief claims it's a good idea for cops to break the Code now, but white male officers bow down to Gates's picture every morning and sabotage the new chief every chance they get. My information is, Taggart's been hated and despised for a long time for breaking the Code. Am I correct on all of this so far?"

Kate stopped at the end of the block, turned back toward the condo. No way would she be trapped into a lengthy conversation with this woman. "No comment," she said.

"What do you mean, no comment?"

"I mean, no comment. It's police business."

"Golly, am I ever uninformed," Lanier said acidly. "The last time I looked, you cops were fully accountable to the public you serve."

"I repeat: no comment."

"My information is, Officer Luke Taggart is being run out of LAPD. My information is, he's been brought up on charges in a frame-up because his fellow officers want him out, if not preferably dead. My information is, he believes his partner was shot by homophobe cops as a warning to other gay cops because Tony Ferrera was going to commit the ultimate betrayal. My information is, Tony Ferrera was going to come out as a gay man and expose how many gay cops actually inhabit the macho world of LAPD and who they are, including a particular one very high up in the ranks. My information is, you were shot because you too are gay."

Stopping in front of her condo, Kate said faintly, "Please tell me you're not going to put all that in the paper."

"Not in tomorrow's edition," Lanier said in an amused tone, watching Kate.

This reporter would need verification, and lots of it for a story like this, Kate assured herself. She asked, "So who are your sources for all this?"

"Other police officers—"

"Like who?"

"Like I've guaranteed them the same confidentiality I'm offering you."

Kate knew that reporters worked the same bluffs that police officers and deputy district attorneys did, but she had no way of gauging how much of a bluff Corey Lanier was running.

Lanier continued, "Another source is an *Advocate* reporter—"

"Matt Brazelton."

Lanier looked surprised. "If you know Matt, you're pretty well informed about the story I'm working on."

"I'm *not* well informed about your story," Kate retorted. "And I don't know the man. He tried to contact me and I blew him off."

"You don't blow Matt Brazelton off any more than you blow off a pit bull. He'll keep coming till he gets you. I ought to know. He's been on my case for months to dig out this story."

"What is it that you want from me?"

"To help me get at the truth."

Kate couldn't resist saying, "I've read enough newspaper accounts of my own cases to know that the press has its own peculiar notions of truth."

"Did it ever occur to you that you might bear some

responsibility? That you could make a difference in the level of accuracy if you yourself ever talked to reporters?"

Kate looked at her without replying. Only a police officer with a lobotomy would believe such garbage.

"Don't be a total cynic, Detective Delafield. I think we both want the same thing. Chief Williams means well and he's making some changes, but LAPD is still so rooted in homophobia it might as well be run by Jesse Helms."

"Tell me something I don't know," Kate said.

"Okay. LAPD's always had gay cops and they're at every level. You do know that. You're one of a significant number of lesbian cops. You do know that. I'm a reporter who happens to be a lesbian, which you didn't know, but you know it now."

"I presume you're going to tell me what I'm supposed to do with this information," Kate said quietly.

"You can decide for yourself what you do with it. What I'm telling you is, some of us aren't going to sit back anymore and let the people paid and trusted to protect us be gay bashers and killers."

"Look . . . Corey," Kate said, deciding to use the reporter's first name. "What you're telling me is unsubstantiated rumor and gossip. The information you're giving me about Officer Taggart isn't proven fact. You're taking the uncorroborated word—"

"Fuck that," Lanier said heatedly. "I mean, fuck it. I don't need any more police PR. I need somebody who'll give me the raw meat. I'm going to my editor with everything I've got *before* Taggart's Board of Rights hearing. I guarantee you I'll make damn sure enough of this story gets out to insure saturation press coverage."

Kate took the tape recorder out of her shoulder bag and handed it back to Corey Lanier. "This conversation is over," she said.

"As a lesbian police officer, Detective, what are you doing about your own coming out?"

Kate met her gaze and said evenly, "My personal life is not your concern. It's not part of what is accountable to the public I serve."

Corey Lanier held Kate's gaze. "Bullshit. You're a senior homicide detective who's in the closet. If the men and women at high levels in LAPD don't come out, who can? Or will?"

Kate turned away and marched into the lobby of her building. Easy for people like Corey Lanier to pass judgment. Outsiders never had an ounce of understanding of how things worked in the professional or personal life of a police officer.

"I'll see you around, Detective," Corey Lanier said and stalked past Kate and out into the garage.

"Hi honey," Aimee called from the living room as Kate walked wearily into the condo. "You've had some calls."

Kate groaned. Shrugging out of her jacket, she made her way into the living room and deposited the jacket and Taggart's computer on an armchair, then slumped down on the sofa beside Aimee. The cat climbed out of Aimee's lap and eagerly onto Kate. "Sorry I'm so late," Kate said to Aimee. "It's been a full day."

"No phone call from Torrie," Aimee said, "before you ask. Louisa from the insurance company called again about your hospital bill. And that guy from the *Advocate* checked in again." Aimee sat with a foot up on the coffee table, law briefs stacked all around her; she had been watching television.

"Miss Marple," Kate said, stroking the cat, brushing the fur under her chin, "could we trade places for a while?"

Aimee tucked an arm around Kate's waist. "Tough day?"

Kate released a long sigh and let her head sink down onto Aimee's shoulder. "The officer I'm representing is telling me maybe twenty percent of what he knows and even that little bit may not be the truth. I have not one but two reporters after me. I'm dealing with a pair of detective goons I'm ashamed to call my peers. I've found a witness who's telling me things I don't want to hear. I have another appointment tomorrow with a psychologist who's taking a can opener to my psyche. I probably have to go back and canvass a neighborhood in Hollywood. And my shoulder hurts."

Aimee reached a hand up and massaged Kate's temple. "How about dinner and a pain pill?"

"Wonderful. I'll trade the pain pill for scotch. What did the *Advocate* reporter want?"

"Didn't say. Just to tell you he called, and he'll be catching up with you again."

Kate moaned.

"I'm sure glad you've got this time off work to get yourself mentally and physically healed," Aimee said.

Kate's eye was caught by a black-and-white image on the television program Aimee had been watching: a still photo of John F. Kennedy and Jacqueline Kennedy in the limousine in the fateful motorcade in Dallas, with dotted lines and arrows superimposed around them.

"God, not the assassination again." Ever since Aimee had seen the Oliver Stone movie she had become fascinated by the historical event that had taken place two years after she was born.

"This just started. It's different—really interesting. They're taking a whole new look at the film that guy took—"

"The Zapruder film." Kate would never forget that film or the name of the man, Abraham Zapruder, who had taken it.

"Yeah. Back then they couldn't do a lot of the tests they run today, and they've got some new answers about how one of the bullets that hit Kennedy could go through him and into the governor of Texas."

Aimee released Kate and got up. "Sit still, relax, I'll get you a drink."

Kate picked up the remote control to put on *Headline News*, but then was caught by the narrator's voice: "... *referred to as the magic bullet. But Governor Connally was positioned exactly right when this bullet exited from beside the president's backbone* . . ." She found herself watching the slow-motion analysis of John F. Kennedy's death, emotion slowly building into something close to what she had felt that November day in 1963 . . . Beginning with when she had assembled in a high school auditorium with her schoolmates to watch in amazement the principal run onto the stage . . . And then to hear Mr. Hayes say, "The President has been shot in Dallas." And then Mr. Hayes sobbing, "School is dismissed—" and unable to utter another word, and being led off the stage by another teacher—an event almost as impossible in concept as the one he had just announced. She had wandered the schoolyard with her milling, aghast schoolmates and then had gone home to sit, mesmerized, in front of the television set beside her father over an entire weekend, mourning with the rest of the stunned nation an unthinkable tragedy that was not supposed to happen in America. It had been the second unthinkable tragedy of that year for Kate: scant months earlier she had lost her mother to leukemia.

Usually, programs about the Kennedy assassination were scheduled around its November anniversary, allowing Kate to easily avoid them. But as Aimee put a drink down in front of her and murmured something about getting a casserole out of the oven, Kate scarcely noticed, so lost was she in a mixture of memory and the nebulous formulation of a theory about distinctly current events.

After dinner and three scotches, Kate tossed aside the new issue of the *Advocate* she had been glancing through in an idle search for Matt Brazelton's byline and turned off the channel five news. It was too late now to hope that Torrie would call.

The printer in the den continued to grind away, chugging out the product of Aimee's day's work. Aimee was slouched in the desk chair where she had been since dinner, holding the phone to her ear as she made notes and spoke low-toned legalese with a colleague, going over in minute detail one of the many points of contention in the lawsuit that her firm was engaged in defending. Aside from political contests, Kate reflected, her profession and Aimee's were unrivaled in their production of paper to arrive at a basically simple up-or-down, win-or-lose resolution.

Damn it all, why hadn't Torrie called? She wanted to share with Torrie Luke Taggart's absurd insinuation that something sinister lay behind the bullet wound in her shoulder, she wanted to hear Torrie scoff at his overactive imagination, at the very notion that any of Kate's team could possibly want to harm her. It would be the perfect inroad to clearing the air over what had happened in that hallway at Gramercy—and how it had actually come about that she'd been shot.

Yes, Torrie might be up to her eyeballs working a case, but that wasn't a valid excuse for not calling—not when Kate was the D-3 on the homicide table, even if she was technically off duty. Torrie should have the good judgment to keep her up to date on new cases and to give progress reports on ongoing ones, especially the Wilkens stabbing they'd been working together before this all happened.

Kate stalked out onto the breezy balcony. She *needed* to talk to Torrie. Damn her for not calling. Her usually faithful remedy of scotch had also failed her tonight; neither it nor the pain pill had been a palliative for her angry and restless mood.

The desert wind whipped strands of her hair into her face and was a rasp against her skin, electrical currents rippling up her arms and under the bandage on her shoulder. A jasminelike fragrance subtly edged the dry gusts, and she leaned over the balcony, peering into a darkness patterned by twisting, dancing branches of trees, punctuated by rectangles of light from neighboring windows. The warm wild night held a palpable erotic charge; Kate felt it invade her as a raw ache.

She heard Aimee come out onto the balcony; then arms slid around her from behind, pulled her back from the railing. Aimee said playfully, "Just in case you're thinking of jumping."

"Too chicken," Kate joked back.

Aimee released her. "You're no chicken," she said seriously, moving to stand beside her at the balcony. "You wouldn't take a chance on surviving a jump. You'd want something sure, like a bullet."

Wondering what on earth had brought this on, Kate turned to face her. Aimee's violet eyes were luminous, her white T-shirt and shorts iridescent in the eerie night. Suddenly Kate did not want to challenge her; something in this erratic devil wind would seize her words and spark a conflagration between them. Aimee's face was shadowed sculpture against the angled backlight from the condo, and Kate instead focused on the beauty of her.

Aimee leaned to Kate and kissed her neck, at the edge of the bandage, her wind-flung hair a silken lashing across Kate's face and throat. Kate brushed the hair back from Aimee's forehead, kissed her lightly. "Finished for the day?"

"Actually, just beginning . . ." Aimee's lips touched her neck. "Or did you mean work?"

The warm moisture of Aimee's mouth was balm on the aridity of Kate's skin. Conscious of the restriction in her shoulder and arm, Kate murmured, "You have me at a disadvantage."

"I know." Again Aimee's arms slid around her. "Unaccustomed as I am . . ."

Aimee's lips stitched kisses down Kate's neck and across her wounded shoulder, her bare legs fitting between Kate's, her body sealing itself against Kate. "Tell me if anything hurts."

Even cloaked by darkness and the rattle and clatter of the wind, this patio was too public a place, Kate thought. But after all the shocks and emotional upheavals of the day, she wanted to be touched, needed to be reassured—to be cherished, and as Aimee lips drank in her throat, all reluctance faded.

It was after Aimee moved her to the chaise lounge, knelt beside her, took off her own T-shirt to expose her breasts, then began to lay bare Kate's body one piece of clothing at a time, that Kate understood this was a different kind of touching from the choreography created between them over the years. Aimee was composing a design of her own, holding her body away from Kate's, her hands almost convulsive in their gripping of the muscles in Kate's hips and legs, her lips unpredictable in where they would caress and where they would pause: inside her elbows, across her hipbones, between and under her breasts. Her mouth became devouring, her teeth pulling at Kate's flesh not quite to the brink of pain, her tongue tasting, savoring.

If Aimee had never touched her like this, the effect was the same: a firing of want, and tension stretched so taut that Kate's nerves seemed to sing with it as Aimee's mouth moved down over her bare stomach, as Aimee's hand caressed her throat. Aimee's fingers stilled over the pulse in Kate's neck as she kissed Kate's thighs.

Her breath warm on the hair between Kate's legs, Aimee murmured: "I'm going to take a long time."

Her mouth was as warm and voluptuous as the gusts of wind buffeting Kate's body—quickly bringing her to a height hovering on orgasm—but just as erratic, taking no direction from Kate's responses or her pleasure, ceasing its rhythms. Fingers leaving her, mouth leaving her, Aimee moved down, her tongue entering Kate to stroke within. Then back, the passion of her mouth again engulfing Kate in paroxysms of pleasure. Again Aimee leaving her, again and again.

"Please," Kate finally uttered in an agonized whisper of pure need, spasms of pain in her shoulder a new counterpoint to her rapture.

As if galvanized by the word, Aimee obeyed with fierce strokes of her fingers and tongue. Gripped in a quivering intensity, Kate hovered at a dazzling edge and then surged over it.

Aimee still did not take her mouth away; and as Kate's heartbeat quieted and her shoulder settled into a dull throbbing, she could feel wetness on her thighs in single hot splashes.

She drew Aimee back up to her. Aimee's eyes were red with tears, her entire face wet.

"My darling," Kate whispered, gently touching her face.

Aimee bowed her head, her tears continuing to fall on Kate's breasts. "I had to," she wept, "I'm so glad you're alive. . . ."

13

THE next morning, Kate idled over her coffee and the newspaper, meditative, her body still holding echoes of the night before, and of the deliciously sensuous hour this morning with Aimee. Aimee had dashed out the door, mug of coffee in hand, to drop off work at her office and to pick up more to bring home.

Finally, faced with the option of calling Luke Taggart to learn the name of the liquor store where Tony Ferrera had been killed or alerting Hollywood Division that she was interested in the case, Kate made the obvious choice. But as she picked up the phone and punched in Taggart's number, she became irrationally wrathful at how gratified he would feel at her question. However, he answered simply, "Silverlake Liquors and Sundries, block and a half south of Sunset," as if she had called a company for information about its hours of business. He added: "They open at ten."

She realized that if Taggart was in communication with Corey Lanier, he knew exactly what conversation had taken place with the reporter yesterday. Maybe Taggart had been the instigator for Lanier sitting in wait for her here. Mindful of the reporter and her attempted intimidation and sensational accusations, she asked Taggart, "Where does Tony Ferrera's family live?"

"What do you want with them?"

She vented some of her antagonism with sarcasm. "You did want me to look into his death, didn't you?"

"Ferdie's family—they've been through hell."

"Have they? That never occurred to me."

"Sorry, Kate. That was really dumb. You see more grieving families than anyone should. I just don't know what you'd want with Ferdie's—"

"Maybe nothing at all," she said in a more cordial tone. Taggart was not the only one who could play cards close to the chest. "I'd like to know how to reach them if I have a question."

"If you have questions about Ferdie, I hope you'll ask me."

Sure, she thought. Especially when you've been so forthcoming with what you know, such as a *Los Angeles Times* reporter who claims Tony Ferrera was a gay man. Where had Corey Lanier obtained that information? From Tony Ferrera's family? From *Advocate* reporter Matt Brazelton? Or from Luke Taggart? "Are you going to give me the information," she said to Taggart, "or do I have to call—"

"No reason to get your buns in an uproar," Taggart said. "I was just getting it out of my address book."

"Fine." She did not believe a word he said.

"Anna Ferrera—everybody calls her Mama—" He rattled off an address on Cicero Avenue in the Silverlake area, adding a phone number and some sketchy directions. "Roberto, that's Ferdie's youngest brother, he lives with her. Pete, that's her other son, he and his wife live three blocks away, at the end of Dillon Street." He gave her Pete's address and phone number.

"Tony didn't live very far from them," she remarked.

"No. Like I said, the family's real close. Another brother, Joe, runs a roofing business out in Kingman, Arizona. He comes in all time to see Mama Ferrera. There's one sister, Theresa's at college over in Tucson. Do you want their numbers?"

"This is enough for now. Thanks." She would give him his due—once he had decided to be forthcoming, he had been generous with information. "Where did Tony live?"

He recited an address on Quintero in an angry tone. "The bastards rented out his place the minute we moved his stuff. They had the For Rent sign out before Ferdie was cold."

"I've got a lot to do today—"

"Like what?"

With a touch of malice, she ignored his question. "I'll be in touch," she said and hung up.

Parking on Wheeler Avenue, Kate took her Polaroid camera out of her trunk and then walked across the street to look up at the apartment building west of Apparition Alley.

Ida Wilson sat in her window; Kate waved to her. The old woman smiled, then raised her crippled hands and managed to give Kate an approximation of a double thumbs-up sign. Ida must be watching lots of MTV, Kate thought, grinning all the way across the street to Apparition Alley.

Rosie the bag lady again lay back in the dark, grimy depths, in the same barely breathing posture as when Kate had first seen her. Kate walked over to her. "You okay, Rosie?"

Rosie cast a single glance up at Kate. "Hot day," she muttered, then faded back into her daydream.

After satisfying herself that Rosie seemed all right, or at least what passed for all right for Rosie, Kate went about her business. She crouched over the taped outline of Julio Mendez's body and shot a number of photos across it to the side and back walls, laying the photos on her shoulder bag as they developed. Rosie's head came up and she opened an eye. "People take pitchers of jus' anything," she commented.

Chuckling, Kate went to the back wall and photographed it, then again in smaller sections, including the excavated bullet holes. She packed up her camera and collected the photos.

"You got another one of thosh fiversh?" Rosie asked.

Kate crouched down beside her. "Rosie, I'll make a deal with you." She took a ten-dollar bill out of her wallet and held it up. "I'll give you this if you promise never to come into this alley again."

With grave suspicion, Rosie looked at the bill, then at Kate. "Why the hell not? Shump'n good in here?"

Kate took out her identification, held up her badge. "I'm a police officer. This place is very dangerous." She pointed to the taped outline. "People die in here."

"'Zhat all," Rosie said indifferently. "Okay, whatever." She snatched the ten dollars from Kate's fingers, folded it, and tucked it under the ribbon holding her hair. She struggled to her feet.

"Remember, Rosie, you promised."

Waving a hand, Rosie shuffled off, pushing her shopping cart. She'll buy booze and be back, Kate thought resignedly.

Silverlake Liquor and Sundries presented a bright, clean storefront with numerous neon beer signs. Kate pulled into one of half a dozen parking spots in front, thinking that the liquor store was an unlikely choice for a holdup. On a busy street, it was public and accessible and highly visible. But then, criminals were not known for intelligence—or at least the ones who got caught.

She entered the store, empty of customers at this ten o'clock hour, and went up to the counter. From here a clerk would have a clear view of the parking lot and street.

A young, slender, light-skinned African-American man was bent over cases of liquor, slitting open cardboard tops with practiced efficiency. He glanced up at Kate with pale green, long-lashed eyes that ranked with Aimee's for the most beautiful Kate had ever seen.

"Help you?" he inquired in a soft voice.

Displaying her identification, Kate introduced herself. "Are you the owner?" she inquired.

"I wish," he said, standing to his full height of what she estimated to be six feet-four. "That's Mr. Matsimoto. I'm Jeff Daley, one of the peons. Don't tell me this is about that cop's death again."

"It is." He looked so crestfallen that she added, "I realize you've been through a great many interviews."

"I can tell my story in my sleep. Mr. Matsimoto says to give you people full cooperation since it was a cop that got killed here, but I've told what happened so many times—"

"You were on duty that night?"

"Yeah. I quit the same night it happened, but Mr. Matsimoto talked me into staying on and working days to see how it goes."

"It was a pretty terrible night, I guess."

He shook his head, as if to dislodge the memories. "No way I'll work nights again anywhere." He had placed his hands on the counter, pressing them into the glass and then moving them, big hands that left moist fingerprints in their wake.

Kate said sympathetically, "Could you just walk me through what happened, Jeff?"

He shrugged. "Hey, I think it bothered me less when I was talking about it all the time. You seem a lot more laid back than the other cops. How come they make you work with that bum arm?"

She joked, "I'm better than the rest of the boys with one arm tied behind me."

He grinned. "That night—I never saw so many cop cars. A helicopter over the whole neighborhood for hours and hours. They really did a job looking for those guys."

"The night it happened, Jeff, what was the first thing you noticed?"

"Him driving up in his red Camaro, that big engine, you could never miss it."

"The victim, you mean."

"Yeah, the cop."

"And no one else was in the store," she said, remembering this detail from Taggart's recounting.

"Nobody."

"Wasn't that a bit odd?"

"For seven-thirty at night, you mean?"

She nodded. She had meant that she assumed this was a very busy store most of the time, but she was grateful Jeff Daley had volunteered the time of the shooting; he would have wondered about her association with the case had she needed to ask.

"Yeah, it's a busy time, evenings always are," he said, "but you'll get a quiet patch anytime for no reason at all. Just damn lucky nobody else got killed by those creeps, including me."

"Will you explain and show me how it all happened?"

He came out from behind the counter and led her to the glass double doors at the front of the store. Kate had parked her car to the right of the doors; Jeff Daley gestured to the left. "The Camaro came into that parking spot. No more than ten seconds later, a Ford Ranger pulls in right next to it—" He pointed to the parking spot to the left of where he said the Camaro had been. "—just as the cop is out of his car and coming toward the doors here. I know it was a Ford Ranger because my brother-in-law has one. I don't remember anything about the truck except it was a light color and dirty and the side panel had black splotches all over it."

Jeff Daley was relating details with the precision of a good observer who had told his story many, many times. Kate listened carefully as he continued, "From where I am, I can see right away the guys in the pickup have white ski masks on. Other than that, nothing else unusual about them—they wore jeans and jean jackets, that's all I remember. I don't know about their hair color, the masks covered it, I couldn't tell you what race they were either. They jump out of the truck and the driver has a gun in his hand, I can see it, but the cop can't because he's walking away from them and anyway the Camaro's screening them off.''

He walked outside the store and pointed to a spot on the pavement. ''One of the guys comes up behind the cop, right about here, maybe five feet away from him, and says something because the cop sort of jerks around like this to face him—'' Daley demonstrated with a quick movement of his long lean body.

''Like he was surprised?'' Kate asked.

''Yeah, sort of like that. Then a couple of seconds later, the guy blows the cop away. And no, before you ask, I couldn't tell if the cop said anything back to him or if the cop had a gun in his hand. He was right here in front of the door and he had his back to me.'' Once more Jeff Daley turned his body in illustration.

''You watched the whole thing from behind the counter?'' Kate asked. ''You didn't—'' She searched for a tactful phrase.

''Hit the silent alarm? Dial nine-one-one?'' he supplied. ''I was frozen. Frozen like a statue.''

''I can understand that,'' Kate said.

''It was like I was trapped in a horror movie and it got worse and worse,'' Daley said. ''The other guy, the passenger, he's running toward the cop's body, and he calls something to the driver and the driver runs to the door and points his gun at me and let me tell you I all but peed my pants. He fires a shot and I hit the floor, I think for sure I'm a dead man, in the next minute they'll be in the store to finish me off.''

Daley turned and walked rapidly back through the glass doors, Kate following. Leaning against the counter as if needing it for support, he pointed to the floor behind the counter. ''I'm lying there with my arms around my head waiting to be shot. Next thing I hear is the sound of an engine roaring, the pickup backing out onto the street. Except I don't know it's the pickup. I get up on my hands and knees and crawl to that end of the counter here, figuring if they're in the store, maybe I can make a run for the door. I see the truck's gone. But I'm still too scared to stand up. So I crawl to the door. And when I don't see any sign of the guys in the masks, I still can't get up because my legs are jelly. So I crawl out the door to see if I can do anything for the poor bastard they shot."

Jeff Daley turned away from her and leaned fully on the counter, his hands and fingers splayed, his head down. "His gun's near his right hand and his eyes are wide open and he's got this look of absolute—" His voice broke. "This is the worst. They shot him in the forehead and the horror in his eyes, I'll never forget it so long as I live."

Involuntarily, she reached to him, gripped his arm. He lifted a hand from the glass and placed the hand, cold and clammy, over hers. "Thanks, I'm okay," he said, and straightened his body to its full height. "By then, people are coming from everywhere. I get to my feet and go back in the store and hit the alarm, call nine-one-one, and tell them a cop's here dead. And that's it."

He had told his story so completely that she had few questions to ask him. "You said you told nine-one-one a cop was dead. How did you know Officer Ferrera was a cop? Had you seen him before?"

"Oh yeah, lots of times. A cool guy, I really liked him."

Kate asked in keen interest, "He came in here a lot?"

He nodded. "Every week. Good customer, a nice man. Bought lots of stuff just for his family. I felt really bad. Talk about the wrong place at the wrong time. And here he was a *cop* and all. Him being somebody I knew—it made it all the worse."

"Only one man did all the shooting?"

"Yeah. The driver."

"You said the driver had a gun in his hand. His accomplice, did he have a gun?"

"I can't say I saw one. I saw him get out of the truck, saw him running toward the cop after he was down. When the guy shot the cop and then came at me, that's all I was looking at."

"I can sure understand that," Kate offered. "Jeff, by now you've had a good long time to think about what happened that night. Is there anything at all that seems in any way . . . odd to you?"

"Well . . . yeah. I mentioned this to the detectives, and the cop that used to be the dead guy's partner. I don't know why those two creeps didn't finish the job, why they didn't come in and take the money."

"You've been robbed before?"

"Not me personally, but a couple of years back we had a strong-armed robbery, the clerk got kicked around. That's when Mr. Matsimoto pulled down some bushes that blocked the store from the street and put in more lights and alarms. But it'd take all of two seconds for those guys to come in here and grab the money. Three grand I had in the drop under the drawer, nobody else in here, they had those masks on, they knew I'd seen them shoot that guy, they knew I wouldn't give them any trouble. Anyway, once they blew away the cop, they could just as easy take me out too."

"Maybe when Officer Ferrera drew down on them they panicked."

"You tell me—why do you draw your piece if somebody's got one pointing right at you?"

Instead of answering his question, she suggested, "Maybe something spooked them. Maybe they saw a cop car coming along."

"I thought about that too, you know." He shrugged. "Could be. Took no time at all for the first ones to get here, including two detectives in plainclothes."

"Really? Do you remember who the detectives were?"

He shook his head. "Kind of Spanish or Italian names. I might remember if I heard them."

"Mussino? Morales?"

"That's them."

Kate heard this uneasily. "When Officer Ferrera's partner talked to you, I imagine he was pretty upset."

"Pretty upset is right. Took me through every single detail, every single second of what happened, like, twenty times. The guy was, like, obsessed."

And it was Luke Taggart, Kate told herself, who might well have put the idea in Jeff Daley's head that there was something wrong about a simple attempted robbery gone bad.

"Thank you, Jeff," she said. "You take care of yourself."

"You too," he said. "Take it easy on that arm."

The small, midblock house where Tony Ferrera's mother lived took up all of its treeless lot except for an impeccably groomed scrap of front lawn beside a driveway that led from the street through the carport and into a white frame garage in the rear. The house stood out from its prosaic neighbors with its sparkling white stucco finish and prominent bay window, and its extravagant ivy climbing up one side of the front door onto a Spanish tile roof that extended over the carport. On this warm, cloudless day, large windows neatly outlined in dark green trim were shuttered by venetian blinds.

The woman who flung open the door to Kate's knock wore a floral-pattern housedress that seemed a costume on her firmly fleshed girth. Gray hair, pulled back and fastened with an elastic band, accentuated the strength in her face and the self-assurance in her dark eyes. Meeting the woman's shrewd gaze, Kate displayed her identification.

"I'm Detective Kate Delafield, LAPD . . ." About to add a caution about the danger of overconfidence in opening a door without first identifying the caller, she was sidetracked by the yeasty aroma wafting from the house. "Bread," Kate said. "You're baking bread."

"Aren't you the lucky one to arrive at just the perfect

time. Come in." The woman's voice was youthful, vibrant.

"You're Mrs. Ferrera?"

"I am."

Kate followed the energetic strides of Tony Ferrera's mother into a shaded living room with a beige carpet brightened by throw rugs. Amid standard furnishings, one wall was almost entirely filled with family photos; a simple wooden cross was the only adornment on another wall; on another, the tortured body of Christ hung from a large crucifix alongside a small, gold-framed print of the Virgin Mary and Child.

Contemplating Kate, Mrs. Ferrera pursed her lips. "Another minute or two and I'll need to get that last batch out of the oven. Would it be rude if I asked you to come back to the kitchen?"

"I'd be delighted," Kate said.

She was not surprised to see a farmhouse-style kitchen reminiscent of her grandmother's—a big room with a linoleum floor, lots of cabinets, counters crowded with bottles of olive oil and canisters and a pasta maker, a family-size table with a vase of yellow daisies on a red-checked tablecloth. Gleaming copper-bottom pots and pans hung from a wrought-iron bar over a large, black stove, along with mesh baskets filled with herbs and root vegetables and cloves of garlic. The stove looked old; the side-by-side refrigerator and freezer and the dishwasher looked new.

"Sit," Mrs. Ferrera said, and Kate obediently took a chair at the table. "My name's Anna. Most everybody ends up calling me Mama."

Taggart had told her the same thing, but it had lacked the impact of the word coming from this woman. Kate had called her own mother Mama up until she was ten, when she had decided it was too babyish and switched to Mother; but her father had playfully taken it up, calling his wife by that name until her death at the age of thirty-nine. Anna Ferrera looked to be somewhere in her sixties, but something about her, and this house filled with the aroma of baking bread, was bringing back childhood memories to Kate with gale force.

Anna poured two mugs of coffee. "You look like a no-nonsense woman who takes it black," she said to Kate.

Kate smiled. "You have me pegged, Anna." She noticed two bicycles on the glassed-in porch behind the kitchen, and two shelves of baseball bats and gloves and children's toys.

Anna lifted a cheesecloth and removed a braided loaf of Italian bread and placed it on a cutting board. "With that arm, I'd better cut this for you." Without waiting for a reply, she whacked off three huge slices and delivered the bread, a tub of butter, a knife, and a napkin to Kate. "You eat as much as you like."

"You're a generous woman, very kind to strangers," Kate said.

Watching in simple joy as the butter melted into the warm, fluffy bread, Kate thought that this might be a home emptied of young children, but Anna Ferrera had learned how to cure empty nest syndrome: she had made the nest her baby birds had left so inviting that they returned willingly, and, judging by the amount of baked bread under the cheesecloth, often.

"How did you hurt that arm?" Anna asked, opening the oven door and checking its contents.

"Wrong place at the wrong time," Kate said as Anna removed the tray of golden loaves and placed it on top of the stove. "Trying to make an arrest. The suspect came out of another apartment. I happened to get in the path of a bullet."

She had made the explanation in a light tone, but Anna Ferrera closed the oven door and then bowed her head; she braced her hands along the edge of the stove top, in the same way that Jeff Daley had leaned for support on the counter in the liquor store. "You police," she said. "I don't know why any of you want to do such a job."

Kate cast a poisonous thought toward Calla Dearborn. This reaction from Anna Ferrera, a woman of evident fortitude, was proof positive of why police officers kept details of their jobs to themselves. "Anna," she said softly, putting down her slice of bread, "I was at your son's funeral. I'm truly sorry."

"Did you know my Antonio well?"

"No, I didn't. I wish I had."

"Why don't you come with me for just a minute. Bring that coffee along if you like."

Leaving the coffee behind, Kate followed Anna Ferrera toward a room at the end of a hallway lined with more family photographs.

It's a shrine, Kate thought, before her eyes picked out further details in the murky gloom of the small back room.

On a dresser draped with an American flag, two votive candles flickered before a three-foot-high statue of the Virgin Mary. Beside the blue-and-white figure stood a silver-framed photograph of a handsome young police officer in full-dress uniform, his face solemn except for the eagerness in his brown eyes, highlighted by the flame from the candles. The flag, Kate knew, would be the one that had covered Tony Ferrera's casket at his police funeral. He would have been buried in that full dress uniform. Two other photos flanked the larger one, one of Tony Ferrera holding a football and crouched in a three-point stance on an emerald-green field, the other of him shaking hands with Police Chief Daryl Gates as Gates handed him his diploma from the Police Academy. Several letters of commendation, preserved in plastic, lay in a fanlike arrangement. Off to the other side of the Virgin, on a white crocheted doily, was a bronzed baby shoe.

"People tell me I should thank God I have four other children," Anna Ferrera said, touching the photos of her son. "As if your living children could ever make up for a child you lose. No mother loves each baby in the same way. He was my sweet boy, my special boy."

Kate said huskily, "From everything I know, he was a fine man, a fine person, a fine police officer."

Without replying, Anna turned and led Kate back into the kitchen. Kate again sat at the table and tucked into another slice of fresh bread; Anna lowered herself with effort into the chair opposite her.

"I wish they'd sent a woman police officer when this first happened," she said. "I was too upset to talk to the police officers very much. My son Joseph flew right in from Kingman, all my children were here—" She gestured with both hands all around her. "My boys take care of this house now that Antonio's gone, they never let me want for anything. But it's hard, you know, and there are still so many questions . . ."

"I wasn't on the scene that night," Kate said, "but if you have questions, I'll do my best to answer, and if I can't, I'll try and find out for you."

"The terrible thing is, there isn't any worldly answer to the hardest question. Why did it have to be my Antonio? I pray every day to the Virgin to bring me peace, I know God has a purpose in all He does—"

She broke off and looked at Kate acutely. She got up from the table and took a roll of aluminum foil from the cupboard, removed the cheesecloth from the loaves, and began to wrap them. "You're here because you have your own questions. Tell me what you want to know."

"What you remember about his behavior." She chose her words carefully. "Did he seem . . . his usual self up to . . . that night?"

"It's odd you should ask that. I would have formed it into a question to you, except you say you didn't know my son."

Anna Ferrera paused over the wrapping of her loaves, looking down at her hands as she said, "Antonio called me every single day. Every Tuesday and Saturday night without fail he came to see me. He loved me, he loved his sister and brothers. We all loved him. But we didn't know him. He held himself back from me, from all of us. What's in that room back there is all I have. And now he's gone, and I'll never know what I didn't know. And so my answer to your question is another question. The way he held back from us, did it have something to do with his being a police officer?"

Kate heard Anna Ferrera's pain with an anguish so keen that she wondered if it showed in her face. Tony Ferrera's conduct was completely consistent with a gay man who had hidden his real self from his family. Who knew better than she did? If Tony Ferrera had felt as exiled from home and hearth as she had from her own family, then he too had closed off an essential part of himself. She answered, "I honestly don't believe it had anything to do with his being a police officer."

It had not occurred to Kate until now to wonder: Had her own parents gone to their graves as perplexed about her withdrawal from them as Anna Ferrera was about her son's?

"Anna," she said, "I wish . . ." She did not finish; she had no right to share her guessing and theorizing with Anna Ferrera.

Carefully watching Kate's face, Anna Ferrera finally nodded. She placed a wrapped loaf on the table in front of Kate. "For you to take with you," she said.

"I thank you," Kate said.

"This is my comfort," Anna said. "He called me to tell me he was coming to see me that night—"

"He was on his way over here when it happened?"

"Yes. And he seemed very happy. Very . . ." She groped for a word, working her fingers rapidly.

"Energized?" Kate supplied.

"Energized." She examined the word. "Yes. In high spirits."

"Do you know why?"

She shook her head. "He died in November, and he'd been happy in that way since spring. I asked Roberto and Peter, but they just said he was acting crazy."

"Is there anything . . ." Again Kate chose her words. "Is there anything about the investigation of your son's death that in any way . . . disturbs or dissatisfies you?"

"So that's what this is all about," Anna said. "You're checking up on the way all those officers and detectives did their jobs."

"Not exactly—" Kate began.

She heard a vehicle roar up the driveway to the house, the shriek of brakes. Moments later the front door of the house opened. Anna said, "I'm not expecting—" A dark-haired, wiry young man burst into the kitchen. "Roberto, what are you—"

"Hi, Mama," he said, and demanded of Kate, "Who are you?"

"You're rude, young man," his mother scolded him. "This is Detective Delafield of the police. Detective, this is my son, Roberto."

He was walking toward her. "What do you want with my mother?"

"Roberto, stop right there. Stop. You apologize right now. No son of mine has such manners."

"Sorry, Mama," he muttered. "Sorry, you're right, Mama. I apologize."

"What's come over you?" Anna intervened before Kate could reply to Roberto. "I've made her welcome. She's following up on a few things. I'm not upset, everything is *fine.*"

"I'm glad to hear that, Mama. I meant no offense, Detective."

"You can just wait till the detective is finished with her work here. Sit down. Have some bread and milk. I raised you with manners, and I want you to show them to the detective."

"Yes, Mama," he said in an even meeker tone, gazing at Kate in frustration.

This was a mother, Kate thought, who would never become a prisoner of her children, who would always rule her roost. Curious about Roberto's agitation at her presence here, fairly certain that he would follow her out of the house, Kate glanced at her watch and made the excuse, "I have to leave anyway, Anna." She picked up her loaf of bread and tucked it inside her shoulder bag. "Thank you for your great hospitality."

Roberto said, "I'll see the detective to her car."

"Of course you will." Anna looked sharply at her son. "You mind your manners."

"Yes, Mama."

Kate said to Anna, "I hope you find your answers, and your peace."

Anna Ferrera nodded. "Be careful of yourself."

Outside the house, Roberto Ferrera gestured to an old canvas-top Jeep parked in the carport. "If you don't mind," he said.

Kate climbed into the car. Luke Taggart had called this young man to tell him she was looking into his brother's death. He must have. Roberto's shirt and tie were clearly business attire; he had left his job to come home. There was no other reason for him to be here at eleven o'clock on a weekday morning. For a man who had asked her to be his defense rep, Luke Taggart was hurling every obstacle he could find into her path.

Settling himself in the driver's seat, his dark eyes boring a path into her, he started the Jeep. "We need to get out of here or Mama will come out to see what's going on."

He parked at the end of the street and turned to Kate. "The reason I came home is I'm real concerned about you upsetting my mother. I need to know what you said to her."

If Roberto was any indication, Mama Ferrera's sons operated boldly only when they were out from under her gaze. "I didn't upset her. Check for yourself. What she's upset about is misguided protection from her sons."

"Please tell me what you said to her."

He was, she thought, as tense as a violin string. Meeting his anxious stare, she said, "I take it you want to know whether I mentioned that Tony was gay."

"Oh my God." His hands clutched the steering wheel. "Please tell me you didn't say that to her." His Adam's apple was working as if he were strangling. "Did you tell her that?"

She said calmly, interested in his agitation, "Is that all that matters to you about your brother's death—that your mother not find out he was gay?"

"Jesus." He jerked back from her as if he had been slapped. "Of course not. Try and put yourself in our shoes, okay? Mama doesn't deserve to suffer any more over Tony, okay?" Spreading his hands, he said pleadingly, "Look. She raised all five of us kids by herself. She went through hell for us. I'm telling you she belongs on the goddamn calendar of saints. Tony was her baby, her pride. She doesn't ever have to know he turned himself into shit. All we want is for her to keep the pride and the good memories of Tony. Is that too much to ask?"

"Roberto, what your mother grieves about most is that Tony kept his real self from her."

"His real self," he repeated bitterly. "You can't tell me being a fag was his real self. The guy that got hold of Tony, I'd like to get my hands on the faggot son of a bitch. He turned Tony, twisted him around into something that wasn't him—"

Kate said, "You don't know that."

"I know him one hell of a lot better than you," he said intensely. "You don't know one damn thing about Tony."

"You're quite right. I don't." It was far more strategic not to argue. "There was just the one man he was ever involved with?"

"Some bastard named Matt."

She heard the name in astonishment. It had to be Matt Brazelton. It could be no other.

"Wait a minute." Roberto was staring at her. "If you

say Mama knows Tony kept his real self from her, then she doesn't know for sure what that is, and you didn't actually tell her. Right? Am I right?"

"You're right. I didn't tell her anything about Tony. Let me ask you this, Roberto. Don't you think she'd be more upset by Tony's former partner saying cops killed Tony?"

"Tony's dead. I don't know how anything could make her more upset. Luke tells me you're looking into this, and we finally got a decent detective. I hope he's right. What are you finding out so far?"

"I'm just beginning to look into it," she said cautiously. "What do you think happened to your brother?"

"Cops." He spat the word.

"Why do you think so?"

His next words issued in a gusher: "Because Luke thinks so, and that's good enough for me. He's on the inside. Who'd know better than Luke? Cops in this town won't have faggots wearing blue, and Tony proves it. Tony turned faggot and cops killed him for it. The way you cops cover for each other, nobody's ever gonna go down for it. Four months Tony's been dead—it's a goddamn cover-up. Even if you find out who did this, nothing's ever gonna come of it—"

Kate said grimly, "If police officers did this to your brother, I intend to see—"

"What good will it do? Luke's gone nuts over trying to find who did Tony. The bottom line is, Tony's gone, nothing can bring him back. All I'm asking here is that you leave my mother in peace."

Kate opened the door of the Jeep. "Your mother is a strong woman—"

"I know that better than you," Roberto said.

"I believe she's a lot stronger than you think," Kate said doggedly. And she got out of the Jeep and returned to her own car.

14

EVEN in sunlight, the dilapidated building that housed the crime lab's Firearms Analysis Unit looked worse, if possible, than the last time Kate had seen it—a year ago January, during a downpour. That day, the technicians, still wary after a rain-caused roof collapse of several years ago, were more concerned about protecting their equipment and themselves from their leaking roof than they were about discussing test results with detectives. Entering the building now, she could see that nothing had changed; stain rings in the ceiling confirmed that the roof still leaked.

Forlorn in every sense of the term, a satellite lab in a remote Highland Park location, shabby, rat-infested, understaffed, underequipped, the lab was out of sight and out of mind to the budget movers and shakers entirely focused on the politically rewarding goal of hiring more patrol officers. Firearms cases had tripled in four years, but personnel to cover the work remained the same, and the lab's constant backlog was the curse of officers and detectives waiting for results from ballistics tests. Kate's advantage today was that the unit's highest priorities continued to be trial cases and officer-involved shootings.

In criminalist Harvey Gaviland's bleak cubbyhole, Gaviland stood to his full five-foot height and leaned across his paper-laden desk. His thick white eyebrows lowering themselves under the rims of his glasses, he demanded, "You *did* see the report, Detective?"

"I saw it, but I have some—"

"Detective, it's all in the report." He spread his hands meaningfully across his stacks of paper.

Kate pulled the Polaroids of Apparition Alley out of her shoulder bag, as well as her copy of the autopsy report on Julio Mendez. "Harvey, I have important questions."

"Say something original. That's what you all say." Gaviland sank back into his chair and flung open the file folder in front of him. "Allan Dershowitz couldn't touch this one. It's textbook. Comparison shots nailed the class characteristics dead bang. Lands and grooves, rifling—they match Taggart's Beretta 92F dead bang. Antimony percent in the projectiles matched the batch of Remington NM 115-grain semijacketed hollow points they came from dead bang. It was Taggart's duty weapon dead bang." He crossed his arms in front of him on his desk. "What do you want, the Pope's blessing?"

"First of all, Harvey, you didn't visit the crime scene—"

"Who the hell has time—*why* in hell would I visit the crime scene?" His bushy eyebrows seemed to come down to his eyelids as he glared at her. "We got the shooter dead bang."

"You say the slugs were deformed—"

"Intact, with extreme deformation in the nose, as you would expect." Gaviland shook his head as if he were dealing with someone hopelessly obtuse. "Detective, it's in the—"

Kate handed him the autopsy report. "Both wounds in the victim were through and throughs—"

"Gee, I guess that's why they found lead in the wall," he said, snatching it from her.

"Slug number one severed the upper spinal cord as it passed through the victim, paralyzing him in place." Getting up and leaning over his desk, she indicated the sketch on the autopsy report where the pathologist had diagrammed the wounds. "Slug number two, cause of death, went through the victim's jugular vein."

"So what?" He jabbed the autopsy report back at her.

She took it and placed the stack of Polaroid shots in front of him, along with her own diagram of the crime scene. "Harvey, I want you to look at exactly where the body fell. And exactly where the slugs were extracted from."

Sighing, Harvey picked up the photos. As he sifted through them, he scrutinized each one more slowly than the last. Then, heedlessly stacking paper to make space on his desk, he laid each one out in a design of his own. Then he sat quietly and examined the pattern, and Kate's diagram.

Finally, he looked up at Kate. He scratched his head. "It's impossible."

Kate grinned. "Dead bang, Harvey."

She pulled her tape recorder from her shoulder bag. "Tell me all about it."

Fifteen minutes later, sitting behind the wheel of her Saturn, Kate picked up her mobile phone.

Mike Bodwin's first question when she reached him was, "Kate—how's the shoulder?"

"All but healed. I have a situation, Lieutenant," she said. "I'd like to discuss it with you. Personally."

Bodwin chuckled. "I doubt you're quite that healed, but it's typical you'd say so. Pretty damn chaotic around here without you, but we're fine, Kate."

Clearly, he had misinterpreted her phone call as a declaration that she was ready to come back. "This has nothing to do with my job, sir. But since you mention it, if somebody doesn't put the arm on my therapist, I'll never be back. She's using my head for a soccer ball."

Bodwin chuckled. "Are you in the area, Kate?"

"Close enough."

"I'm bogged down with appointments and clearance reports. I'll see where I can work you in."

The necessity for this kind of activity was exactly why promotion to his level did not interest her. Paper-pushing and politics were not her idea of police work. "I'll leave my mobile phone on, sir."

Next, she searched her shoulder bag and found the slip of paper with Matt Brazelton's number on it, and punched it into her phone.

"This is Matt," he answered in the assured baritone she remembered from when he had called her at home.

"Detective Delafield," she said crisply. "I'd like a meeting."

"Great," he said immediately. "Where are you?"

"Highland Park, heading for Hollywood."

"How about we meet at a restaurant?"

The *Advocate*'s offices were located in Hollywood; she would not have agreed to meet him there. "Fine."

"I know someone at Musso's, I can get us in. How about . . . half an hour?"

"I'll be there," she said and disconnected. Then she dialed information.

The wood-paneled booths in the main room of the Musso & Frank Grill were famous for the studio power players who lunched there daily amid homage from table hoppers, and so Kate was not surprised to be seated in the side room of the clubby, storied old Hollywood eatery. Surrounded by an energized buzz of conversation, she studied the man across the snowy tablecloth from her, peering at him over the restaurant's extensive menu.

He was handsome, tanned, and young, appearing to be in his mid to late twenties. His coarse dark hair was crimped, like short bent grass on a golf course; his mustache was neatly trimmed. He wore a blue-checked shirt partially buttoned over a white T-shirt, which was tucked into crisply pressed jeans, and cowboy boots. She had noticed on the way to the table that Brazelton was short in stature, his slender body tautly muscled.

After several attempts at pleasantries to which Kate gave minimal response, he said, "I do appreciate the meeting, Detective. I guarantee you it's off the record."

"I'm not worried," she said.

He raised his eyebrows. "That wasn't the impression I got when I called you."

"Let's cut to the chase, shall we? Tell me what you know about Tony Ferrera. And Luke Taggart."

His eyes narrowed. "Fine. But let's get something understood. I also get to know at least some of what you know."

"And what are we having here," said a gruff voice at Kate's elbow.

She looked up at the white-aproned old man standing imperiously with his hands on his hips. Some of Musso & Frank's waiters, she had heard, were old-time communists who disdained the wealthy capitalists they served. She had not really looked at the menu, nor, she suspected, had Brazelton, but she left it to him to court this waiter's scorn by saying so.

"Cobb salad and a Coke," Brazelton said hastily.

"Corned beef on rye, iced tea," she said.

His face impassive as if withholding reproach for their choices, the waiter nodded curtly and withdrew.

Brazelton said, "The waiters here . . ."

She nodded.

"To return to our conversation," Brazelton said. "Cops killed Tony Ferrera."

She said dryly, "I assume you have names. Badge numbers."

"I have corroboration. From cops inside LAPD."

Just as Corey Lanier had claimed. "Like who?"

"I've guaranteed them confidentiality."

Just as Corey Lanier had claimed. "That was good of you."

"You seem really flip about all this," he said. Ire had crept into his voice and his eyes. "I don't get it. I don't get where you're coming from."

She took a sip of her water before she answered. "I'm tired of being jerked around by people telling me half truths and nontruths. People like you."

"What the hell are talking about?"

"Your claims of corroboration, your off-the-record guarantees. There is no record to be off of. Because you're no reporter."

He picked up his knife, balanced it across a knuckle on his index finger for a moment, then dropped it back onto the table. Not meeting her eyes, he asked, "How did you find out?"

"I'm a detective."

He looked at her, intensity in his gaze. "Yeah, but Corey Lanier's a reporter and she bought it, and I didn't think anybody could be more suspicious than she was. What tipped you off?"

"When I called, you didn't offer to meet at the *Advocate* offices—"

"It's lunchtime," he protested.

"—plus I didn't remember ever seeing your byline in the pages of the *Advocate*, and Brazelton is a name I'd remember. I don't have a photographic memory, but I tend to remember what I read. Lawyers make me very sorry if I don't. So I called the magazine."

He nodded, rueful respect in his face.

She would not admit to him that she hadn't been all that clever nor even suspicious. Had she not put the two facts she had just given Brazelton with Roberto Ferrera's mention of a Matt as a boyfriend of Tony Ferrera's, she'd have been taken in by Brazelton just as the *L.A. Times* reporter had been.

She asked, "So what do you actually do for a living?"

"I'm an agent. With Creative Advocates. We handle screenwriters mostly. A few literary authors."

"You seem pretty young," Kate commented.

"Not hardly. Not for this town." He smiled weakly. "So when I say I work for the *Advocate*, it's not a complete fabrication." She couldn't be bothered arguing this witless point, and he continued. "I use a private line into my office when I need to be a reporter."

"How did you come into contact with Tony Ferrera?"

"On a Hollywood movie shoot about a year ago. He was part of the security detail. I had a new screenplay that needed some input about correct police procedure. I thought he was beautiful in his uniform, and it gave me an excuse to talk to him."

"The cop movies I see," she said, "nobody cares a hoot about correct police procedure."

He smiled. "I guess nobody should. The film never got made."

"So you and Tony Ferrera met and became lovers." It was hardly a guess—but let him think she was omnipotent.

"It wasn't nearly that simple. I found so much in Tony besides a beautiful body in a uniform . . ." He had retreated to some deep interior place and she sensed, rather than saw, his grief.

There was obviously much more to this particular story, but she pressed on. "How did you arrive at the belief that Tony was killed by one of his own?"

Brazelton snapped out of his brooding. "He was about to expose LAPD for the homophobic fraternity it claims it isn't. He was going to come out as a gay police officer. And he had a list of the hundreds of gay and lesbian cops at LAPD, and he was going to take everybody on it out with him."

Their food arrived. The waiter ceremoniously set down her plate and Brazelton's, turning each one until they achieved an angle of presentation that met his satisfaction. Then he picked up and set down the condiments on the table, readjusting them, fussing as though he could read Kate's mind that she needed this time to reassemble thoughts that had been scattered by Brazelton's dismaying confirmation of what Corey Lanier had told her. If Brazelton had been Tony Ferrera's lover and confidant, then there could be substance to the allegations of homicidal police misconduct she had heard from Taggart, Brazelton, and Lanier.

Abruptly, the waiter nodded and withdrew, and words spilled from Brazelton as if pent up: "Tony knew how much shit would hit the fan, he knew he was dealing with men whose masculinity's all tied up with their uniforms and guns. He knew he might be killed."

"And you supported him?" She could not remotely imagine ever agreeing to such a course of action by a partner of hers. "You went along with that?"

"No way in hell. Are you kidding? I begged, I bargained, I threatened, I did everything. He kept telling me he'd planned the whole thing out to protect himself."

Jabbing at his salad with his fork, he stopped and looked up at her. "I came out when I was thirteen—the minute I knew I was gay. When Tony was thirteen, he knew he couldn't be gay—he thought it would destroy his family. When he became a cop, he knew he couldn't be gay—he thought it would destroy his chances for any kind of police career. When he met me, I don't know what happened to the guy, but he looked at the twenty years he'd crapped away, and I reaped the whirlwind. There was nothing I could do with him. I've been a radical since my UCLA campus days, but all of a sudden, Tony embraced his gayness like—he was like a convert who believes more passionately than anybody born into a faith. Except he had the discipline to control himself."

Kate said thoughtfully, "I never, ever heard along the pipeline that he was gay."

Brazelton asked with a faint smile, "Do you know everyone at LAPD who's gay?"

"Not by a long shot, not even the ones who belong to the Golden State Peace Officers Association. Some are so deeply closeted . . ."

"Tony was close to people in GSPOA, but he didn't join. He was so deep in the closet he was part of the paint. He came out to Luke, but Luke was closer to Tony than anybody except me. And there was one other cop, somebody he trusted—his prime source for information. A cop Tony called Deep Throat.''

Kate laughed in spite of herself. "Quite a name for a gay male cop informant."

Brazelton looked at her soberly. "I know Deep Throat's not a guy. In fact, I'm betting it's you."

"You *what*?"

Forking salad into his mouth, Brazelton shrugged. "That's *absurd.*"

"Whatever you say. Deep Throat swore Tony to secrecy, so I don't expect you to admit it."

"Look—it's absolutely, definitely, positively not me."

"Whatever."

Any further attempts to convince him appeared to be futile. She asked, "Tony never told you who this person was?"

He shook his head. "Too many dangerous people— the less we knew, the better. That's what Tony said."

Kate bit into her sandwich. "This alleged list of gay and lesbian cops—where is it now?"

"I think you probably know."

She said with irritation, "And I think you're trying to run another one of your bluffs. I think you probably have some sort of an agenda all your own. I think this list is a figment of your imagination."

Brazelton said, "If you don't think there's a list, how do you think Luke Taggart knew to call you?"

She shrugged. "Granting your contention that there is a list, then I have to be just one of many names on it."

"Like I told you: hundreds. Hundreds and hundreds of names on it. But your name is at the top of the list. And no, I don't know why," he said as she gaped at him, "not with all the cops in far more senior positions than yours. Do you want me to name some of them?" he challenged.

"No." Astounded by his statement, Kate only vaguely

tasted her corned beef. "This list—you actually saw it."

Brazelton nodded. "On Tony's computer screen. He was always working on it, adding names, updating it as gay and lesbian cops promoted or retired."

"Who's got the list now? Corey Lanier?"

"She wishes. I wish she did, too. Tony died because of that list. Luke claims he doesn't have it, has never seen it. All I know is, it's gone."

Taggart had had possession of Tony Ferrera's computer. The list would have been done on that computer—the computer now in her possession.

As if reading her mind, Brazelton said, "Believe me, I thoroughly searched Tony's computer, the one Luke's got. And the computer I've got at my apartment, in case he put it on that one. My guess is, he worked from a floppy and never risked copying it onto a hard disk anywhere. I ransacked his place—mine too. Nothing. But that disk of names is out there—somewhere."

Kate put down her sandwich, ate a bite of dill pickle, barely tasting its sourness. Brazelton, fork poised over his salad, was looking at her carefully. He asked, "How do you feel about that, Detective? About somebody publishing a list of gay and lesbian cops with your name at the top?"

"I'm not sure," she said.

"Are you in favor of it?"

"I'm not sure," she said.

"When will you be sure?"

"I'm not sure," she said. "Tell me this. Why did you call me?"

He said with a trace of impatience, "Because your name was at the top of Tony's list. I figured you were Deep Throat. What else would I think? I figured you were the one Tony might have sent the disk to."

Kate stared at him. "This is crazy. *Crazy.*"

"Luke—he thought for sure you'd help us find Tony's killers at LAPD."

"All I can do is guarantee you I have nothing to do

with any list. Has it occurred to either one of you that if your theory's correct about cops being Tony's killer, then one of those killers could be the closeted gay or lesbian cop Tony came out to? Who decided against being the fall guy who set up fellow officers for Tony Ferrera's personal agenda?" *Just like I've been set up for everybody else's personal agenda,* she thought angrily.

"This whole thing's a lot larger than anyone's personal agenda," Brazelton argued. "The original Deep Throat gave the crucial information about Nixon because he wanted to be part of the battle but didn't want to be the target of all the spear chuckers. So if you're Deep Throat, I can relate to you, I understand why you won't admit it."

"I guess I have no way of making you believe me, but I'll tell you again: I am not Deep Throat. How does Corey Lanier fit into all this?"

"I knew she was a lesbian. I called her when LAPD swept Tony's death under the carpet. She understands there's a big story here. But she needs more before she can break it."

"So Luke Taggart thought involving me would improve the odds of the story getting out. But when I narrowed my focus to the death of that man in Apparition Alley—"

"Luke called me, and I got into the act. And I got Lanier into the act to up the ante even more."

"It's only a matter of time before Lanier runs into a journalist who knows damn well you're not an *Advocate* reporter."

Brazelton shrugged. "I'll cross that bridge when I come to it."

"Does she know your true relationship with Tony Ferrera?"

Again he shrugged. "I didn't happen to mention it."

Picturing the combative *L.A. Times* reporter, Kate thought that she would not like to be in his shoes when

Lanier discovered the depth of his deception. "But Taggart, he knows."

"He knows."

One other minor little item that Taggart had neglected to tell her, she thought in disgust. "How many people in Tony's world know of your existence? His family—did any of them meet you?"

"That was the next stage in the plan, but it didn't happen. They knew Tony was involved with someone—that's all."

Correction, she thought. Tony's mother didn't know a thing, and his brothers knew about a man named Matt, and possibly more than that.

"You keep mentioning Tony's plan. What exactly was the plan?"

"It was in phases, for safety. Phase one, come out to his sister and brothers. Phase two, come out to his mother. Phase three, the press: notify key people in the gay and mainstream press, some of the tabloids. Phase four, LAPD: notify everybody on the list that they would be identified, then notify superior officers. Phase five, universal publication: put the list out on the Internet."

Kate contemplated the sandwich in her hand. "And the time frame?"

"For all five phases? No more than a week, all told."

She put the sandwich down, abandoning all attempts to eat her lunch.

Brazelton said, "He'd just started to set everything into motion. Somebody killed him because of that list. And maybe the somebody's got a lot less compunction than Tony had about what to do with it."

"At this point it seems more likely that the somebody killed him to get the list and prevent its publication."

"Other things can be done with that list besides publication."

"You're right," Kate said softly.

"All I know is, cops killed Tony. I'll tell you the truth—at this point, I don't care about the damn list. I only care about finding who did this to Tony. Whether they were gay or straight, it's equally monstrous. One way or the other, the truth needs—"

Kate's mobile phone rang. As Kate fished it out of her shoulder bag, Brazelton commented, "You fit right in here with all the power players."

As Kate expected, the caller was Lieutenant Bodwin. "I've got some clear space in about half an hour, Kate."

"I'll be there, sir. Thank you."

Kate stuffed the phone back into her shoulder bag and fished money out of her wallet, dropped it on the table. "Enjoy your lunch, Mr. Brazelton. Mine too, if you like."

"I'll be in touch, Deep Throat," Brazelton said.

15

DRIVING down Highland Avenue, Kate pulled over in order to use her mobile phone, cursing the shoulder that so curtailed her ability to function normally. She punched in a two-digit code, hoping that Aimee had returned home by now.

"Yes, hello," Aimee answered in a tone that combined exasperation with preoccupation.

"Hi, it's me."

"Hi, honey." Aimee's voice sharpened to affectionate attentiveness, but the audible, rapid click of computer keys in the background meant that she was holding the phone to her ear with her shoulder. "What's up?"

"Sweetheart, when you get a few minutes, could you do me a favor? Could I call on your computer expertise?"

"Could you make it a different favor? I need a break from this damn thing." The clicking of computer keys continued unabated.

"That computer I brought home—"

"I'm using it right now. It's faster, has lots of power." The typing ceased. "Just borrowing it, okay?"

"No problem. It's about that very computer. When you get a chance, could you see if you can spot a file somebody might've hidden somewhere?"

"Computer skullduggery?" Aimee hummed the theme from *The Twilight Zone*. "What am I looking for? Give me a clue."

"A list of names, with mine at the top."

"As it properly should be," Aimee said. "Is this, like, a recent file?"

"I'd guess . . . maybe last November."

"If it's not password protected, I'll find it. When's the appointment with your therapist?"

"God, don't remind me. Four-thirty. I'll check in with you later."

"Love you, bye," Aimee said cheerily.

Kate parked in the lot behind Wilshire Division and made her way toward the station feeling as if she were returning after an absence of months.

Self-conscious about her immobilized left arm, she felt even more awkward as uniformed officers besieged her at every step, asking "How's the shoulder?" or exclaiming "Good to see you back." Neither Fred Hansen nor Alicia Perez, who had been with her in that hallway during the shooting of Darian Crockett, appeared. She wondered if they were off duty—or avoiding her as Torrie seemed to be doing.

Outside the detectives' squad room she paused, a hand on the door, wondering who would be at the homicide table if she went in there; then she turned decisively toward Lieutenant Bodwin's office.

He was on the phone, but beckoned for her to come in, soberly scrutinizing her as she closed his office door after her. Pulling a chair away from the table where Wayne McMillan and Jim Phillips had interviewed her what seemed to be weeks ago, she positioned it in front of Bodwin's desk and made herself comfortable. Idly listening to Bodwin argue dinner arrangements with his wife, she noted that the single area on Bodwin's desk clear of paper was, as usual, his in-box. She respected his ability to handle paper—and problems—quickly, but organization was not an accompanying virtue; every surface in his office was a chaos of reports, memos, correspondence, files, notebooks, bulletins.

The list, she thought, shifting in her chair. What if that list of names were actually published? What if it were being disseminated this very moment? What would be made of the fact that her name was at the very top of such a list? Maybe she should launch a preemptive strike before all hell broke loose; maybe she should come out to the man sitting across from her. No. No, she would wait till that particular bridge came a little closer before she decided how she would try to make her way across it.

Bodwin hung up and then hunched over his desk toward her, leaning on his elbows. "You look a damn sight better than the last time I saw you."

"Yes, they washed the blood off," she quipped.

After a quick grin he sat back, pulling his tie loose from the neck of his white shirt. He said ruefully, "You make me nervous when you come in and close that door, Kate. The last time, it meant the end of Ed Taylor as your partner."

And this was a lot more serious than that, she thought. "You know of course that Luke Taggart's asked me to be his defense rep."

He looked at her grimly. "I hope to hell you're turning him down, Kate. You don't want your name associated with defense reps. That section—they're a collection of losers, no cop there is worth shit. They take a phone call and go out and drink lunch—that's their idea of a tough morning's work. They're defense reps because nobody else'll have them."

She was not surprised by his animus. Defense reps were the natural enemy of the brass, a major roadblock for an administration looking to rid LAPD of problem cops. "Sir, I've felt it's my duty to at least look into things surrounding this officer."

"Kate, listen to me. Dump any notion of repping this guy. You have a spotless package, you're highly respected throughout LAPD. If you might ever decide to move beyond D-three, don't do this. Don't ruin your promotability by having this business attached to your name. And let me remind you, by the way, your paid time off is for you to rest and heal—"

"I'm fine, sir," she interrupted. "I need to talk about my involvement with Officer Taggart. I need advice from someone I trust."

He looked taken aback. "I appreciate your confidence in me, Kate. But this is a clear conflict of interest."

"I've considered that, sir. But there's more to this than meets the eye—and in some ways a lot less. I have a pretty good idea of how I want to proceed from here logistically. I could use some feedback. And some help."

Bodwin got up from his desk. "I think I need to get us some coffee."

An hour later, Kate was again in her car, once more driving toward Hollywood. She checked her watch: three o'clock. She had plenty of time to see Mouse Mussino at Hollywood Division and then to head downtown.

Images of Bodwin's face crowded her mind, the range of his reactions to her narrative of the events of the past four days, the increasing grimness in his eyes as the specter of police misconduct emerged from what she had uncovered about the Mendez and Ferrera homicides. She had omitted two facets of the story: Tony Ferrera's sexual orientation, and Matt Brazelton's claim of the existence of Ferrera's list of gay and lesbian police officers.

Immediately pointing out that Internal Affairs needed to be notified, he had conceded that the situation was too volatile and fluid at this point to commit to paper. About Max Mussino's conduct he had commented with clear disdain, "I know him. I worked with Mouse years ago at Hollenbeck. LAPD's come to a sorry pass when a Mouse Mussino becomes a D-three."

When she had called Mussino from Bodwin's office to request this meeting, his response had fully lived up to her expectation: "Give me one fucking reason why I need to look at your face again."

"Detective Mussino, it's in your best interests—"

"Bullshit."

"Let me put it this way," she had snapped as Bodwin grinned at her. "You will be one sorry-ass detective if you let me go to the Board of Rights with what I've learned about Luke Taggart's case."

Max Mussino was waiting for her in the station lobby. He led her into the same interview room where she had pored over the files on the Julio Mendez homicide. She could still smell, faintly, cigar smoke.

She let Mussino choose his chair, the one at the head of the Formica-top table; then she lowered herself into the chair adjacent to him, placing her shoulder bag on the floor between them. Mussino, in a mustard-colored shirt and dark brown jacket, seemed more rodentlike than ever with his big ears and small, bristling mustache.

Rearing back on two legs of the metal chair, he hooked his thumbs through the straps of his shoulder holster. "Try not to waste more than two minutes of my time."

"The Mendez homicide," she said calmly. "There's nothing in the file about interviews of anyone at the Burger King on Hollywood Boulevard where Taggart said he was."

He snorted in disgust. "Who gives a fuck?"

"You arrested him for murder. His account of that evening included the fact that he'd just come out of the Burger King and saw a drug deal going down. And there's nothing in any of the reports about where his patrol car was parked."

"You gotta be absolutely fucking kidding," he said incredulously. "You came here to tell me that?"

"I take it that means you didn't interview anyone at the Burger King, and you don't know where his patrol car was parked."

"It means I don't give a flying fuck. What else you got?"

"Did you interview tenants in the buildings adjacent to Apparition Alley?"

"What kind of a question is that? You saw the FIs."

"The field interviews are filler. In the two adjacent buildings, no police officer or detective interviewed anyone in the three days after the evening of the murder and before the case went to RHD."

"Bullshit."

Kate said quietly, "I did my own interviews, Detective."

He was only momentarily disconcerted. "Big deal. So what? RHD talked to them and did all that other stuff too. It's covered."

"Did you talk to Ida Wilson?"

"Who the fuck is Ida Wilson?"

"Only a woman in the front apartment of the building west of Apparition Alley with a clear view of the street."

"Oh, her. Yeah, Oliver from RHD got on my ass about that one." He shrugged. "Okay, you maybe got a point, I maybe should've talked to her. But some batty ninety-year-old—you think her story about four shots is any less crazy than Lucy Taggart's? Who's gonna believe her? Or Taggart, for that matter? We got bullets that fit Taggart's gun, we got Taggart sticking to some wild-ass story that doesn't match up with anybody's idea of logic. Who needs witnesses when we got evidence that doesn't lie? The guy who did Mendez is Lucy Taggart."

"Ida Wilson—you're drawing conclusions about a woman you never even talked to."

"So kill me," he said witheringly. "Kill me for not talking to a crazy old bat I didn't need to talk to."

"Did you examine the ground in the alley or the walls for other bullets in addition to the ones you extracted from the wall?"

"We got the only two bullets that matter. What are

you, some kind of obsessive-compulsive? You on lithium or something?''

"I saw nothing in the Mendez file about notification of his next of kin.''

"For chrissake, the guy was a fucking useless wetback dope pusher with a rap sheet. He was a piece of shit. Anybody that gave a damn, they could read about it in the fucking paper.''

"Did you furnish photographs of the crime scene to the Firearms Analysis Unit or have them come out to the scene?''

He rolled his eyes. "That's the stupidest goddamn thing I ever heard of. Get to the point or get out of here. What's all this about?''

"It's about Luke Taggart not being the killer of Julio Mendez.''

Mussino sat forward on his chair, its front legs thumping onto the floor. "You're outta your fucking mind.''

"And when he's exonerated, which he will be, you've got nothing to fall back on, Detective. Because in the three days it took for the case to go downtown, you did nothing, and you misled Robbery-Homicide into thinking you had done a complete preliminary investigation. Any witnesses who might establish a lead to the real—''

"Piss on them.'' His small dark eyes were cold with hostility, his struggle for composure visible in his white-knuckled fists. "For the sake of argument, let's say you're right. Let's defy all the laws of reason and say Lucy Taggart's as pure as the driven snow. That means somebody else did it, which means some drug-pushing scum blew away another piece of drug-pushing scum.''

"Detective, because the Mendez murder went downtown to Robbery-Homicide, your lieutenant and your captain didn't do their normal oversight. You showed me the Mendez file without running it by either one of them because you didn't want them to see what's not in that file. All you wanted to do was to nail a man you despise—''

"Attacking procedures, attacking me—it won't work," he sneered. "Because your client's guilty as sin. Even the fucking civilian on the board is gonna see right through you. Are you gonna sit there and tell me you're gonna defend a rotten cop by taking me down over a file that's not as neat and tidy as you'd like it to be?"

"I'm telling you what's in those files does not begin to establish a case against Luke Taggart."

"Oh, Christ." He tipped his head back and gazed at the acoustic tile ceiling. "Tell me I'm dreaming."

Kate did not reply.

"Look. Work with me on this."

"How is it that you want me to work with you?"

"If there's holes in the file, let's sew them up."

"It's up to you to sew them up, Detective."

"Are you gonna sit there and tell me you're actually gonna take me down in order to defend a rotten cop who took out his own partner? Who the hell are you loyal to?"

"Loyalty is no reason to excuse lousy and lazy police work."

"Fuck, I'm dealing with Mother Teresa. Wilshire Division must be a fucking convent. Let me get this straight. You're telling me you're gonna shit all over me at a Board of Rights hearing when we got a bad shooting by a bad cop, and we got that cop by the balls. Is that what you're telling me?"

"One last time, Detective Mussino. Luke Taggart did not kill Julio Mendez. I've got the evidence you couldn't be bothered finding."

"All right. Okay. Evidence such as what?"

"Evidence you can find by doing your own footwork."

"You think I'm some dumb cabbage patch cop? You think I'm gonna fall for a bluff like that? What are you looking for, some kind of a deal? Exactly why the hell did you come here?"

"To try and prevent some blood from spilling on the floor."

"Okay, okay." He raised both hands. "You got something? Give it to me."

"Go get it yourself."

"You know what I think? I think we got Lucy Taggart cold, and you're just a dyke bitch out to bust a pair of balls you wish you had. If you do one thing to take me down at that Board of Rights hearing, you better watch your dyke back because I got friends. You fuck with me and so help me God . . ."

He pointed at her, sighting along his finger as if it were a gun. "You fuck with me and it won't help you if you crawl downtown and suck the black dick off of our jungle bunny police chief. That bullet in the shoulder is a pinprick compared to what could happen. You do anything to deep six me, you're gonna be in worse trouble than your worst dream."

Kate got up from the table. "This conversation is over," she said with icy formality. Picking up her shoulder bag, she left the interview room.

Outside the station, assembling her composure, she glanced at her watch. She had just enough time to report in to Lieutenant Bodwin before heading into Calla Dearborn's clutches.

16

MAKING herself comfortable in the chair in front of Calla Dearborn's desk, Kate noted that the surface of the desk was clear of paper or pen.

The psychologist peered at her with narrowed eyes. "What have you been doing with your time off?"

"Sitting around, relaxing."

"You don't seem relaxed. There's tension in your face and body. You seem quite distracted today."

"I do?" Kate said innocently.

Elbows on her desk, Dearborn knitted her fingers together and gazed over them at Kate. "I wish we had more time for hide and go seek, Kate, because you're quite a challenge—you're a most interesting woman. But we don't. And so you must pay very strict attention today."

"You certainly have my attention. What's up?" Will I be released from protective custody? she wanted to ask.

"Today I'm going to talk more than listen. The reality is, therapy for you police officers bears as much resemblance to conventional therapy as battlefield surgery does to conventional medicine. So I'm going to cover as much ground as possible in the time I have with you. You can take out of it what you want to. All I ask is that you listen."

"Gladly," Kate said. This turn of events looked promising.

"You may not be so glad when you hear what I have

to say. I'm a detective of sorts too. The difference between us is that I don't necessarily have to be suspicious of you—I can believe anything you tell me. What we have in common is we both form hypotheses from pieces of information. From what I've managed to glean from you—or maybe I should say tugged out of you—I've put together some hypotheses. The first one is that your life is completely shrouded by death."

The conclusion was so obvious and so artfully phrased that Kate smiled. "That's quite a metaphor."

Dearborn's dimple appeared with her smile. "An appropriate one. For your age, you've been touched by an uncommon number of deaths. I'm talking now about your personal life. The loss of your mother before you were out of your teens. The loss of your father in your early thirties. The loss of a mate after a happy, twelve-year relationship before you were out of your thirties. The death and loss you saw in Vietnam. All of that, added on to the death you deal with every day in your professional life, the fourteen years you've spent in homicide."

Kate was struck by the assessment. These basic facts of her own life had never been laid out in such a fashion.

Dearborn said, "You rely almost entirely on your own self-sufficiency. The truth is, it's a blind spot. And you've invested a lot of capital in sustaining the blindness. The truth is, you're incomplete as a person."

Kate sat up in her chair, animosity building along with stiffening resistance.

"The truth is," Dearborn said, "I'm incomplete too. We all are. But most of us grope for what's missing. If you stayed with me long enough, I could help you risk reaching out for what's missing in you, but we both know that's not going to happen. The truth is, Kate, you've turned yourself into a stranger to yourself. You're a woman who continually sabotages opportunities for connection with other people—and with yourself. Because you've already lost so much, everything you do is framed by the need to lose nothing further."

With a prickling between her shoulder blades, Kate absorbed this information silently.

"It all stems back to your mother," Dearborn said.

Kate eased back into her chair. Even with her limited knowledge of psychology as a discipline, this seemed to be one of its staple findings.

"I'm sure you're thinking that this is what every therapist says. But consider these facts. You say you were closer to your father than your mother—not unheard of, but unusual between most mothers and daughters. And quite understandable in your circumstances. Relatives constantly reminded you that your birth destroyed your mother's health. Any child carrying such a burden of guilt would distance herself from her mother. Then you lost her to death when you were only seventeen. All your life you've carried around the burden of thinking you were responsible for your own mother's death."

To her horror, Kate felt tears welling up.

Dearborn said, "I seriously question whether your birth had anything at all to do with her health in later life. What did she die of?"

"Leukemia," Kate managed to say.

"Then I doubt that her death had anything at all to do with you, and you should doubt it too. It's helped make you a person whose potential for connection is buried by a fear of doing fatal damage to the other person. Your reluctance to answer questions about your deepest self is a way of deflecting anyone's attempt at connection with you, it's a way of deflecting your fear."

Shaking her head, Kate murmured, "I know better than anyone that there are no guarantees about anything in this life."

"Lip service. You're speaking from your intellect, Kate, not your emotions. You conduct your life as if you're trying to guarantee what can't be guaranteed. You spend your present guarding against a future that's rooted in your past. Every day of your professional life reinforces that.''

Again, Kate shook her head. ''I don't agree with you. But maybe I don't completely understand what you mean.''

''I mean that death is what orients you. Every day on your job you witness the emotional cost of someone's death on the living. Because of what's happened in your past, every day you learn all over again that you need to shut down to protect yourself from any more pain. Your intimate knowledge of the cost of death has closed you down. And that leads to my second hypothesis—that you need to continue therapy. Not with me, perhaps, but with someone.''

Never, Kate thought. ''You know, I think I'm basically okay. I feel like you're trying to turn me into a victim. I feel like this whole thing is victimization.''

Anger engulfed Dearborn's face, drawing her eyebrows together behind the steel-rimmed glasses, the darkness in her eyes seeming to spread into the almond of her skin. ''‘Victimization,''' she repeated wrathfully. *''Think* about that latest bit of jargon, Kate. It's the smug new buzzword, the newest rationalization for privileged people to turn their backs on people with no advantages. Dare give voice to legitimate grievances, and you're indulging in ‘victimization.' Dare sympathize with other people's legitimate grievances, and you're accused of being ‘politically correct.' ''

''I never thought to look at it that way,'' Kate said.

''Exactly what those people intend. But we're off the subject, which has nothing to do with any view of you as a victim. I think you're a strong and moral and admirable woman, but I also know that at this point in your life, you urgently need to take on some alternative survival techniques.''

''I'm listening to everything you say, but I have a pretty good life. I seem to be surviving just fine—''

''Are you telling me you never get depressed? Never

drink too much? Never get irrationally angry?"

Kate said cautiously, "I stay pretty much on an even keel . . ." *Except for not being able to relax without the help of a drink,* she conceded to herself. *Except for flying into a rage these days at the slightest provocation . . .*

"Kate, you wouldn't admit it if you were ready to leave this office and leap off the building." Dearborn added with exasperation, "You police officers are all alike. Your reluctance to ever admit—"

"Look. If I told you I was depressed, which I'm not, God knows what could happen. Your department's run by LAPD—I know from what I've seen that it has no confidentiality, and I don't care how much you deny it. I know about officers who said they were depressed and ended up on the rubber gun squad—minus their gun and on modified duty. Officers who've lost their jobs and their pensions."

Dearborn calmly asked, "Are you carrying a gun now?"

"Of course."

"And you carry that weapon with you twenty-four hours a day. It's right there, it's part of you. It may be your best defense, Kate, but it can turn into your worst enemy. Do you actually expect me to allow a seriously depressed police officer to have a weapon at her finger-tips when she's going through her darkest hour? If I have evidence to the contrary, I can't give armed police officers a carte blanche benefit of the doubt. It would be different if you yourselves would reach out for help. But you always have to be macho tough authority fig-ures, you can't break down, you always have to be in command."

"Of course we do. It's how we're trained. It's how we *want* to be trained. It's what we do. It's what we're paid for."

Dearborn waved her hand in dismissal. "That's your police culture talking. We expect you to perform during the shift you're working, not twenty-four hours a day.

The problem is, you don't even try to help yourselves, you don't even confide in each other. When one of you kills himself, you say he permanently retired or blew out his brains or ate his gun or cashed in his chips or called it quits—you cops have more ways of referring to suicide than men do to their penises. Have you ever heard another police officer utter the word *suicide?*"

"No," Kate said.

"Suicide. Your great taboo. Suicide is the ultimate weakness for a cop, isn't it? Cops who commit suicide don't get that big police funeral with the police chief and all the brass in attendance."

"You're not a cop," argued Kate. "You have no police experience."

"So you question how can I make valid clinical judgments about any of you, is that it? Let me say that if you take anything at all out of these sessions, I hope you'll use it to help other officers. It was unlucky you were shot. But you're damn lucky to get even a few minutes of therapy." Dearborn's index finger was punching repeatedly at the desk as if it would dig a hole. "Because every one of you should be in here getting at least one hour of counseling every few weeks to care for your mental health, to ground you, to remind you that the image of police as men and women of steel is only an image, that you're neither heroes nor villains, you're people who deal with the same problems as everybody else."

"I suppose you're right," Kate conceded.

"You're damn right I'm right. The street today is a war zone and some of you suffer from post-traumatic stress disorder just like any war veteran. You specifically worry me, Kate. You're in a high-stress job that takes an enormous emotional toll. Over fourteen years, you've become enclosed in a small, tight container. You're like a root-bound plant. You need a funnel leading out of you somewhere, to let the horrors escape. All that said, I'll give you the real bottom line."

As she paused, Kate instinctively braced herself.

"You're a textbook candidate for alcoholism. And every day that you wall yourself off from a partner you love, you jeopardize your relationship with her."

Kate did not respond. She could find nothing to say.

"Tell me, Kate. What if your police career ended tomorrow? What if that bullet had done severe nerve damage or taken out a kneecap instead of hitting you in the fleshy part of the shoulder? What would you do with the rest of your life?"

"I don't know," Kate said.

"Have you ever imagined being anything but a police officer?"

"No," Kate said.

"I had one of you in here about five years ago who also wanted nothing more out of his life than to be a police officer. But he lost his moral compass. He made the mistake of buying into some macho idea of what his status justified him doing, and Internal Affairs got hold of him, placed him on restricted duty, and sent him to me for counseling. In one single day of his life, his entire sense of self-sufficiency broke down. Sudden and total loss of face, disgraced in the sight of his police family. Then he had his Board of Rights hearing and lost his badge, gun, uniform—his whole identity was taken away."

Bud Avery, Kate thought. *She's describing Bud Avery to a T. She must be the psychologist who treated Bud Avery . . .*

"I was new here. I had excellent training but limited experience. I followed departmental guidelines, but I was following the usual textbook methods of mental etiquette to treat police officers. I didn't have the full context of a brutally hard profession performed by fiercely dedicated men and women one slender thread away from breaking down completely. By this police officer's lights, he had nowhere to turn to find the profession he'd lost. He had a life he no longer considered worth living. And I couldn't help him.''

Kate could hear grieving in Calla Dearborn's voice. *She's never forgiven herself for Bud Avery.*

''There was no way you could help him,'' Kate said. ''Trust me when I say there are some things I know and you don't. Believe me when I say that if you don't want me to blame myself for my mother, then don't blame yourself for Bud Avery.''

Calla Dearborn stared at her.

''I know you can't say anything more. Thank you for telling me what you did. You're right about police culture, and you're right that it's very hard for me to talk about personal things.''

Dearborn nodded wearily. ''You can't even answer the question about the worst thing you've seen as a police officer.''

Kate said softly, ''It was when I was in Juvenile. This would be back in seventy-eight. Homicide took a child-murder suspect in for questioning.''

She paused, swallowing painfully as the image of Victor Schmidt's bearded face penetrated her defenses and flooded her mind. Calla Dearborn sat in still, rapt attention, and once again Kate realized that she was a gifted listener.

''The case detectives had a hunch and some circumstantial evidence—not nearly enough for probable cause and a search warrant. The suspect told Pierce and Rollins he wouldn't talk to anybody but me. I don't know why he chose me. I have no idea. He was a neighbor of the family, he'd seen me at the home when we were first called in, when the little girl was still missing. The ground rules for him talking to me were, I couldn't take notes, there could be no recording device of any kind. We met every condition, agreed to an unwitnessed interview hoping it would lead to a formal one—because he'd raped and tortured to death a nine-year-old girl.''

''Was this man Victor Schmidt?''

"Yes," Kate said in surprise. "You know the case?"

"It's in the literature," Dearborn said softly. "My God, I can't believe you actually talked to the man. Go on."

"Then you know how much we wanted to get this monster. They put the two of us in an interview room. I spent two hours and fourteen minutes with him. It took him that long to describe every physical detail of what he did to that little girl, all her excruciating pain and screams, over the five-hour period that he let her live. He had an erection the entire time he talked to me."

"Oh God," Calla Dearborn breathed.

Kate's voice dropped to a whisper. "The whole time, all I wanted to do was kill him. I was sitting in there with this beast . . ." Kate coughed, found her normal voice. "I needed to kill him. I needed to go out of that room and get my gun and blow his brains out, I needed to empty my gun into him and reload it and empty it again and again . . ."

"Yes," Calla Dearborn said.

"He knew it. He sat there reading me like a book. Afterward I had to write down everything I could remember. Everything he said. He denied it all. We collected enough evidence based on what he said to arrest him. He pled not guilty. My conversation with him was admitted into evidence, so I had to go through it again, I had to recite all the detail of what he told me. The family elected not to attend the day I testified, but Schmidt was there, and I just know the whole time I was on the stand he had an erection as he sat at the defense table just like he did the day he talked to me. All the time I testified, I pretended I was handcuffed because all I wanted on this earth was to draw my gun and exterminate him."

Dearborn said gently, "I recall he was killed before the case went to the jury."

"Yes. Knifed by another inmate. If the case is in your

literature, then . . ." Kate tried to smile. "I guess I don't need to get into what Schmidt told me."

"You told me how you feel. That's what's important. That's what you need to talk about. It's good. It's important that you told me what you did."

"Victor Schmidt is why I took full advantage when LAPD was forced to open its detective ranks to women. I'm not all that ambitious, but I knew I couldn't survive dealing with crimes against children."

"I hope what you've told me is the beginning of what you'll be willing to share with your Aimee."

Kate smiled, this time with much less effort. "I'm not really all that self-controlled, you know. If I were, I wouldn't have fallen in love with a woman. Twice."

Dearborn smiled back at her. "Well, nothing mocks our best-laid plans like sexuality. Who we love seems to have very little to do with logic or life circumstance. Fortunately, unhappiness is not a moral obligation. At least not in my book."

"Mine either," Kate said.

"As you may have gathered, I'm releasing you as of today."

"Thank you," Kate said, feeling an instant surge of regret at the loss of contact with this deeply intelligent and compassionate woman about whom she knew virtually nothing.

Dearborn said crisply, "I assure you, it's not because of the pressure that's been applied from your lieutenant and captain. I'd keep you here if I felt it was necessary. You're quite right, you know, in your self-assessment that you're basically okay. You are. It's not your present I'm worried about—it's your future. Do we understand each other?"

"We do," Kate said.

"I assume you have physical therapy scheduled for that shoulder?"

"Yes. Beginning next week."

"The statement I'll be giving your captain is that I'm

releasing you as of today to resume your duties on a part-time basis to be determined by you and your physician."

"Fine."

"Do you think you might take up my suggestion of seeking additional therapy?"

"I'll think about it," Kate said.

Calla Dearborn shook her head ruefully, then got to her feet and extended a hand. "I wish you the best of luck with everything in your life, Kate."

Kate clasped her hand. Covered it with her other hand. "Thank you, Calla."

"You make me wish again that I had some way of measuring exactly whatever it is that I accomplish."

"Believe me when I say please don't leave this job. We need you."

"Believe me when I say that as much as LAPD needs you, Kate, you need to leave the job each day and live your own life."

Then Calla Dearborn's dimple appeared with her smile as she touched Kate's cheek with a warm, gentle hand. "You be careful out there."

17

AGAIN Kate drove down Hollywood Boulevard, following it onto Laurel Canyon Boulevard, thinking what an absurd misnomer "rush hour" was when cars crawled antlike in a tightly packed column up the winding two-lane road and through the Santa Monica Mountains to the San Fernando Valley.

Exiting the main road, she navigated the same hairpin turns through trees and bush as the last time she had gone to Luke Taggart's house, passing the same battered Volkswagen van and rickety, falling-down shack, again pursued by the four slavering Dobermans. As before, clothes hung on the line strung between two pine trees, but the fat woman was nowhere to be seen.

Pulling off the road in front of Taggart's house, Kate edged open her car door and extended the back of her hand for the fiercely barking Turk and Dreamer to sniff; both dogs subsided into a tail-wagging welcome.

Taggart's gray Range Rover, bathed in orange-lemon light in the waning afternoon sun, was parked in the gravel driveway beside the house. Receiving no answer to her insistent knock, Kate marched around the side of the house, following the sound of opera music. She found Taggart weeding a flower bed alongside the deck, his bare shoulders gleaming with perspiration, his khaki shorts patterned with damp.

"We need to talk," she commanded over the music.

"I guess we do." He leaned his hoe against the deck.

"*La Traviata* again. I seem to need to listen to tragic opera these days." He turned off the portable CD player. "Get you something to drink?"

After a day like today, I deserve a fifth of scotch served by the glassful—and to hell with Calla Dearborn's prediction of alcoholism. "Nothing," she said.

"Well, I need something myself," he said. "I've sweated off about two quarts. Be right back."

She climbed the four stairs to the deck. A GTE mobile phone, its power-on signal blinking, lay on the table. She flipped it open and pushed Recall. The number illuminated on the display was one she had dialed earlier to reach Matt Brazelton. She cleared the display and refolded the phone. No doubt Taggart had been in communication with Tony Ferrera's brothers as well, and God knew who else as part of his arsenal of methods to keep track of and interfere with her attempts to uncover the facts of his case.

Her glance falling on the hoe leaning against the deck, she remembered the bullet hole Taggart had shown her in his bedroom window. He couldn't be too worried about being shot from ambush if he was working out here in the open, half-naked, with opera music impeding his sensory awareness of his surroundings and no gun in sight for protection. Undoubtedly he had staged the bullet hole for her benefit.

A bird chirped from the deck railing, but she sealed off any appreciation for her rustic surroundings, focusing on how she must deal with this deceptive, infuriating man.

Taggart reappeared, a polo shirt over his shorts. He placed two glasses of lemonade on the table, one of them in front of her. "In case you change your mind," he said, easing himself down across from her and crossing an ankle over a knee.

For a moment, she enjoyed a vision of picking up the drink and dashing it into his face in reciprocation for his hypocritical courtesy. How appropriate that he would offer an acidic drink to combine with the corrosive taste in her mouth.

"I know what you did, Taggart."

" 'Taggart,' " he repeated. "So it's no more Ms. Nice Guy."

"What I don't know," she continued, "is why."

Taggart said easily, "Why don't you explain what it is you claim I did."

"You've told everyone involved with this case a truckload of lies. You asked me to help you and then proceeded to fabricate everything but your name. You've managed to torpedo my every step."

"Tell me about it," he said.

So he was going to slide down this cliff with his fingernails dug in. "I found a witness. With a perfect view of what happened on Stewart Street the night Julio Mendez was killed."

He nodded. "Robbery-Homicide told me about her."

"Ida Wilson saw your patrol car."

He shrugged. "If you recall, I did tell you I looked into Apparition Alley every night on patrol."

"You did. And you told me it was ten-fifteen when you came out of the Burger King and began the foot pursuit that led you to Apparition Alley. Ida Wilson saw your car at nine-forty-five."

"She could be wrong."

"She's not wrong," Kate snapped. "You stopped at Apparition Alley at nine-forty-five and saw the body of Julio Mendez—maybe you were in the area and heard the two shots Ida Wilson hoped were backfires. You saw Mendez had just been fatally shot. And that's when you made your decision to abandon your sworn duty as a police officer. Instead of reporting a homicide, you left the scene."

Taggart did not respond; he sat calmly drinking his lemonade. Turk moved to him, the dog's paws making clicking sounds on the deck; Taggart inclined his powerful body slightly and ruffled the shepherd's coat.

"You parked your patrol car south of Hollywood Boulevard," Kate said, "and called in code seven because you needed to take yourself off duty. You went into the Burger King because you had an idea about the nature and position of the dead man's wounds, and you wanted to work out your idea, think out your next steps. At ten-fifteen, you left the Burger King and began carrying out your plan."

His eyes distant, his face impassive, he asked, "How did you arrive at this deduction?"

"For one thing, if I were a police officer accused of murder and out on bail, I'd be so anxious to clear myself I'd interview every witness I could find to support my version of events. You didn't lift a finger to fight the murder charge against you. It would take a very stupid detective not to notice that."

"Mouse and Moron didn't notice it," he offered.

The amusement lightening his face intensified her ire. "You didn't even get yourself a lawyer. You probably couldn't be bothered hiring one to enter your plea."

"I did bother. I'm hardly qualified to negotiate my own bail."

"When you described your pursuit of the drug suspect, I asked if he could have dragged his female hostage into one of the buildings flanking Apparition Alley. You told me those buildings were locked. But they aren't. The front door of each building opens into a small entryway with mailboxes. The door beyond that unlocks with a key."

"So that explains what happened to the guy I was chasing."

She wanted to go over the table at him. "God damn you Taggart, stop playing me for a fool." *Hold your temper,* she told herself. But she snapped off her words: "There never was any drug suspect. There never was an Indian woman hostage he dragged into Apparition Alley. There never was a drug deal on Hollywood Boulevard. You made everything up. And you deliberately made it all so preposterous that no witness could possibly corroborate it."

Again Taggart's face lightened with amusement. "If you recall, I did swear that I never shot Julio Mendez."

"It's the only thing you've told me so far that's the truth," Kate said, leaning wrathfully toward him. "I should have made you swear to every single statement you made to me. You invented a scenario that matched nothing at the scene—"

"Which was?"

"You ran up Stewart to Wheeler, past Ida Wilson's window to Apparition Alley. You drew your weapon, lined up your sights over Julio Mendez, and precisely placed two shots to correspond with the ones in the dead man's body."

Her anger spiraling out of control, Kate picked up the lemonade. Its cool tartness quenched some of her heat and calmed her. "You told your crazy story about chasing a man with a hostage to the investigating officers because you knew they'd be only too willing to suspect you. The cops at Hollywood Division blame you for Bud Avery's suicide, they hate your guts for your accusations about them over Tony Ferrera's death. Mussino loathes you so much he'd leap at a chance to take you down on a murder charge, he'd do anything to finish you off. You took full advantage of that—"

"Anybody could take advantage of Mouse Mussino. Mouse and Moron are a sick version of Abbott and Costello. How the department could—"

"What's really sick is a holier-than-thou act coming from you, Taggart. After what you've done."

"What else tipped you off?"

Kate gestured toward the house. "Your library. All those books on the techniques of police work and forensic science. Including a reference book on firearms." It occurred to Kate that he had assembled that library because he had once dreamed of advancing in his police career. "Your big roadblock was Robbery-Homicide and ballistics. According to Harvey Gaviland, Oliver and Moynihan found and collected two other bullets from the scene. But no one called on a firearms examiner to visit the crime scene, and the lab's focus was to match up your gun with the bullets you fired. Oliver and Moynihan did a decent investigation, but they were understandably inclined to accept the conclusions of Mussino's biased investigation and the ballistics report. So no one put anything together about the logistics of the crime scene. You were home free."

"Home free," he said ironically. "Accused of murder."

"You knew you could extricate yourself any time with ballistics," Kate retorted. "The autopsy report shows faint stippling around the wounds. The victim was killed at close range. But you knew test results on your Beretta would show no blow back in the barrel, no evidence of blood or flesh. Distortion of course in the bullets, but no microscopic particles of bone or blood."

Idly stroking Turk's head, Taggart responded with a nod.

"And if any of that should prove too subtle for anybody's brain, you could always fall back on bullet trajectories. Straight over Julio Mendez, lined up perfectly with his wounds. Proof positive you didn't fire the shots that killed Mendez."

Kate quoted firearms examiner Harvey Gaviland's words as best she could remember them: "The angle of incidence doesn't apply to bullets. A projectile hits something, its shape is altered, and so is its path. It either sinks from lessening velocity or deflects off at a different angle, or both. Slugs from a Beretta striking and passing through the flesh and bone of a victim would take any trajectory except straight into a wall twenty feet behind that victim—where your slugs were found. Harvey Gaviland told me there's a remote possibility that one slug might continue with minor deflection—the one that went through the victim's jugular—but both would deflect, especially the slug that struck the bone of the victim's spinal cord."

"You're pretty knowledgeable about ballistics," Taggart commented.

Kate shrugged. "Not really. I heard about an FBI case when I was at a profiling seminar in Washington. A bank robbery victim shot in the head point-blank with a .357. The bullet deflected inside her skull and circled her brain. She lived to identify her attacker."

"You did quite a job of detective work," Taggart said. "As I expected."

She did not reply. It had been lucky detective work, and detectives always needed some degree of luck in any investigation. She might have been just as misled by those bullets as any other detective, had it not been for Aimee's choice of that TV program about the John F. Kennedy assassination and the slow-motion replaying of the Zapruder tape of the motorcade in Dallas. Had it not been for the program's discussion of the "magic bullet" that had exited Kennedy's body and penetrated Governor Connally's wrist and then his leg, she would never have taken those photographs of Apparition Alley. And she would never have gone to Harvey Gaviland had it not been for the narrator intoning, ". . . *today we have computerized models of bullet trajectories, today we know there was nothing magical about that bullet. Because the trajectory of a bullet after striking an object is, by its very nature, virtually unpredictable . . .*"

But, she thought, casting a poisonous glance at Taggart, all that deduction should have been unnecessary. She said, "What I don't understand is why."

"Are you wired?"

She looked at him in surprise, and with a degree of guilt because she had considered suggesting it to Bodwin. "No," she answered. She had good reasons not to use a recording device for this conversation.

"You guarantee I'm not being recorded and this is not entrapment?"

"I guarantee you are not being recorded," she said, understanding why he had been so taciturn. With his devious and supple mind, he might have made quite a good detective. He might have even been in Mouse Mussino's job had he not been so marked a man over the death of Bud Avery.

He said, "I did everything you say I did. I did it to get Ferdie's killers and maybe salvage what I could of my self-respect."

"I don't understand," Kate said.

"I'm not sure I do myself, altogether." Leaning his elbows on the table, he rubbed his hands tiredly over his unshaven face. "All I knew for sure was Ferdie's death had been swept under the carpet. And after I shot my mouth off about cops killing Ferdie and Robbery-Homicide had to check everybody's weapons, I was dead meat. I called every radio, TV, and press reporter I knew, but I couldn't prove my story and I couldn't get them to look into it. They all acted like my next stop was the psych ward."

His half-grin looked effortful, and he gazed off into the trees as if to compose himself. "When I saw Mendez's body, it came to me like a flash—how I could maybe use this. I knew I'd end up being fired, but I figured what difference did it make. I could be more at peace about not being a cop if I could get it out in public about Ferdie. I could live with myself if I did something about one of my two dead partners—especially Ferdie."

"The whole thing could have come apart in two seconds," Kate pointed out. "All it took was a decent investigator—"

"Hell yes. Sure it was a high wire act—but look at my advantages. Mouse and Moron were the investigating detectives. And Julio Mendez—low priority all the way. Everybody knew the guy was a dirtbag, plus Mouse hates Latinos. I had nothing to lose. Even if the whole thing came apart, I'd go out with a bang and it might get me some press attention and I could get somebody to listen about Ferdie."

"You really did love Tony," Kate said, conceding him that much.

Pain etched Taggart's face, deepening the lines around his mouth and eyes. "I never knew anybody like him. The first month as partners I flat-out knew he was the one person in my life I could trust with everything. I told him my secrets, trusted him with my life. His payback was to trust me with his biggest secret, his whole damn career. He told me he was gay. We let it all out with each other, told each other everything. About girlfriends, boyfriends. I mean, even what we did in bed. He told me he felt closer to me than his whole family put together, and I believed him because I felt the same way about him. The things he taught me . . ." He said huskily, "Yeah, I loved him."

Rejecting a surge of sympathy for him, she said sternly, "Doesn't it matter to you that the real killer of Julio Mendez is still walking the streets?"

"It matters." He looked at her, his green-blue eyes hardening. "But not for the reasons you think. Mendez had a BOLO all his own. You know what the be-on-the-lookout applied to? Schools and kids' hangouts. Julio Mendez pushed dope on kids."

Kate shook her head. Hollywood Division so far had lived down to her lowest expectations.

Studying her face, Taggart said, "Everybody knew the bastard. Any one of us at the station could have dropped the cyanide on him at San Quentin and walked away whistling. Which is another reason everybody thought I did it. But his killing was a hit. Anybody looking at the crime scene with any objectivity could see the triggerman was a pro. I'm betting some Mexican Mafia godfather-type up the dope pusher chain found out about Mendez's little sideline of selling to kids and put out a hit. So yeah, theoretically, I want the real shooter. But everybody involved in this thing is a member of Slime-bag Incorporated."

"You've committed felony obstruction of justice," Kate pointed out.

"Felony obstruction of justice," Taggart repeated, and smiled faintly. "You think the chances of finding Mendez's hit man are any better than slim and none?"

"It doesn't matter, you're still facing felony obstruction charges."

"I like my chances of explaining it all to a jury."

She doubted it would ever come to that. She asked the question whose answer she had come here to learn: "Why involve me? What was my part in all this grand design of yours?"

"To kill not two but three big birds with one stone." The smile that slowly spread over Taggart's face was so self-satisfied and contagious that Kate had to prevent herself from joining in. He extended one finger after another as he made his points. "A good detective with a reputation for integrity would take an impartial look at Ferdie's death. I could prove Mouse Mussino makes Inspector Clouseau look like a genius. And you and I would carry out Ferdie's legacy."

"Ferdie's legacy," she said, misgiving spreading through her.

"Yeah. Ferdie's legacy. The list. Your part in all this is still very much your part. I figured you'd want to continue doing this with me. I figured you'd want to help me expose once and for all through Ferdie's death why cops like you and Ferdie are forced to stay in the closet. Ferdie's gone, but you can still put a stop to all the homophobe cops waiting in the weeds for any police officer that dares to say they're gay."

"What do you mean, I can still do this, I can continue being a part of this?"

"Meaning it's turned out to be pure genius—my getting Deep Throat to be my defense rep."

"*I am not Deep Throat!*"

Turk made a sound in his throat, raised his head, and cocked his eyebrows. Dreamer trotted anxiously over to Kate.

"Okay, okay," Taggart said calmly. "Matt told me he was sure you were Deep Throat because your name is at the top of Ferdie's list. I didn't buy it—and when I met you the first time at that restaurant and we talked about Ferdie, I didn't pick up any sense of you having any connection with him. But I still wasn't sure. I figured even if you weren't Deep Throat, you probably knew who she was. Then you came to my place and tossed out a hint about borrowing the computer Tony used for compiling the names. I was sure you had to be in on it. What else was I supposed to think?"

Petting and soothing the fretful golden retriever, Kate fumed, "I borrowed the computer for exactly the reason I gave you—I needed the use of one. How did you get your own hands on that computer if it was Tony's?"

"I had a key to Ferdie's place. After I talked to the clerk in the liquor store where Ferdie was shot and figured out what was going on, I went into his place and took it."

"Matt Brazelton says you've never even seen this list."

"That's right."

"Then how can you be so sure it exists?"

"Matt saw it and did everything but turn himself inside out to get Ferdie to deep-six his plan. It exists, Kate. The proof is that Ferdie died for it."

"Why didn't you tell me the truth about this right from the start?" Kate demanded.

"If you were Deep Throat, you wouldn't come near risking exposure. If you weren't Deep Throat, then you'd be like everybody else—you'd figure I was an obsessed nut and walk away."

He was right about that, she conceded. "You didn't even tell me that Tony was a gay man."

"That particular piece of information I figured you'd already know." Complacently, Taggart finished his lemonade. "If you were Deep Throat, it was too dangerous for you to overtly try to identify Ferdie's killers, but I could give you perfect cover. I could give you the opportunity to investigate without looking the least bit suspicious. And if you weren't Deep Throat, then the only way you could be convinced about why Ferdie died was if you started with a clean slate, looked at everything, and saw how shady it all was just the way I did."

"This is crazy. I never met Tony Ferrera, I never even heard of him until I went to his funeral. I'm not custodian of any list. I don't know why my name is at the top of such a list—"

"Kate, if you're not Deep Throat, then it was Deep Throat who put your name there. She must know you pretty well."

"I don't know who the hell she is. I tell you, I *don't*. Tony never told you who this woman is?"

Shaking his head, Taggart said bitterly, "The one thing Ferdie keeps from me and look what happens. I wish to hell I'd dragged the information out of him. Look, we can make a deal. All I want is the list. I want it out there. It's Ferdie's legacy. I've got nothing to lose by carrying out his plan. If you're Deep Throat, I can understand why you're spooked. You can continue being Deep Throat—nobody ever has to know about you."

"I'm *not* Deep Throat. Look . . ." It was futile to keep denying it, and she subsided into frustrated silence.

"I know you're pissed about all this. But my plan worked, didn't it?" Taggart said. "You did find inconsistencies in Ferdie's death."

"Any decent investigator would. I can't imagine that Robbery-Homicide didn't find the same inconsistencies."

"Which proves there's a cover-up. They know something they aren't telling."

A thought suddenly occurring to her, she uttered, "But we know something we're not telling—that Tony was gay."

"True." Taggart hunched over the table, leaning on his elbows. "I figured I had no right to do that to Ferdie's family, have it in the papers and all. He talked all the time about finally being honest with his mother, facing her and explaining about himself, telling her the truth. If Ferdie's plan about releasing the list couldn't come to pass, I knew he wouldn't want Mama Ferrera to find out that way."

Kate thought: *Then Robbery-Homicide didn't have all the information you and I have.*

"What are you going to do now, Kate?"

Call Mike Bodwin the minute I leave here, she thought. Beyond that . . . She said, "I don't know."

"You're still with me on this, aren't you?"

"Taggart, has it never occurred to you that Tony's list is none of your business? You're a straight man. This is a matter that involves the gay community."

"You're a lesbian cop, your name is on the top of a list of hundreds of other names. That's the reason I involved you in this. It's Ferdie's legacy," he said stubbornly. "And you're now custodian of his list."

"No, I'm not. Taggart, believe me—I don't have anything to do with this."

"If you don't have it, you have access to it. So how can you be a lesbian cop and not be with me?"

"You're no longer a cop of any kind, Taggart, you're an anarchist." She added, getting up from the table, "And you've made a total shambles of my life."

He grinned up at her. "That's what we anarchists do."

18

KATE came back down through the hills into Hollywood, this time driving on the side of Laurel Canyon
Boulevard comparatively free of traffic; cars coming up
the Canyon road still crawled along in a tight caravan.
She pulled over and dialed Aimee on the mobile phone.

"Where are you, honey?" Aimee asked cheerily.
"How did it go with Dr. Demon?"

"I'm on Sunset in Hollywood. Dr. Demon's released
me."

"Did she retract her teeth and claws? Or did you have
to shoot your way out?"

Chuckling, Kate said, "I think she actually did me
some good."

"Sounds like I should go see this woman for some
pointers," Aimee said. "Three sessions with you and she
gets into you more than I have in six years."

"Sweetheart, that's ridiculous," Kate protested. But
there was an element of truth in what Aimee had said,
and a disturbing tone in Aimee's voice. Maybe there was
substance in Calla Dearborn's warning about her behavior endangering this relationship. Then again, maybe
there wasn't. She asked, "How's your work going?"

"Thanks to you, it'll be another hour before I can
turn off this blank-faced monster. Hunting that file was
one hell of a challenge—the hard disk's loaded with
programs."

"I really appreciate you taking the time to look," Kate said apologetically.

"At least it was worth it."

Kate almost dropped the phone. "You *found* it?"

"Yeah," Aimee said buoyantly. "Tucked away *very* cleverly, let me tell you. The computer's got an old version of Word along with Lotus Notes and Excel and tons of games and other shit, so after I looked there and everywhere else, I went into File Manager for the old Word program and found a dot EXE file. I'd never have picked it out of all the other EXEs except this one was dated November third, and all the other files were July of ninety-four, the date they were loaded. I can't get into an EXE file of course, so I converted it into a dot doc and lo and behold, here was this humongous list of names, and lo and behold your name led all the rest."

Stunned, Kate did not even try to comprehend Aimee's technical explanation of how she had located the file. Until this moment, she had hoped against all logic that the list had been a figment of Luke Taggart's fertile imagination, that Deep Throat had somehow been another ploy on the part of Matt Brazelton.

"Honey, are you there?"

"Yes," Kate managed to say.

"Thought I'd lost you. Is this some big deal? Did I stumble on the coded list for the location of our nuclear silos?"

Just about, Kate thought. "It's some evidence," she said.

"Is that right," Aimee said, the phrase she always used to convey polite curiosity about a topic in which she had lost all interest. "Want me to save it onto a floppy?"

"Don't touch it," Kate said more sharply than she intended.

"Hey, okay. What's the big deal here?"

"It's evidence in the Luke Taggart case." She dared say nothing more over an easily monitored mobile phone connection—even if she wanted to.

"Is that right. I'm absolutely beat, I bet you are too. Why don't we order in some pizza tonight and have a nice bath together and catch up on the last couple of days?"

"Sounds great," Kate said, her mood lifting in spite of herself. "I have just a couple more things to do, and I'll be home."

As she disconnected from Aimee, the phone rang in Kate's hand.

"Kate, it's Lieutenant Bodwin. I've set up a meeting at Parker Center at nine A.M. tomorrow. By the way, it turns out the OIS team handling the Tony Ferrera case are familiar faces to you."

He had to be referring to the two detectives who had interviewed her regarding the death of Darian Crockett. "McMillan and Phillips?"

"The very ones. I don't know McMillan, but maybe Jim Phillips mentioned to you that he and I go back a ways."

"He didn't happen to mention it, sir."

"Understandable, under the circumstances of how he met you. He's a good man," Bodwin said in a satisfied tone.

She recognized this as a signal that not only did Bodwin's rank give him access to information closed off to her, his acquaintance with one of the case detectives had heightened the candor and accuracy of that information.

"Jim's just as troubled by the Ferrera homicide as you are, Kate. RHD's had their suspicions all along about this so-called robbery gone bad. They've interviewed everyone within a wide radius of the crime scene, checked into Ferrera's personal life—canvassed his apartment building and neighborhood. They haven't found a thing beyond his being a dedicated police officer and very close to his family and very generous with them money-wise. They've checked out felons he arrested, everybody he ever worked with, including a real close look at Luke Taggart. They're still working the case, but they've got no suspects and no real leads beyond one witness who saw the Ford Ranger leaving the scene and caught a partial on the license plate. But there's thousands of Ford Rangers in this state, and two digits out of seven—that doesn't narrow it down at all."

"I appreciate the briefing, sir. I believe I have new information for the case detectives, and also a possible hypothesis . . ."

Kate pulled off La Brea and drove up the steeply rising driveway to the shrubbery-lined parking lot shared by the Nightwood Bar and the Casbah Motel. Sprightly Turkish music drifted across to her from the motel's restaurant, but she exited her car cautiously, palm on the handle of her gun, thumb on the snap of her holster. She had been careful in this parking lot ever since the investigation of Dory Quillin's murder years ago, when she had found herself embroiled in a chaotic brawl with two drugged-out gay bashers.

In the years since that investigation, except for a thickening of the firs fronting the coffee-brown building, the Nightwood Bar had been for Kate an unchanging, enduring oasis. The neon lavender script letters in the front window welcomed her into a enclave as familiar and comfortable as her living room.

Under dim track lighting, half a dozen women occupied the bar at this early evening hour, two of them playing pool under the lemony glow created by a Tiffany-style lampshade. A tough-looking, sixtyish woman in greasy overalls sat at a table drinking a beer and reading the paper; two other women in T-shirts and cutoffs were bent over a Scrabble game at the table in front of the bar's bookcase. Kate recognized Patton by the ancient blue yachting cap tilted back on her head; she stood at the bar making jocular conversation with bartender Maggie Schaeffer.

Patton drained her drink and pocketed her change;

turning to leave, she spotted Kate. "Hey, it's Murder Incorporated." Moving quickly toward Kate, raising a hand, she slammed palms with Kate. "How's that shoulder doing?"

"No problem," Kate said, ignoring the pain reverberating through her from the enthusiasm of Patton's greeting. "I'll take you on at pool anytime. You still with Monica?"

"Yeah, she's my one and only this week," Patton said. "I gotta get home to her. Take care of yourself—you're still my favorite pig next to Babe."

Behind the bar, arms crossed, Maggie stood grinning in front of a kidney-shaped mirror encircled by lavender lights. On the curved, dark wood bar sat the same glass bowl with the same sign, AIDS PROJECT L.A., that had been there the first time Kate had walked in here, and Kate, as was her habit, dropped all her one-dollar bills and loose change into it.

The one thing about this bar that had changed was its owner, Kate reflected as she hoisted herself onto a stool. Maggie, wearing a rainbow shirt tucked into white shorts, was thinner, her tanned skin more leathery, her hair gone to pure white; and the cigarette that had once been a permanent component of her right hand had vanished. Cigarettes had been absent from Maggie's life for well over a year, along with the cigarette machine that had once reposed alongside the jukebox.

As Maggie pulled a bottle of Cutty Sark off the bar to pour Kate her usual drink, Kate said, "I'm on duty."

Maggie stopped in mid-motion to stare at her. "You're pulling my leg," she said in the soft voice that belied her authoritarian appearance. "How the hell can they have you on duty with that shoulder?"

"You're right," Kate said. "How can they? I'll take that scotch."

"How you doing, Kate?"

"Cleared to return to duty."

"You fucking scared Aimee and me to death. A hospital bed doesn't become you."

"What's been going on around here?"

Maggie set the drink on a napkin in front of Kate. "Got another one of those damn wish-you-were-here postcards from Raney and Audie."

Kate nodded. The two long-time bar regulars were off on a three-month trip to Africa. Maggie said, "So what's behind this claim about you being on duty? Looks to me like you might have something on your mind, Detective."

Maggie always read her with more shrewdness than anyone. And discussed what she read with unsparing bluntness and affection. Which was why she was the closest and most trusted friend Kate had ever had, and why Kate had immediately come here with the burden she now carried.

Kate took a sip of her scotch, then glanced around to reassure herself of the privacy of their conversation. She lowered her voice to draw Maggie closer to her. "Imagine you're a member of Congress."

"Do I have to be Newt Gingrich or Bob Dornan?"

"Be serious, okay?"

Picking up her bar rag, industriously swabbing the bar, Maggie said, "Okay, I'm a serious member of Congress."

"Let's say you're also a long-time member of Congress."

"Right. No term limits here."

"Right," Kate said, gritting her teeth. "Let's say you were accidentally made privy to a plan to do something highly visible—"

"Don't tell me you've uncovered a government conspiracy to pass health care reform."

"Maggie, I give up."

Maggie raised her hands in surrender. "Okay, okay, I'm done. I'm all seriousness."

"Okay, this is the deal. Let's say that as a seriously

long-term member of Congress you've accidentally learned that two other members have compiled a list of all the closeted gays and lesbians in Congress and the Senate and in the Cabinet and on the Supreme Court. Their plan is to disseminate it nationwide.''

Maggie pursed her lips and let out a soft whistle.

Kate continued, "Let's say that something's happened to one of the two members and this list has been bequeathed solely to you. Let's say you've been asked by the other member involved in this to carry out the plan. What do you do?''

"Call everybody from Peter Jennings to the *National Enquirer*,'' Maggie said.

Kate took a deep swallow of her scotch. Maggie's answer had not been unexpected, but nevertheless Kate admonished her: "It's a very serious question.''

"I'm giving you a very serious answer, my friend,'' Maggie said.

"Give me the reasons why you'd choose to expose all those unsuspecting men and women.''

Maggie leaned across the bar, her hooded dark eyes searching Kate's face as she answered. "There's only one reason, Kate. Every time we say it's okay for someone to stay in the closet, we practice our own version of homophobia. We agree that there's something wrong with us, we agree with all the people who claim we're inferior, we agree with their excuses to despise us and persecute us, we agree that we deserve to hide our true selves away from anybody who doesn't like us.''

"It's not that simple,'' Kate said.

"It isn't? Either we join those of us out there living honestly and trying to make it better for all the gay and lesbian children coming after us, or we stay in the closet and collaborate in keeping the status quo.''

"It's not that simple,'' Kate repeated.

"No? Then explain to me how complicated it really is.''

"We shouldn't force people to come out.''

"I've never met anybody—I've never even *heard* of anybody who ever regretted coming out of the closet."

"That may be true, but you're talking about people who've made a personal choice about it, not people flung out whether they wanted to be or not."

"Are we talking about an actual list of high government people?"

Kate hesitated a fatal moment over her answer, and Maggie said, "I thought not. We're talking about something much closer to you, aren't we."

Kate did not answer.

Maggie said, "Something needs to be done about the bigoted bullies with uniforms and guns at LAPD who hate gay people, Kate, and outing everybody en masse looks like a very good way to protect all of you."

Kate looked at her.

Maggie shrugged. "This isn't like the don't ask, don't tell abomination they've foisted on the poor bastards in the military. You can't be fired."

"Not legally. Not today, at least," Kate muttered.

"I think you should help whoever it is and release this list of gay and lesbian police officers—that's my opinion plain and simple. What's yours?"

"I agree with what you've said. But I don't know what I should do, Maggie. I don't know that I can or should do what you want me to do."

"I haven't said a thing about what I want you to do, Kate, only what *I* would do. But now I *will* tell you what to do: take all the wisdom of your life and vote your conscience. Do what you can live with."

Kate nodded.

Maggie put her hand over Kate's. "Nobody can really help you with this. What does Aimee think?"

"I haven't talked to her about it."

"She's a wise young woman," Maggie said.

"She is," Kate replied. "But the operative word is *young*. She hasn't traveled the distance you and I have . . ."

"Good God, are you telling me you're not going to talk to her about this?"

Weary to the center of her bones, Kate picked up her scotch and finished it. "I don't know what I'm telling you."

"I think you're afraid of her opinion."

"Maybe I am, Maggie," Kate said. "Right now, I just want to go home and have some pizza and a bath and go to bed."

"Good plan. And then what?"

"Tomorrow I'll make my decision."

19

STEPPING out of the shower the next morning, Kate peeled the moisture-preventing plastic from her bandaged left shoulder, scowling at her thickening midsection outlined in the steam-shrouded mirror. Aimee pushed open the bathroom door and handed Kate the portable phone. "Your lieutenant," she said in stage whisper. "Urgent."

Mouthing a thanks, Kate wrapped a towel around herself, then took the phone. "Yes, sir."

"Kate, I'm in my car, on my way in to the station. I suggest you call Officer Taggart and have him meet the two of us there."

"Yes, sir. Is it—"

"Yes. I just got a call from Jim Phillips."

Forty minutes later, in an interview room at Wilshire Division, Kate sipped hot strong coffee from a Styrofoam cup. Along with Mike Bodwin, she awaited Luke Taggart, who was still making his way through morning traffic from Laurel Canyon. Bodwin, between drinking coffee and munching doughnuts, had concluded his briefing of her, and Kate, weighted down by a deep and inchoate mixture of anger and grief, had taken refuge in silently consuming her scalding brew.

Bodwin did not share in her downward spiral; he was obviously gratified that his involvement in a homicide case had led to the breaking of that case. Finishing off the last of his three doughnuts, he said buoyantly, "Mc-Millan and Phillips did a great job, but the key lead was checking out the truck and the license plate with Arizona DMV like you suggested."

Kate nodded numbly. She would be conducting the conversation with Taggart, and she had begun the necessary process of gearing herself up.

Taggart, shaven and neatly dressed in a white shirt and a blue tie that matched his slacks, was ushered in by the assistant watch commander.

Bodwin nodded to him. "Good morning, Officer Taggart. Please sit down."

"Good morning, Lieutenant," Taggart responded with a deferential nod. "Thank you, sir."

In her phone call to Taggart to request his presence here, she had merely repeated the statement Bodwin had made to her, and that she was on her way in to Wilshire to learn further details. Now his eyes searched her face for clues as he settled himself into a chair.

"Officer Taggart," Bodwin said coolly, "this conversation is not being recorded." Bodwin's use of this room instead of his office and his aloof courtesy told Kate that in his mind, Taggart was already an outsider, already banished from the police family. Sitting back in his chair, Bodwin nodded to Kate.

Kate began formally. "We've called you in to advise you that Robbery-Homicide has made an arrest in the death of your partner, Officer Tony Ferrera."

She held his unwavering stare as she delivered the bottom line: "They've placed Roberto Ferrera under arrest. Joseph Ferrera has also been arrested in Kingman, Arizona. He'll be extradited."

She watched the blood drain from his face, his tan become yellowish.

"Ferdie's . . . *brothers?* Roberto . . . Joe?"

"The investigation is ongoing, but at this point, it appears that all three brothers may be involved as coconspirators.'' She added, ''Roberto Ferrera signed his confession this morning.''

''I . . .'' He leaned his elbows on the table, kneaded his eyes with his fingertips. ''I don't know what the hell to say.''

Kate said with profound sympathy, ''I know, Tag.''

Then his head snapped up. ''I do know what to say. I fucking don't believe it.''

''You will,'' Bodwin said complacently.

Kate said, ''The liquor store clerk described a light-colored Ford Ranger with black splotches on the side panel. A witness identified the same vehicle leaving the scene at high speed.'' She gained more control of her emotions as she continued her recitation of details. ''The witness was able to provide two digits from the license plate. A tan Ford Ranger containing those two digits is registered to the Ferrera Roofing Company in Kingman, Arizona. The truck was located and impounded last night by Kingman PD. They report it has tar splotches on its side panels.''

''Fine work all around,'' Bodwin contributed, ''especially by Detective Delafield. The case detectives were looking in California for that vehicle. She was the one who pointed out that Joseph Ferrera ran a roofing company in Kingman and had them check whether he had a Ford Ranger registered in Arizona.''

Kate welcomed neither the interruption nor Bodwin's remarks, which she knew had struck Taggart in the heart. Horror was dawning in his eyes as he fastened his stare on her again.

''Go on, Detective,'' Bodwin urged her.

With effort she said, ''Using the information that Tony Ferrera was a closeted gay police officer, a number of facts pointed directly to his brothers. Opportunity, for one.''

She glanced at her notebook, again trying to compose herself. ''Officer Ferrera's mother told me he visited her every Tuesday and Saturday without fail. Jeff

Daley told me Tony was a regular at the liquor store—
that he came in all the time to buy various things for his
family. The fact that Roberto Ferrera lives with his
mother meant he knew the pattern of Tony's habits: the
evenings he visited, exactly when he arrived at the house,
where he bought his gifts of drinks and snacks—"

Taggart muttered, "You mean to tell me Joe drove in
that night from Kingman . . ." He did not finish.

Kate nodded. "You were right about the intent to
make Officer Ferrera's death appear accidental—a two-
eleven gone bad. Everybody thought Joseph Ferrera was
in Kingman. He and Roberto disguised themselves in ski
masks, they used one of the roofing trucks to lessen the
possibility of it being traced. They followed Tony from
his house to the liquor store and killed him. Joseph Ferrera waited for word from Roberto on his mobile phone
when police officers made official notification to Tony's
mother. Then he timed his arrival at his mother's house
as if he'd flown in from Kingman." She paused, pain
squeezing around her heart at her next topic.

But Taggart broached it himself. "Why." He spoke
the word as if motive were not a question, but a bizarre
concept he was turning over in his mind to examine
from all angles. "Why."

From her own life experience and point of view, motive was the most obvious aspect of this homicide and
had led her to its solution. She said quietly, "Because
Tony came out to his brothers and told them about his
plan to reveal himself as a gay police officer with the
highest possible public visibility. Because they considered it another family disgrace."

She leaned toward Taggart, wanting to somehow
lessen the impact of her next words. "Remember when
you told me how rough it was for Tony growing up? How
Tony's father stole from friends and relatives and disgraced the family, how the family was left to face all
those people?"

"Yeah, but . . . I mean Jesus Christ, this isn't anything like that, Ferdie wasn't a thief, he was only—"

"I know. But when Tony warned you two days before he died about the possibility of his being killed, I think it was his brothers who'd threatened him. Tony's brothers realized Tony wouldn't abandon his decision, wouldn't postpone or change his plans, so they . . ." She found herself unable to continue.

Bodwin said, "The big reason Roberto Ferrera broke down and confessed is because he's convinced the murder of Officer Ferrera is justifiable homicide. He claims the stresses of Officer Ferrera's job drove his brother crazy, and his brother had to be killed to protect his reputation and to protect their mother."

"Christ in heaven," Taggart uttered.

Kate experienced an aftershock of her own emotional earthquake when Bodwin had made the same statement to her. She remembered Jeff Daley at the liquor store telling her that the gunman had spoken to Tony Ferrera before he killed him, she remembered Daley talking about the horror frozen in Tony Ferrera's eyes. Tony Ferrera had known that his killers were his own brothers.

Bodwin said, "Detective Delafield expressed the opinion to me yesterday that Roberto would likely break under questioning, and she was right—"

"Roberto's always been the crazy one, a real hothead," Taggart said. "He was in Juvenile Hall for assault—"

"We know." Bodwin looked displeased by the interruption. "He's graduated from fists to guns. The case detectives took him into custody last night and this morning he gave up his brother Joseph as the triggerman. But we believe Roberto's the killer and Joseph's part in carrying out the scheme was to place Officer Ferrera's gun in his hand after he was shot by Roberto."

"This is . . ." Taggart was staring at Kate. "How could they . . . How could they murder a brother? How can you kill your own brother—even if he's gay? This is way beyond homophobia. This is Cain and Abel. How could they possibly believe Mama Ferrera would rather have Ferdie dead than . . ." Leaning over the table, he gripped his head between his hands as if the thoughts within were threatening explode it.

Bodwin looked at him sternly. "Officer Taggart, in view of your earlier accusations against police officers in the death of your partner—"

"Yes, sir," Taggart said without lifting his head. "I owe a lot of apologies. I was wrong."

"Any questions?"

"No, sir."

Bodwin glanced at his watch and got to his feet. "Detective," he said to Kate, "you and I and Captain Delano have an appointment at Parker Center."

She replied, "If I could have a few minutes to discuss with Officer Taggart the options now open to him about his own case . . ."

Bodwin's expression was a mixture of annoyance and disapproval. "We'll meet you downtown." He strode from the room.

Kate leaned over and placed a hand on the cuff of Taggart's white shirt. He shook it off. But she knew from his pain-glazed face that he had simply gone into a different plane and needed to be alone with his grief. Like her, he was inside that ivy-covered house in Silverlake; he too was in that shrine of a room with the statue of the Virgin Mary and the photograph of a dead son in a police uniform. He too was looking into the face of a woman who had given her life to raising her four sons, and had now lost them all.

After Taggart left the interview room, Kate gave herself five minutes to gather her composure, her grief so heavy that she could not get up out of her chair. However hard it would be, she had to see Anna Ferrera soon and offer comfort, however meager it would be in the face of such tragedy. Calla Dearborn was right: There were things about her profession that were simply too hard to try to carry alone.

As she summoned willpower to get to her feet, there was a soft rap at the door; it edged slightly open. "Kate . . ."

"Come in, Torrie," Kate answered, recognizing the voice of her partner.

Torrie entered the room tentatively, pulling at the sleeves of her dark green blazer. Kate resisted the impulse to glance at her watch. She needed to be downtown. But confronting her partner had greater urgency than keeping the brass waiting at Parker Center. Anyway, she told herself, the meeting there could only go so far without her.

Torrie sat down at the table, again pulling and smoothing her jacket into place. The sight of this familiar, obsessional personal tidiness cut through Kate's rancor, afflicting her with acute homesickness for her messy, inefficient department and for this woman whose funny little phobias and quirks had acquired the familiarity of a family member's.

Torrie said, "I guess I don't have to ask how you are— we heard the news you're coming back."

You could ask anyway, Kate thought. You could have and should have asked days ago. She said evenly, "I have a doctor's appointment on Monday to see what limitations they'll place on me."

"Kate, I can't tell you what I've gone through without you—how much I've missed you."

Her mind suffused with images of the agony she had just witnessed on the face of Luke Taggart, Kate compared what Taggart had sacrificed in loyalty to his partner to the gutless performance of Torrie Holden. She said savagely, "You couldn't take the time, you couldn't even be bothered to call."

Her cheeks flaming, Torrie looked away. "Anything you want to say to me, I have it coming. I just didn't know what on earth to do after what I . . . after what I knew."

"What is it," Kate asked coldly, "that you knew?" Had Taggart actually been right? Had Torrie been complicit in concealing someone's intent to harm her in that hallway on Gramercy? Had Hansen been nursing some grudge and seized an opportunity to square accounts? Had Perez reacted in fury when Kate had hurled her aside? Did Torrie herself have a hidden agenda?

"You know they wrote me up for—"

In her impatience to cut to the answer to her question, Kate said sharply, "Yes, I know what they wrote you up for. What did you actually do?"

Torrie jerked back in her chair as if lashed by Kate's words. "It's what I didn't do, Kate. If I'd had my weapon out—"

You and me both, Kate thought, instantly reliving the slow-motion horror of ripping her gun from her holster as that hallway erupted in gunfire.

"I didn't cover you," Torrie said. Her dark eyes were dry but there were tears in her voice. "I not only didn't back up my own partner, I might have been the one who shot you."

As Torrie struggled for composure, Kate sucked in a breath and asked, "Who did shoot me?"

"We don't know. They dug out lots of lead from that hallway and some of it was too fragmented to match with our weapons."

Kate said, "So it's like the firing squad where no one knows who shot the live round."

Torrie looked horrified. "I hope to God you don't look at it that way, Kate. You have no idea how terrible we feel. We wish we did know, none of us wants to . . . to carry . . ." She groped for words, then shrugged her frustration.

Kate too was frustrated. She wanted to know which of the three of them was untrustworthy in a firefight, and now she knew she would mistrust all three. She said, "Why didn't any of you tell me this?"

"None of us knew what you thought. Or how to face you. It's been absolutely terrible around here. People in the department treat the three of us like we've shot Snow White."

Despite herself, Kate burst into laughter. After a moment, Torrie joined in. She leaned over to grasp Kate's hand. Squeezing Torrie's hand in return, Kate felt as if a poisonous boil had been suddenly lanced. Lanced, but not cured. She could have been killed in that hallway, or maimed for life. She had been lucky.

Kate said, "I'm glad you told me, Torrie. I'm glad we finally talked."

"Hansen and Perez want a chance to talk to you themselves." Grinning wanly at her, Torrie said, "They sent me in here to promise we'll never do it again."

"A few more weeks of healing, I'll be as good as new." Not quite that good; the doctors had told her she would always have residual stiffness and intermittent discomfort. "Tell them we'll talk more about this, okay?"

"We all know we need to," Torrie said firmly.

Kate finally looked at her watch. And leaped to her feet. "Good God, I'm supposed to be at Parker Center right now. Bodwin will kill me."

"Kate, what on earth is going on?" Torrie accompanied her out the door and trotted alongside her down the hallway toward the parking lot. "We've heard all kinds of rumors about you repping some cowboy cop from Hollywood."

"I looked into his case. I don't think he'll need anyone to rep him. Tell you about it sometime over a beer."

She would tell her *some* of it over a beer. Torrie Holden was no Luke Taggart. Would she ever be blessed with a partner like Luke Taggart? she wondered.

Dashing through the parking lot to her car, ignoring the jolts of pain in her shoulder, she thought: I'm back.

Thank God I'm back and things may even have a chance to get back to something close to normal.

Her police family was her police family again. Dysfunctional though it might be.

20

STILL cursing the five minutes she had wasted circling the lot in search of a parking place, rushing toward Parker Center, Kate almost collided with Mouse Mussino. He had planted his short, rotund body in her path just outside the lobby of the building.

"You . . ." His eyes glittering with hatred, his mustache jerking and twitching with his effort to either find or form words, he finally flung out both arms in disgust at his incoherence and stalked past her.

"Same to you," she called after him, and strode on into the lobby.

Ushered immediately into a boardroom by a uniformed officer waiting for her at the elevator doors on the sixth floor, Kate apologized to the seven people assembled around the long table: "Ten minutes just trying to park out there," she exaggerated, trying to reassemble her composure.

She noted that the brass were clustered together, Assistant Chief Paul Henderson occupying the head of the table, with Captain Seymour Thomason of Hollywood Division and her own Captain Eric Delano flanking him. Bodwin scowled at her from his seat next to Delano.

"Parking's not the half of it," Assistant Chief Henderson said. "They can't tear down this goddamn antique quick enough."

"I guess they're actually going to do it," Delano observed, looking pleased by the idea.

"The budget shenanigans in this town, I'll believe a new headquarters when I see it," Henderson retorted.

Kate shared brief handshakes with Detectives Roy Moynihan and Robert Oliver of Robbery-Homicide, who looked twinlike in their dark blue suits and their doleful expressions. Then she reached over for the hand of Detective Helene Rodgers of Internal Affairs.

Recalling that this woman had been identified to her as a lesbian, Kate took note of her. A blonde wearing a severely simple black jacket and skirt, she offered Kate a smile that did not come close to reaching her glacial gray eyes.

"How's that shoulder, Detective?" inquired Henderson.

With his crewcut and curtain rod–straight shoulders, he reminded her of a Marine Corps drill sergeant, and the image put her at ease. "Good as new, Chief," she answered.

He waved her to the seat at the other head of the table. "Saved the best chair for you. You make yourself comfortable, Detective."

"Thank you, sir."

As Kate took her seat and pulled out her notebook, Rodgers turned to her. "We interviewed Detective Mussino."

"So I gathered. I saw him in the reception area."

"Looking over his future assignment, was he?" growled Henderson, and the group around the table, including Captain Thomason of Hollywood Division, guffawed.

"He didn't have much to say to me," Kate said mischievously.

The group laughed again. Helene Rodgers said, "Our officers seized the files on the Julio Mendez homicide and brought Detective Mussino in this morning. We played the tape recording of your last conversation with him. Actually," she amended, "we played the part where he says that if you fuck with him it won't help you if you crawl downtown and suck the black dick off of our jungle bunny police chief. By the time we got to his threat about the bullet in your shoulder being a pinprick compared to what could happen to you, he'd turned a very interesting shade of green."

None of the grinning inhabitants of the room looked particularly startled or offended by Rodgers's offhanded quotes, not even African-American Roy Moynihan. Kate surmised that there had considerable denunciation of Mussino before her arrival.

Clearing his throat, Henderson said, "I'd say that if Detective Mussino chooses to contest the charges—"

"He'll return to Hollywood Division the day Betty Grable comes back to life," Thomason growled.

Rodgers said, "Working the desk downstairs, bowing to the Chief—what could be more appropriate for soon-to-be-ex-Detective Mussino?"

Kate was gratified by what she saw in the faces gathered around the table: sparks of anger mixed with contempt.

Clasping his wiry hands together on the table, Thomason said, "Detective Delafield, Lieutenant Bodwin's filled us in on the entire, ah, remarkable story concerning Officer Taggart. The question now is, what do we do about Officer Taggart's involvement in the Mendez homicide?"

"The real question," Henderson said, "is how we handle the damn vipers from the press."

Her tapered fingers extending over her notebook as if to protect its contents, Helene Rodgers said, "Just for starters, even with dropping the bad shooting charge, we've got a laundry list on Taggart. Obstruction, neglect of duty, falsification of evidence and reports—conduct unbecoming goes without saying."

Kate said, "If I may state Officer Taggart's position . . ."

Robert Oliver jerked to attention. "His position? What do you mean, his *position?*"

"Go ahead, Detective Delafield," Henderson said.

"Officer Taggart is willing to tender his resignation in exchange for dismissal of all charges against him."

"In exchange for—" Oliver rose partway up from his chair, yanking on his tie as if it were choking him. "Is that asshole trying to offer us a *deal?*"

"Fucking lying bastard," Moynihan snorted. "We have a dirty cop making us an *offer?*"

Kate looked at the Mendez case detectives sympathetically, knowing they spoke out of the mortification of having been deceived by both Mussino and Taggart.

She raised her voice over a hubbub of conversation rising around her: "If I may state an opinion . . ."

Henderson slammed a hand on the table, and silence abruptly descended. "Go ahead, Detective."

Kate spoke carefully. "Based on the facts of this case, Officer Taggart is responsible for all the charges outlined by Detective Rodgers—which of course show good cause for his dismissal. At the same time, Officer Taggart could provide a detailed, plausible—and highly public—explanation of his motivations at a Board of Rights hearing. Based on the facts of this case, my opinion is that Officer Taggart is not a dirty cop. The facts of this case, in my opinion, prove that Officer Taggart is a police officer who's been made a victim of the Code of Silence and has been completely destroyed by it."

"Bud Avery's ancient history," Helene Rodgers objected, her voice rising sharply over those of Oliver and Moynihan. "Bud Avery was five years ago, he's a closed chapter—"

"The Code of Silence is no longer acceptable," Captain Delano interjected, as Kate expected he would. "We have a police chief enforcing zero tolerance for officers covering up for one another."

Kate said cautiously, "Among the rank and file, sir, it's still a matter of conjecture whether that's actually true. But I'm not talking about that particular Code of Silence. I think everyone in this room knows there's more than one Code of Silence at LAPD. I think everyone knows which Code of Silence I'm talking about. If Officer Tony Ferrera had felt any measure of safety, much less acceptance as a gay police officer at LAPD, this whole cycle of events would never have been set into motion, possibly including Officer Ferrera's death."

The room settled into a prolonged stillness.

Finally, Henderson ruminated, "The way it looks to me, that don't ask, don't tell policy is working okay for the military."

What planet was he living on? Kate wondered. Then she answered her own question: the planet Heterosexual. She said, "With all due respect, I believe many gay and lesbian people in the military would tell you the new policy's made matters worse. In any case, at LAPD, the general perception about gay and lesbian officers is not don't ask, don't tell, it's don't dare tell or we'll make your life a living hell."

"We've appointed a new liaison to that particular community, a lesbian officer, and we're working on all those concerns," Henderson said, his dismissal clear and resonant.

"This alleged list that Officer Ferrera had compiled of gay and lesbian police officers," Helene Rodgers said in a casual tone. "Does it actually exist? Have you seen it?"

"I haven't seen it," Kate said truthfully. She met Rodgers' gray eyes and held them. "But yes, I'm absolutely convinced it exists."

Henderson cleared his throat. "Fact is, we need to tamp this down, figure out how to take care of it expeditiously."

Bodwin spoke for the first time. "It seems to me the first recommendation to the Chief should be to release a statement that reinterpretation of ballistics tests has exonerated Officer Taggart of the shooting charges pending against him, and the Mendez homicide has been reopened and returned to Hollywood Division for further investigation.''

"Done," said Henderson. His frank blue eyes settled on Oliver. "Give Captain Thomason every scrap of paper you have on Mendez. Today."

"Yes, sir," Oliver responded glumly.

"As to the rest of it," Bodwin said. "Under the circumstances, thinking about accepting Officer Taggart's resignation—"

Bodwin broke off as a sound came from Oliver.

Henderson barked, "You have a problem, Detective Oliver?"

"No, sir," the detective replied.

Bodwin repeated, "Thinking about accepting Officer Taggart's resignation, I'm wondering if a possible disposition of the situation could be made via complete disclosure of all the facts in a miscellaneous memo."

Kate pondered his idea. Miscellaneous memos allowed some internal investigations to be closed without being noted in the personnel records of the officers involved, but the procedure was seldom exercised and narrowly focused when it was.

"Discussion," ordered Henderson.

"Will it fly?" Thomason wondered aloud.

"To determine that," Henderson said bitingly, "is the objective of this discussion, Captain."

"I can tell you the thinking of Commander Miller," Helene Rodgers said of her superior officer, the head of the Internal Affairs Division. "Commander Miller would rather pick up a rattlesnake than sign off on a miscellaneous memo."

"And Chief Williams would rather lunch with the Ku Klux Klan," agreed Henderson.

Kate knew that miscellaneous memos were coming under severe scrutiny by police watchdog groups because no matter how thoroughly and rigorously documented an internal investigation might be in such memos, there was suspicion that LAPD used the device to sweep its embarrassments under the carpet.

She also knew that every person in this room wanted to put a judicious if not humane end to Luke Taggart's case.

Everyone, especially closeted lesbian Helene Rodgers, knew the risks of having Taggart's connection to Tony Ferrera and his list of gay and lesbian police officers become public: He would become a cause célèbre in the media. Bringing Luke Taggart up on charges would permanently blight the records of Oliver and Moynihan because of their misreading of evidence in the Mendez homicide, and it would further stain the elite Robbery-Homicide Division after the O. J. Simpson debacle. Captain Thomason would be left with the continuing canker sore of a case which had already ruptured morale at Hollywood Division. Because of Kate's involvement in the case, Delano and Bodwin would be forced to continue with their peripheral role in a mess that was none of their making.

As for Assistant Chief Henderson, his perfect military bearing was appropriate to his basic mission: to protect as best he could yet another flank of an organization that every day seemed to suffer a new assault on its reputation and prestige. As for herself, her own stake was as basic as Henderson's: to stanch the blood of a compounded tragedy, to help a man who had lost everything meaningful to him salvage whatever he could of his life.

"Given everyone's distaste for a miscellaneous memo," Henderson said to Rodgers, "think you might be able to explain the wisdom of this one to Larry?"

Rodgers' gaze settled on Kate for a moment. Then she said to Henderson, "Yes sir. I believe I can present a convincing case to Commander Miller."

"And I'll talk to the Chief." Henderson added reflectively, "Maybe this mess doesn't fit any definition of what should go in a miscellaneous memo, but maybe this mess doesn't fit anywhere else, either."

He leaned forward over the table. "Detective Delafield." He locked eyes with Kate. "Detective, in the interests of inflicting the least amount of damage on innocent people both inside and outside of LAPD, we'll take Officer Taggart's offer under advisement. This meeting is over."

Outside the boardroom, as Thomason, Delano, and Bodwin went off for a private meeting with Henderson in his office, Helene Rodgers said to Kate, "I'll walk down with you."

The two women did not speak until after they exited the lobby of Parker Center.

"I'd say it's odds-on you won't have your Lieutenant Bodwin at Wilshire much longer," Rodgers said. "That was a very impressive performance from him."

"I agree," Kate said.

"I'd say it's also odds-on your offer is a done deal, whatever way they figure out how to do it." She added, "Henderson's impressed with you, too."

"He is?"

"He is. You brought a solution he could work with to the table, and you saved the two captains from embarrassing themselves with stupid suggestions. But he was impressed before you walked in. Anybody who comes in late to one of his meetings, he tears their flesh off piece by piece. You can go places with Henderson in your corner."

"I don't want to go places," Kate said.

Helene Rodgers' laugh was incredulous. "An unambitious police officer. In this building, they're on the endangered species list."

Kate shrugged. She had seen enough of what had gone on in that room upstairs to reinforce her conviction that she wanted no part of the higher echelons and political whirlpools of LAPD.

"Think Tony Ferrera's list will ever surface?" Rodgers asked.

"I do," Kate said.

"I do too," Rodgers said. "It's only a matter of time before all of us wake up and find glass doors on our closets. Gather rosebuds while ye may, say I." Her tone changed. "Henderson's not the only one who's impressed with you, by the way."

Kate looked at her.

Rodgers said softly, "I think you're impressive indeed. Maybe we could have a drink together sometime."

"I'm in a relationship," Kate answered, flustered by the blatancy of her approach.

Rodgers shrugged. "So what?"

One sexually aggressive woman at a time in my life is quite enough, Kate thought, much less one in Internal Affairs. "I'm in a relationship," she repeated.

"If that's all you can say . . ." Helene Rodgers smiled. "Good luck, Detective. Keep me in mind. I could be a useful woman for you to know. And vice versa, of course," she added, then turned and walked back into Parker Center.

21

FOOT firmly on the accelerator, Kate sped along the Santa Monica Freeway as if she were fleeing Parker Center, weaving the car aggressively in and out of traffic. Exiting onto La Cienega Boulevard, she pulled over to the curb and leaned her head against the headrest. The ache in her shoulder seemed to be spreading throughout her body. Heartsick and weary to the bone, she picked up the mobile phone and dialed a number she now knew by rote.

"Tag," she said, "it's Kate."

"How are you doing," he said in a perfunctory tone.

A million times better than you, she thought. "It appears a deal will be worked out to put an end to all this."

"Thank you," he said.

"Chief Henderson—"

"Spare me the details."

She made no attempt to conceal her sigh. "Look—"

"Don't worry about it," he said. "Right now I'm tossing a few clothes together. A friend of Lindy's is coming to stay at the house, she'll look after Turk and Dreamer. I'm going to go sit on a beach in Mexico for a while."

"I think the department might prefer you to stick around till—"

"Fuck that. Fuck what the department might prefer."

"You're right," she said quickly. "A beach in Mexico is just the ticket." But she could not prevent another sigh. "Anything I can do, Tag?"

"You did everything you could, Kate. And more. You've been as good a partner to me on this one as anybody could ever ask."

"Tag," she said fervently, "If I could ever have someone like you for my partner—" *And if I could only have you now for a friend. If only there were some way I could be a friend to you now* . . . Tears leaked from her eyes at the sheer impossibility of it all. For the sake of his own mental health, he needed to leave behind LAPD and everyone associated with it.

She could hear the quaver in her voice as she said, "I've never had a partner good enough to polish your badge."

She heard an exhalation of breath and then he said, "Thanks, Kate . . . I really appreciate that."

Holding the phone braced with her shoulder, she pulled Calla Dearborn's card out of her wallet. "Promise me one thing."

"Sure."

"One phone call, that's all I ask. Call me when you get back."

"Sure."

"Promise me." He would need help. No matter how long he sat on that beach, he would still need help from someone, and that someone was Calla Dearborn.

"I'll call you," he said. "Kate . . ."

She waited.

"You be careful, my friend," Taggart said, and a moment later the mobile phone buzzed with a dial tone.

As she unlocked the door to the condo, Kate heard the phone ringing, heard Aimee pick it up.

"May I ask who's calling?" Aimee inquired. Then: "Someone's at the door, let me see if it's her."

As Kate walked into the living room, Aimee covered the mouthpiece and whispered, "A woman named Corey Lanier."

Kate closed her eyes for a moment, then took the receiver. Aimee grinned sympathetically and went off into the kitchen.

"Hello, Corey," Kate said heavily, sinking into an armchair and toeing off her shoes.

"Go ahead, yell at me for calling you at home. I hear you get very upset at people who do this."

"I've given up," Kate said.

"Don't tell me I'm talking to a beaten woman," Lanier said, an edge to her voice.

"A tired one."

"I just talked to Luke Taggart. Luke Taggart sounds really beaten. He tells me it's finished, he's done at LAPD, it's over, he has nothing more to say to me. All of a sudden Matt Brazelton isn't taking my calls."

"What do you want with me, Corey?"

"I want to know what the hell's going on." Her tone was sharp with anger. "There's a story here, an important one. I know it in my bones. I'm not going away, I'm going to get this story."

"I'm afraid I can't help you."

"Fucking bullshit you can't help me. I'm sick of hearing that crap from you. You're right in the fucking middle of it. Everybody's in the fucking middle of it except me."

Kate did not respond. Lanier would have her story soon enough—at least a large part of it. She'd find out in a matter of hours about the arrests of Roberto and Joseph Ferrera. Even if plea bargains came down, there would be a press inquisition into this case. And, Kate acknowledged, public dissection by the press of the homophobic murder of Tony Ferrera by his brothers would have its beneficial aspects.

"What did you cops do to Taggart? Take him in and beat the shit out of him? What about you? Is this the big sellout? What kind of deal did you stitch up, Miss Lesbian Detective? You getting some kind of promotion out of this?"

"No," Kate said.

"Yeah, right, you're Miss Integrity all the way through," Lanier sneered. "Are you really dumb enough to think there's anybody at LAPD who doesn't know you're a dyke? And now they know you're a dyke cop who's a sellout. You're worse than the most homophobic heterosexual—"

"You don't know what you're talking about," Kate snapped, goaded into reacting.

"I don't? So tell me you and the brass didn't take Tony Ferrera's list and do a fire dance with it. Tell me you didn't have a ritual burning of that list and Luke Taggart's career in the lobby of Parker Center."

"You don't know what you're talking about," Kate insisted.

"Sure. So Tony Ferrera's list is going to see the light of day, right?"

"I expect it will see the light of day. Deep Throat is still out there somewhere."

Lanier's voice lost some of its stridency. "Detective, would you be willing to swear to me you're not Deep Throat?"

"I would be," Kate said. "I swear to you I'm not Deep Throat."

Aimee had come out of the kitchen with a bottle of Foster's for Kate; she stopped in her tracks to stare at her.

Lanier asked, "Do you know who Deep Throat is?"

"I have no idea who Deep Throat is. I'll swear to that as well."

Shaking her head incredulously, Aimee handed Kate the beer.

"Whoever this person is," Lanier said, "they're turning out to be exactly like the original one." Having incited Kate into talking, Lanier was transparent in her change of tactics; her tone was now conversational. "I wonder if we'll ever find out who it is, even if the list does come out."

"I wonder too," Kate said.

If in fact her own name had been on top of the list because she was Deep Throat's potential replacement for Tony Ferrera, she was no longer in the running. But Deep Throat was out there somewhere, list in hand, waiting for another opportunity. Searching for another Tony Ferrera.

" 'I'm afraid I can't help you,' " Lanier mimicked Kate, her voice bitter again. "Do you mean that literally? Are you really *afraid* to help me, Detective Delafield?"

Pondering the question, Kate set the bottle of beer on the table beside her. Aimee sat down on the sofa, making no pretense that she was doing anything but listening intently to this conversation.

Lanier demanded, "Aren't you even going to defend yourself, Detective Delafield?"

"I'm too tired. And I feel too bad about Luke Taggart."

"God only knows what you mean by that. Bottom line, you'll say nothing on the record about this case."

"Bottom line I can't, Corey, under any circumstances. And you know that."

"That's a cop-out. Pardon my pun."

"No it isn't. Dealing with the press on an open homicide case is not my job under any circumstances."

Lanier sighed. "Look. There's something very important at stake here—"

"I know that," Kate said quietly.

Lanier lowered her voice as well. "I'm not letting this go. You know that, don't you?"

"I know it," Kate said.

"I'll be in touch, Detective."

Kate replaced the receiver softly in its cradle, and rested her head on the back of the armchair.

"Deep Throat?" Aimee asked, standing up, her hands on her hips. "Some lunatic actually thinks you're Deep Throat?"

"Another Deep Throat, not the one who did in Nixon," Kate said.

"What's going on about Luke Taggart? Who in the world is Corey Lanier?"

"The Taggart case is over. Corey Lanier is one of the toughest of the tough new breed of women out there. Not to mention she's an *L.A. Times* reporter."

"She is? And you were practically civil."

Kate smiled, picked up her beer, looked at it, and set it back down. "Very unlike your favorite detective, Jane Tennison."

"You're my favorite detective. Even if you're more mysterious sometimes than any of your cases."

"I promise to try to be less mysterious." Miss Marple trotted into the room and leaped into Kate's lap. Ruffling the cat's fur, Kate said casually, "Tell me what you think about outing."

"Nothing. I mean, it's so passé. The whole subject got talked to death about five years ago."

"Yes, but what's your take on it today?"

"Hell, I don't know. Kick the gays and lesbians out of the closet who're in public office and hurt us with their self-hatred. Beyond that, all of us need to be out, need to be visible, we need to help each other come out. You know that's what I think, it's obvious."

Kate nodded. Young lesbians and gays had so much more certainty and confidence today than when she was growing up.

Aimee continued, "Everybody's got a different story. Some of us come busting out the minute we know, like I did to my Aunt Paula. But look at Inch-at-a-Time Eileen."

Kate smiled at her nickname for a friend who was emerging as a lesbian with great deliberation, telling one person in her life at a time. Kind of like me, Kate thought.

"Hey, as long as Inch-at-a-Time Eileen gets there . . ." Aimee shrugged. "Lots of us take these winding trails through the forest. As long as we all get to the clearing . . . I feel sorry for anybody who never gets there, never gets to stand in the sunlight. Being out is the only place to be."

"Growing up, I never thought I'd live to see the day so many of us are already standing in the sunlight of that clearing," Kate mused.

"Yeah," Aimee said. "So what do *you* think, Miss Closet Case?"

"I think I'm really glad you've got your nose out of that computer. I think it's a beautiful Friday afternoon, and we should ask good old Ben next door to look after Miss Marple and we should get in the car and point it somewhere and go away for the weekend. I think I want to tell you about every single moment of this entire week."

Aimee looked surprised and gratified. "Let's go," she exclaimed. "I'm dying to hear about Deep Throat." She picked up the message pad from beside the phone. "Louisa from your insurance company called again. But not Torrie."

"I talked to Torrie," Kate said.

"Thank God. Let's get out of here. I want to tell you all about the briefs I've been working on too."

Kate swallowed a groan and smiled bravely. She said, "I don't think I want this beer."

Looking astonished, Aimee started to say something, then picked up the bottle and whisked it off to the kitchen.

When she returned, Kate asked, pointing at the laptop which sat on the coffee table, "Would you bring up that file of names you found? Not the list itself, just where you found it."

"Sure. I suppose you have to get this computer back to Luke Taggart."

"I suppose I do," Kate said.

With a few keystrokes and whirring of the computer's innards, Aimee used the mouse pointer to highlight two files on a long list. "There's the original file, and the dot doc I saved it into to make it a readable file. You want to see it now?"

"No," Kate said.

"You want me to save it on a floppy disk?"

"No," Kate said, staring at the two files, the simple gray print highlighted in a stark black band.

Aimee said, "If it's evidence in the Luke Taggart case, I guess it doesn't matter now."

Kate managed a faint smile. "You were right the first time. The list is actually the location of our nuclear silos."

Aimee chuckled. Kate reached for her hand, clasped it hard.

Aimee might understand, might agree with her decision. Or she might not, when all was said and done. Kate would soon find out. But the decision was hers, and hers alone, to make.

Looking at the highlighted files, Kate thought: May all of us on that list manage to find our own way out to the sunlight in that clearing.

Reaching to the computer, she pushed the Delete key.